CHRISTINE MARION FRASER

King's Close

Fontana
An Imprint of HarperCollins*Publishers*

Fontana
An imprint of HarperCollins*Publishers*
77–85 Fulham Palace Road,
Hammersmith, London W6 8JB

Published by Fontana 1992
9 8 7 6 5 4 3 2 1

First published in Great Britain by
HarperCollins*Publishers* 1991

Copyright © Christine Marion Fraser 1991

The Author asserts the moral right to
be identified as the author of this work
ISBN 0 00 647002 5

Set in Linotron Meridien by
Rowland Phototypesetting Ltd
Bury St Edmunds, Suffolk
Printed in Great Britain by
HarperCollinsManufacturing Glasgow

KING'S CLOSE

Christine Marion Fraser began her life in the tenements of the Govan district of Glasgow just after the war. At the age of ten she contracted a rare muscular disease, and has been in a wheelchair ever since. She now lives with her husband in Argyllshire.

A keen reader and storyteller, Christine started writing at the age of five and got the idea for her first novel, *Rhanna*, while on holiday in the Hebrides. Since then she has written six more bestselling novels about the little Hebridean island, including the recently published *Stranger on Rhanna*. She has also published three volumes of autobiography. *King's Close* is the fourth volume in the popular *King's* series, which follows the fortunes of the Grant family, and is set in rural Aberdeenshire and in Glasgow.

'Christine Marion Fraser writes characters so real they almost leap out of the page, so believable you would swear she must have grown up side by side with them.'

The Sun

THE KING'S SERIES

King's Croft
King's Acre
King's Exile
King's Close

For Peter 'extraordinary' Hornby.
Love you to bits.

PART ONE

Winter 1926/7

CHAPTER 1

'That's me finished for the day, Lizzie.' Evelyn placed the last of the groceries on the shelf as she spoke, or rather shouted, for Big Lizzie Matheson was as deaf as a post and frequently had to have everything repeated to her at least once.

She appeared at the kitchen door, a large, well-upholstered woman with a cheery red face framed in two coils of black hair pinned over her ears. Privately Evelyn thought that the 'dinner plates' of thick hair might have a lot to do with Lizzie's deafness for she had a habit of lifting one or the other of them away from her ears when she was listening extra hard to a conversation, but it was a style that looked as if it might have been born with her and was as much a part of her appearance as the high-necked black silk blouse worn ever since Evelyn had known her.

Of course there must have been more than one blouse, in fact there might have been several as there was always one lurking in the clothes basket when Evelyn came to do the weekly washing. Yet, no matter how hard she looked, she never saw anything different in the style; they must all have been the same, even down to the scuff marks on the elbows and the oval faded patch at the neck where a large mourning brooch was pinned when the garments were in use.

In mischievous moments, Evelyn imagined Lizzie diligently rubbing away at the worn patches in order to get them all to appear exactly the same and she would look at the big woman and smile to herself as the ridiculous visions flitted through her mind.

'Did you remember to get the tea?' Lizzie had asked

the same question three times since Evelyn had come puffing in with the basket of groceries, but this time it was a high, thin, piping voice that answered, accompanied by alarming squeaks and rattles as the other member of the household appeared in the doorway.

Fanny Jean Gillespie was a thin little stick of a woman with sparse grey hair, ancient brown molars, and poor eyesight. She was confined to a wheelchair, a huge wickerwork affair which seemed to swallow up her wizened body, but for all her frail appearance she was extremely bossy and imperious and whenever she wanted anything she thumped her stick on the floor till she got attention.

'Of course she got the tea,' she barked. 'She's told you that three times already. The trouble wi' you, Lizzie, is you never listen to anything anybody tells you.'

'Ach, there's no need to shout,' roared Lizzie, who always addressed the other as if she was deaf also. 'I'm the one who has to see to everything, remember, and if you don't get your damt tea in the morning *I'm* the one who has to listen to your moans and grumbles.'

Evelyn was well used to such loud exchanges between the two spinster ladies. Thrice weekly she walked to the drab grey villa in Drumoyne to make beds, light fires, clean rooms and fetch any supplies that Lizzie had forgotten to ask the message-boy to bring. She was required to wear a blue wrapper, white cap and apron in the morning, in the afternoons she changed into her black and whites with long streamers dangling from her cap and apron so that she would look the part when she opened the door and made tea for afternoon callers.

Fanny Jean had delusions of grandeur; her father had been a minister, she told Evelyn, and there had been a cook as well as two maids to keep the manse spick and span. She was most annoyed that Evelyn couldn't live in but made do because she was the best girl she had had working for her since before the war. Yet for all her airs

4

and graces she was not above enjoying a game of cards
with Lizzie, especially on a Sunday evening when all the
church services were over with and she could settle down
at the card table with a glass of beer at her elbow.

Evelyn had discovered this closely guarded 'secret'
when she had had reason to call on the two ladies one
Sunday after tea. Once over the initial shock of being
'found out' they had sworn her to secrecy and had invited
her to join them in their game. They had both argued a
good deal and had talked in loud, excited voices. Fanny
had been inclined to cheat and after that they had been
at real loggerheads and had thrown one another black
looks. Both ladies had consumed three glasses of beer
each.

When the game was over the big family bible had come
out with Fanny reading aloud mournfully and piously,
pausing frequently to sip beer in order to 'wet her dry
thrapple'.

Despite the fact that she was paid only eight shillings
a week for her services, Evelyn liked the two eccentric
ladies and she smiled as she let herself out of the house
and could still hear their voices through the thick mahogany of the heavy front door.

It was cold outside, a damp raw cold that bit into her
bones and made her pull her woollen collar over her ears
as she hurried homewards. Fog curled into her lungs, the
sooty smell of it made her cough and strain her eyes into
the gloom. Even though she had left Drumoyne at four
o'clock it was now almost dark; two streets away a coalman bawled out: 'Co-al! Co-al!'

The lusty voice of a fishwife filtered through the murky
twilight: 'Finnan haddies! Fine Finnan haddies!'

Evelyn intercepted the barrow as it came rumbling
towards her and while she waited for her 'fine Finnan
haddies' she fondled the ears of the horse as he stood
patiently in his shafts.

'Ay, it's me, Dobbie Loan,' she whispered. 'See what

I've got for you.' Into his mouth she pushed a carrot: she always carried one in her pocket, hopeful that she would meet Dobbie Loan pulling his fish barrow. He had taken his name from one of the dark Glasgow lanes where old Fishy Alice claimed she had rescued him from a pedlar 'sodden wi' drink and beating the poor cuddy senseless'. Dobbie Loan had been a young horse then, now he was old, his belly sagged in the middle, his shoulders drooped, his eyes were watery and hopeless, looking beneath matted spikes of hair.

But he was a horse and to Evelyn that was all that mattered. Her vivid imagination could lift him out of the drab Glasgow streets and place him in the wide sweeping parks of Aberdeenshire where she saw him roaming free and wild, dipping his nose into juicy grasses and rich purple clovers. Perhaps some of her visions transferred themselves to him for whenever he saw her he would lift himself out of his apathy to toss his head and give a little snort of pleasure.

'He likes you, does old Dobbie,' nodded Fishy Alice as she handed Evelyn her parcel of fish. Her hands were cold, the roughened flesh was coated with fish scales; a tattered wool shawl framed a coarsely-hewn face; a greasy apron made of sack cloth was draped over a long grey threadbare dress. On impulse Evelyn handed back the tuppence change she had just received and went on her way with 'you're a good lassie, Evelyn Grainger, one o' Jock Tamson's bairns right enough. God bless you, God bless you' ringing in her ears.

A group of men were lounging at the corner of Lewis Street, dipping their fingers into bags of chips they had bought at Greasy Joe's across the way. 'Will you hae a chip, Evie?' they called as she passed. She stopped and helped herself from the nearest poke. The men gazed at her admiringly. At twenty-eight she was more beautiful than she had ever been. She hadn't followed the latest trend of having her hair bobbed, instead the rich red tresses were pinned in heavy coils on top of her neat head giving her neck a swan-like appearance and adding height to her small-boned figure.

'You're lookin' well, lass,' commented a small man with a beery nose and a habit of picking his big teeth with a dirty thumbnail when he was excited. His small, glinting eyes undressed her as he spoke.

This was 'Big Aggie's Man'. When he came into a conversation he was always called that though to his face he was Willie Dick – a reference to his huge liking for women and his boasting about his prowess in that field.

But anyone with a wife like Big Aggie might be excused for indulging in a bit of fantasy for she was a huge monument of a woman with a voice like a coalman and great fleering breasts that wobbled and bounced underneath the flowing peenie that she always wore.

As if on cue she came thundering down the street, looking for Willie, roaring out as she approached the group of men, 'Have you seen ma man? Ay, there ye are, ye wee bugger, chattin' up the lassies true to form. Did ye get the fish suppers? The weans are waitin' fur their tea. And who said ye could bide at street corners eatin' chips oot a poke like a common wee hooligan. Hame this minute. *I'll* get the fish suppers but there will be nane fur you seein' as how ye've already had yer tea.'

Meek as a lamb Willie Dick trotted homewards while his mates didn't dare make a single sound, not with Big Aggie's black eyes upon them and her disdainful 'hmph!' sounding threateningly in their ears.

Evelyn threw them a laughing look and went on her way. She had lived in Govan for almost seven years now, yet still she found the noise and character of it something of a novelty. She loved the people, she admired their

7

courage and the wonderful warm sense of humour that they never seemed to lose, not even now when unemployment was rife after the General Strike. But she could never get used to the drab greyness of the streets nor of the filthy slush that the children lovingly referred to as 'snow'. Her thoughts frequently drifted back to the virgin snowfields she had known in her own childhood and she would remember again the clean, wide parks and houghs of Rothiedrum in Aberdeenshire. That was her home and always would be, no matter how long she was separated from it. She would think of King's Croft, the house of her birth, sitting in its green acres, and a strange kind of fear came to her heart at the thought that she might never see it again . . . And she wondered – would she ever see Gillie again, the only son of Evander and Lady Marjorie Forbes. Eight years had passed since their last meeting but she had never forgotten him, he who had so loved her, who had tried so hard to win her but had in the end known that she would never belong to anyone else but Davie. She would never see him again – never . . .

But no! She mustn't think like that, one day she would go back, she would smell again the rich, loamy earth, she would see the peesies birling and swooping in the great endless skies – and she would see Gillie again . . . striding over the fields to meet her, his dark head thrown back, his face lighting with that warm, wonderful smile she remembered so well . . .

The cold November air brought her back to reality and she stared into the black mouth of the close – 198 Camloan Road – as yet unlit; eerie and dark and unwelcoming. This was her home now, there could be no other, no turning back, gone from her life were the country lanes and the quiet, safe dark of nights that never really grew black under canopies of glittering skies. Here there was never any opportunity to be alone. Always there was somebody, coming or going, a never-ending stream that began in the early hours and went on till the early hours.

The close of 198 was considered a 'good' close with its tiled walls whose shining appearance reflected the pride of the occupants. Mrs Boyle, front close, first door on the right, had come from a plain, plastered close where she had been in the habit of decorating the wall-edges with pipeclay scrolls and she had carried on the habit at 198, her designs being so elaborate they were the envy of the neighbours who came to visit from her previous tenement.

'It makes a close look fit for a king,' she had once told Evelyn with one of her droll smiles, and Evelyn had hoped that the reference to 'king' was because her own father's middle name was such and not because he had once, a long time ago, been a gypsy king. Not that she was ashamed of that fact nor ever would be. In his youth his black curly hair and flashing dark eyes had beguiled everyone he met. Now there was little in his appearance to tell of those days and she had grown afraid of the hurt he might have to endure if the truth about his identity ever became known.

But Jamie was his own worst enemy. Drink loosened his tongue, he was well known and well liked in the various pubs that he frequented and of course he had spoken of himself as a young man: the past was all that really seemed to matter to him now and King Jamie he had fondly, sometimes mockingly, become. Mrs Boyle's comment had been no accident, King's Close stuck and soon became familiar to everyone and in time some even forgot how it first came by that name. It wasn't uncommon for closes to bear the titles of people who lived in them: in Lewis Street there was Macdonald's Close, in Younger Park Street everyone knew Dan's Close even though Dan had been dead and buried for the last twenty years, so if Mrs Boyle chose to dedicate her pipeclay work to Jamie it was better to take it as a compliment rather than see it as some sort of slight on his name.

Some of the dwellers of 198 did not approve of Mrs Boyle's fancy decoration. They thought it was loud and a bit vulgar, 'plain and straight' being their idea of good taste so that where the scrolls ended at the foot of the stairs the pipeclay was continued in straight lines on either side of the steps leading to the upper landings.

But Evelyn liked Mrs Boyle's fancy whorls and when it was her turn to do the stairs she often had to fight the temptation not to add a little squiggle here and there, but then she would have had Mrs Conkey, alias 'Creeping Jesus' to reckon with.

She was one of those 'carpet slipper folk' who came and went as if they were gliding on castors. That was exactly what Mrs Conkey did so that very often you didn't know she had been there on the landing till you saw the furtive closing of her door.

The whiteness of Mrs Boyle's handiwork seemed to leap out at Evelyn from the dark oblong of the close, just like the 'tattie bogles' of long-ago childhood nightmares, and she was glad to hear Leerie the Lamplighter whistling along, holding his flame-stick to the gas mantles. The feeble light sputtered and flickered; for a few moments a greenish-blue glow illuminated the walls before it strengthened and spread till the shadows were banished from the narrow cavern.

Creeping Jesus was coming downstairs, carrying her wringer to put in the wash-house for the morning. Squeezing herself against the banister to allow the lamplighter to pass, she glided away into the dim nether regions at the close back.

'I could swear I saw a ghost just then, Evie,' laughed the lamplighter. 'Or rather, I felt one brushing past me as I came up.'

Evelyn giggled. 'If ghosts carry wringers and smell of soap and polish then you might just be right at that.'

CHAPTER 2

It was warm and steamy in the kitchen. Maggie Grant always did her washing on a Monday morning and the smell of green soft soap lingered for a long time afterwards. Although the gas mantle had been lit the room wasn't as bright as it might have been owing to the lines of washing hanging from the pulley.

Sheets and pillowcases mingled with underwear and nightwear and two pairs of Jamie's combinations which dangled down so low Evelyn had to duck to pass under them as she came inside. Maggie's refusal to use either the backcourt wash-house or the local steamie never ceased to infuriate Davie.

'Do you think you're too much of a lady to use the public wash-house?' he would challenge her, his handsome face set into stern lines. 'I'm sick to death of coming home to a house full of wet washing. It's high time you changed your ideas, Maggie. You've been here long enough to grow into the town ways and to realize that the Maggie Grant of King's Croft died a long time ago.'

'Maggie Grant o' King's Croft will never die,' Maggie would retort, pulling herself up to her full height so that even at the age of sixty-two she looked as regal and as proud as she had done at twenty-two. 'If you think I'm pushing a bundle of washing on a squeaky old pram through the streets like a common washerwoman you have another think coming, my lad. As for the steamie, I have more to do wi' my time than listen to a lot o' cleck and gossip and to have to pay for the privilege o' doing so.'

'The backcourt wash-house, then,' Davie would persist, really getting his temper up as his mother-in-law's pride

11

never failed to annoy him. 'You could take your turn at that and hang your washing out on the lines like all the other women round here.'

At that Maggie's nostrils would flare and Jamie would stay quiet and still by the fire or go ben The Room till the argument was over with, while Evelyn would sigh and wish for the umpteenth time that Davie and her mother would learn to live with one another in peace.

But they had never seen eye to eye and never would. As time went on and the family grew bigger, the clashes between the two were becoming more frequent and Evelyn couldn't help wishing that it was just she and Davie and the children living together.

But she knew it could never be. Her father's drinking bouts had become heavier and more regular since coming to Govan, at seventy-one he was too old to work and Maggie could never have managed the upkeep of a place of her own. Even so she would have tried and died in the attempt if it hadn't been for Evelyn pleading with her to stay.

'I suppose I have my uses,' she would say bitterly, her white head bowed down in despair and longing for the independence that she had once known and clung to so fiercely. 'At least the bairns need me – if it wasna for them none o' it would be worthwhile.'

Evelyn knew only too well the truth of that. She could never have gone out to work the way she did if it wasn't for her mother looking after the children; it was difficult enough as it was to make ends meet. Davie recognized this and though it was a bitter pill for him to swallow he would occasionally relent and make some conciliatory gesture towards Maggie and for a time peace would reign.

But over the matter of the washing Maggie stuck to her guns; every Monday morning saw her up to her elbows in soapsuds at the scullery sink: rubbing cuffs and collars on the scrubbing board, pounding bedding with a big wooden 'dolly', turning every so often to stir the whites simmering away gently in a large, two-handled pan on the gas stove. Later the mangle would be affixed to the kitchen table and Jamie conscripted to turn the handle while Maggie fed the wet washing into the rollers.

If the weather was dry the washing could be hung outside the kitchen window on a v-shaped line that had a pole in the middle to keep the ropes taut, but in winter the pulley was in constant use and Evelyn's heart sank a little when she came home that Monday evening and smelt the steam and the soap and saw all the clothes hanging from the ceiling.

She pictured Davie's face, the lowering of his brows, the meaningful look thrown at her that said all too plainly it was *her* mother and she ought to be able to do something about it.

But Davie wouldn't be home for an hour yet and it was very peaceful in the room. Jamie was working on his last, the solid thump of hammer on leather sounded good and purposeful to Evelyn's ears. It was a well-remembered sound, an echo of long-ago days when he had eked out their meagre crofting livelihood by making shoes and boots for the gentry. He had been a shoemaker to trade and had been so much sought after that often the beat of his hammer went on into the small hours of night.

Childhood always came winging back to Evelyn whenever she heard the ring of his hammer and she looked at him and knew the pain of sadness as she so often did when she visualized him as he had been then and saw him as he was now: his silvery head down-bent, not a single dark hair to show that it had once been as black as a raven's wing.

His shoulders were stooped and old yet once they had carried her high on harvest-home nights, and she had touched the stars and sung his gypsy songs along with him before her heart beat into her throat with thrill and delight as he broke into a gallop and ran the rest of the way down the hay-scented lane to King's Croft sitting warm and lamplit in its moon-shadowed hollow.

The shoes he made now were very different from those he had once fashioned for the gentry's feet yet they were, in every sense, far more beautiful than anything he had ever done before, except perhaps for the soldier lads in the Great War to whom a pair of sturdy boots was a wonderful luxury. But it was little boots that Jamie fashioned now, made to cover the little blue feet of the barefooted waifs in the district.

Both children and parents alike blessed 'King Jamie' for his kindness and the menfolk would take him out and buy him a drink and then he would get a taste for the stuff that had been his downfall for more years than his family cared to remember. Unable to help himself, he would embark on a drinking spree till sodden and ill he might be picked out of the gutters by the police and taken to a cell to sleep off his excesses.

More sober times would follow but even so he could never get through a day without a dram and the family found the bottles hidden everywhere. Recently Evelyn had found one half full, tucked in behind the gas meter in the lobby, but she hadn't the heart to say anything as more and more he had the look of a trapped animal, hopeless and afraid, with no dignity left to him. Part of him had died when he had left Rothiedrum and King's Croft to seek a new life in Dunmarnock Estate in Renfrewshire. It had been a sad time for them all but they had grown to love the Baird family and had enjoyed working for them. Renfrewshire had been so different from the plains and houghs of Aberdeenshire, it was a soft, undulating countryside with lush pastures and little lanes whose banks and hedgerows had burgeoned with wildflowers. In winter, when the woodlands had been blanketed in snow, Gillan had come to stay at Dunmarnock and she and he, together with Andrew and Christine Baird, had played and laughed in the beautiful white world. Grace, her sister, had been there too, lovely Grace whom Andrew had loved from their first meeting. It had been a world filled with love and laughter and then Gillan had gone away back to the war and everything had changed. Davie had come home from the trenches, sick in mind and body, she had given birth to their son, Alexander, and she had felt old beyond her twenty years.

A time of great tragedy had followed, Andrew and his mother had perished in a fire in Dunmarnock's east wing and Sir Richard Baird, unable to bear his sorrow, had rode out one morning to the moors and there he had taken his own life. The Grants and the Graingers had moved on again, this time to Govan where Davie's parents lived: gone was their green world, grey and drab was their new, each of them had left something of themselves behind but Jamie had left the most. He didn't speak very much now of his beloved lands but they all knew that never a day passed but he longed for them.

The only times he seemed to find some contentment was there by the fire with his lasts and the bits and pieces of leather that Davie brought home from the cobbler's shop.

He looked up as his youngest daughter came in, peering at her over the top of his metal-rimmed specs. 'You're home, lass,' he acknowledged, and something came into his dark eyes, pride and love, mingling together, reaching out to embrace her and make her feel special. They had always understood one another, had seldom been anything else but close and protective of each other, and bending down she kissed his brow and said warmly, 'Ay, Father, I'm home.'

'I'm setting the table tonight, Mam.' Rachel Grace rattled the cutlery as she spoke, a smile coming swift to her solemn little face which was framed in a cloud of thick, dark hair. She was so like her Aunt Grace, sweet and considerate, her lovely grey eyes knowing more, seeing beyond her mere five years. Although she was so young her sense of duty to her family was already well developed. Hers was a placid nature but underneath there lay a romantic heart and a turbulent spirit which manifested itself in bouts of trembling anger when she was upset. She was Jamie's favourite grandchild and she loved to sit on his knee, listening to tales of his travelling days. 'There are ten places tonight – ten places . . .' she repeated in awed tones, then she checked herself and looked guiltily at her grandmother as she came through from the scullery to take the parcel of fish from her daughter.

'You're frozen, Evie,' she commented. 'Go you and warm yourself by the fire. Meg, get up and give your mother that seat.'

Margaret Mary, who was usually known as Meg, wrenched her gaze away from the flame pictures in the fire. She had been dreaming of all the things she wanted and could never have – but one day she would, one day she would be seventeen instead of seven and she would have a big yellow ribbon in her hair like Maisie Thomson in school: she wouldn't have to run the messages or polish the brasses and she would have chicken for dinner instead of horrible old fish again . . .

Meg was a plump, easy-going girl who grudged doing anything around the home. Her olive skin, black eyes, and glossy black curls should have made her a beauty but she had no vibrancy in her and wore a perpetually uninterested expression. She was lazy at school and was forever bringing notes home from her teacher complaining about her work. She often played truant and the School Board inspector came regularly to the door. There was a lot of her Aunt Murn in Meg. Murn had wanted none of King's Croft and had set herself firmly on the road to self-improvement. In the end she had become a teacher, she had worn fine clothes, she had cast off her north-east dialect and had altogether done her best to deny her country upbringing.

16

But the one thing she wanted most in the world had been denied her – Kenneth Cameron Mor, the big, red-bearded Highlander of Knobbliknowe who had married Nellie, the eldest of the Grant girls. Murn had fled to Australia to try and forget and she was there still, unmarried, always promising to come home but 'not for a while yet, there's still so much I have to do here'.

But unlike Murn, Meg had no intention of working too hard to fulfil her dreams. 'I'll just marry a rich man,' she would say serenely and smile the oddly sweet smile which was her saving grace. She could be completely charming when she wanted to be and was in many ways a likeable child and a gifted one, for she was possessed of a wonderful rich singing voice and often she, her mother, her grandparents, and Grace had some happy musical evenings there by the kitchen fire with the others listening and sometimes joining in, though quietly since Meg wasn't slow to pick out a flat note and was pertly adept at pointing the accusing finger.

Unwillingly she gave her seat up to her mother who bit back a sharp rebuke at the look on her eldest daughter's face. James Douglas Grainger came toddling towards his mother. Of all her children he was the one who looked most like Davie, with his velvet brown eyes and earth-coloured hair. He was a strange little boy; timid and shy, afraid of the world, prone to fits of violent temper. He found his refuge in Rachel and followed her everywhere, and next to her he adored Jamie. When he was two he had plucked the strings of Jamie's old fiddle, now, a year later, he would tuck the instrument under his chin as he had seen his grandfather do. It was an unusual sight, to see the tiny boy, standing solemn and frowning, pulling the bow over the strings, his touch sure for such an infant.

And Jamie so proud, knowing the boy had taken the gift of music from him, doing everything he could to encourage the child's interest: guiding the small hands to the strings and the bow, grinning daft-like with pleasure

17

when the little fellow finally managed to produce a few recognizable notes. So he had guided Evelyn when she was small, and she would sit and watch and be ready with her smile when her tiny son glanced up for her approval. She wished that Alex, her eldest son, would look at her like that but he was dour, quiet and moody, and seldom confided in her. It had been like that from his beginnings, eight years ago, when she had left him with Nellie at her croft home in Kenneray soon after his birth. Davie had just returned from the war and she hadn't been able to cope with him and a new baby – she hadn't even been married at the time.

Some sense within her told her that he knew of her desertion of him, somehow he knew and he had never forgiven her. Nellie had scoffed at that and had told her she was wicked and sinful to attribute such things to a tiny, newborn baby, but she knew she was right. As for tiny, that he had never been, he had weighed more than twelve pounds at birth and was now a fine, strapping lad with fair hair and strange eyes – one green, the other brown. At school he was known as Marble Eyes which infuriated him and incited him to bunch his fists and start yet another of his infamous fights.

A knock at the door made them all look up questioningly. It couldn't be Davie since he had his own key and it was still too early for him to come home. Evelyn was suddenly made aware of a suppressed excitement in the air; Maggie's face was flushed, Jamie's head turned away. Alex had clapped a hand to his mouth and Rachel put hers over little James's when it seemed he was about to open it to say something.

She looked at the table. Rachel had said something about ten places, normally there were only eight . . .

'Evie, would you get the door?' Maggie sounded very calm and not in the least put about – yet wasn't that a sparkle of anticipation lurking in the green depths of her eyes.

Evelyn went into the dark L-shaped lobby, a surprisingly large enclosure where an assortment of trunks housed the overflow from drawers and cupboards. There was also a big kist in the corner; it had come from King's Croft and had flap-lid compartments at the sides for hats. A variety of Sunday best clothes were kept inside, all carefully folded into tissue paper with some mothballs and bibles at the top. Evelyn seldom passed it without thinking of the days of her childhood when it had contained mostly girls' clothes. It had stood on the landing of King's Croft and hardly a day went past without Murn or Grace, Mary or Nellie rummaging through it for some items of clothing.

The knock came at the door again, slightly impatient and more prolonged this time. For some reason she couldn't explain Evelyn's heart began to beat more swiftly – she knew that knock, surely she knew it! But she must be mistaken – it couldn't be . . .

The pull of the bell made her jump and without more ado she rushed to obey the imperative command that had once sent her heart plummeting to her boots but which now was part of the past that she so dearly cherished.

CHAPTER 3

'Nellie!'

The name was torn from Evelyn as she came face to face with a tall, fair-haired woman whose knuckles were raised as if she was about to rap the door again. 'No!' Evelyn held her hands to her face in mock terror. 'Dinna hit me, Nellie! You know I'm too old for that sort o' thing now.'

'You're never too old to get a good spanking from your big sister,' Nellie laughed, her sharp-featured face alive with the pleasure of the moment. The two sisters gazed at one another for a long time, then Nellie's arms came out to enclose the other in a strong embrace from which Evelyn emerged redfaced and gasping. Nellie had never been one for 'that sort o' palaver' but three years had passed since last they had seen one another and the younger sister felt the glimmer of tears on her lashes.

There was a footfall on the stair and the next minute a fair-haired giant of a boy hove into view, a shy, nervous little smile spreading over his face.

'Col!' gasped Evelyn, unable to believe her eyes, 'Wee Col, my baby brother! It must be eight years . . .' She stuttered to a halt, unable to express herself further.

She had last seen Col on Kenneray at Nellie's house when she had gone there to bring Alex home to Renfrewshire. He had only been a few months old, Col had been no more than ten at the time. Now . . .

The soft closing of the door across the landing brought her back to her senses. Creeping Jesus was listening again and without any more ado Evelyn pulled the visitors over the threshold and into the kitchen.

For the next five minutes nobody could hear themselves speak. Both Jamie and Maggie were overjoyed to see their eldest daughter again. In the old days she had been stubborn and difficult and would have ruled King's Croft with a rod of iron if she had had her way, but marriage to Kenneth Mor had been her salvation and she was now altogether a far more likeable human being.

Evelyn noticed that Alex was pale-faced and trembling amidst the hubbub and that he was staring at Nellie as if he couldn't believe the evidence of his own eyes. He had adored her from the start. When he was just a helpless infant it was she who had nursed him and fed him, cuddled him and played with him, and he had never forgotten. He had only been five on her last visit to Govan but hardly a day passed but he thought of her. When everybody else in his world seemed against him it was Nellie he turned to. She received letters from him that would have surprised his teachers for he was a clever boy but wouldn't apply himself in the classroom and as a result he was forever getting into trouble.

He had never looked at his mother the way he looked at Nellie and Evelyn felt the old pangs of regret tugging at her heart. She should never have deserted him all those years ago. She ought to have been with him when he was so little and helpless and sore in need of his own mother's love. But — she had to admit it — she hadn't even liked him very much as a baby, and as for being helpless, he had never seemed fragile and vulnerable the way a newborn baby ought to be. He had been big and strong and those peculiar eyes of his had known too much. At the back of her mind she wondered — would she and he have been any closer even supposing she had never left him with Nellie? The question had tormented her for years — that and something else she didn't want to think about but which kept slipping into her mind when she least expected it. The place — that strange and frightening place where life had begun for him. The Devil's Door, that great gap in the crags lying way up

21

yonder in the mists of the hill above Rothiedrum. He had been conceived amidst that black satanic pile where long ago, according to local legend, human sacrifices had been offered to the devil . . .

She shivered and cast such dark thoughts from her mind. The kitchen was warm, too warm, and she was glad when her father went to throw up the sash and allow cold air into the room.

There were questions she wanted to ask but they had to wait. Davie came home just when it seemed Nellie must surely be smothered in a tangle of childish arms round her neck and her skirts. Alex had claimed her as soon as he had gotten over his awe, Rachel's hand was trustingly entwined in hers, and little Jimmy, who had only been two weeks old at her last visit, had climbed onto her knee and was staring solemnly into her eyes, his face breaking into grins every now and then. Only Meg remained aloof and watchful, though even she looked as if she might join the throng at any minute.

All children loved Nellie, and even during her angry, uncertain years everything in her had softened and blossomed when in the company of little ones. Her dearest wish was to have babies of her own but the years had passed and still her arms were empty. To satisfy her maternal instincts she had 'collected other folk's bairns', to quote herself, and had made a fine job of raising Calum and Isla Nell, the children of Kenneth Mor's first marriage. When he was just a small boy Col had also gone to live with her. He had fretted and pined so much when she had moved to Kenneray after her marriage, she had taken him away for 'just a wee while' and he had never returned.

He had been born mentally disabled and physically frail. He was Jamie's only living son, twin boys having died in infancy. Maggie had bitterly blamed herself for not producing a healthy son who could have helped

Jamie run King's Croft and at first she had been unable to reconcile herself to Col.

Only Nellie had ever been able to handle the sickly infant and as he grew up he turned to her more and more for comfort so that in the end he couldn't bear not to be near her. He had always called her 'Nella' and still did. The childish name, spoken in his gruff, half-broken voice, was repeated often, as if he had to say it in order to reassure himself that she was near. Although he was tall he was too thin; the knuckles stuck out like marbles in his big, awkward hands, his shoulders were narrow and slightly stooped and his too-loose mouth was wet and gaping. But his red-golden hair was thick and shining and his cornflower blue eyes, while mostly dreamy and vacant, often seemed to hold so much wisdom it was difficult to believe that his intelligence was so limited.

During his early adolescent years he had been martyr to one ailment after another and the doctors had told Nellie that he wouldn't live much beyond thirty. But there was no evidence of his fragility that evening. His eyes were brilliant in his thin face; in the excitement of seeing his family again he tried to communicate too fast and as a result he stuttered and became tongue-tied.

He had never been able to express himself clearly and was prone to making small grunting noises that only Nellie and her stepson Calum had ever been able to understand. Even so, he had long ago learned to stutter out the names of his family and a sadness crept into Maggie's heart when his attention finally came to rest on her and she realized that he had forgotten who she was and didn't know what to call her.

'I'm your mother, Col,' she said firmly. 'You havena forgotten how to say that, surely?'

He nodded vigorously and said nothing and the result was the same when it was Jamie's turn for scrutiny. Looking blank and unhappy the boy turned away from his

23

parents who were saved further embarrassment by Davie's arrival.

'Davie!' Evelyn went to take his arm. 'Would you look at who's here! Och, but you kent fine they were coming, didn't you? And so did everybody else. Why didn't anyone tell me?'

'Because in my letter I told them I wanted to surprise you,' laughed Nellie. 'And it was worth it, just to see the look on your face.'

'You're looking well, Nellie.' Davie welcomed his sister-in-law coolly though there was a light in his brown eyes. He and she hadn't always seen eye to eye but with the passing years they had learned to tolerate one another and even to enjoy the spicy little altercations that passed between them. 'In fact,' he continued dourly, 'I might go as far as to say you're looking very well and not in the least bit Nellie-ish.'

'Well, you're still looking – and sounding – Davie Grainger-ish,' she returned with asperity. 'But then, I dinna suppose you'll ever be anything else.'

'No, some things never change.' He glanced up at the washing as he spoke. 'I would have thought, as you were expecting visitors, Maggie, you might have put washday off for a day or so – failing that, you could have hung it in the backcourt.'

'What? And spoil Evie's surprise!' Maggie retorted ably. 'She would have guessed something was afoot if everything wasna as usual.'

'Tea's ready,' Evelyn intervened hastily. 'Davie, there's hot water for you in the kettle – and dinna be long about it, though see and wash behind your ears or I'll have something to say, my lad.'

Still smarting at Maggie's words he did not appreciate the joke. 'Promise you won't hang me up on the pulley to dry,' he hissed in Evelyn's ears. She burst out laughing and he had the grace to look ashamed. Holding up a brown paper package he said briefly, 'Jamie,' and thrust-

ing it at his father-in-law he retired to the scullery to strip
and lather soap over his body as he did every night when
he came home from the little carpenter's shop where he
worked.

Jamie opened the parcel. It contained an assortment of
leather pieces. The look on Jamie's face suggested he had
just been handed a packet of money and Evelyn went
into the scullery to rub her hands over her husband's
back and whisper in his ear, 'You've made his night, it's
good o' you, Davie.'

'Ach, it keeps him off the streets and I'm damned if I'm
tramping the gutters looking for him again.'

But he didn't mean the harsh words. He and Jamie had
always got on well and though the older man's drinking
annoyed and sometimes disgusted him it worried him as
well and he was the first to go out looking when Jamie
didn't return home from the pubs of which Glasgow
offered a bewildering choice.

Evelyn's mouth tickled her husband's ears. Playfully
he grabbed her hand and whispered, 'How about it, Mrs
G? Right here at the sink? No one would ever be the
wiser, they're all too busy blethering out there.'

'The chips!' she gasped, breaking from his grasp.
'They're burning!'

It was a happy meal with everyone talking at once, catching up on the latest happenings at Kenneray, the gossip
of Govan. The children were well-behaved and mannerly
though Meg was wont to gape round-eyed at her Uncle
Col who had a habit of sniffing everything before putting
it into his mouth. He ate and drank with silent enjoyment
and appeared not to notice the little girl's open, wondering stares. It was therefore all the more startling when he
suddenly half-rose from his seat to put his nose next to
her plate and make a noise like a dog barking.

Meg was so startled she dropped her fork and took a

pace backwards, there only being enough seats for the adults which meant the children, with the exception of little James, had to stand. Tears sprung to Meg's eyes, her round plump face grew so red she looked as if she was ready to burst any minute.

Beside her, Rachel looked at Col with appreciation for having rendered her sister speechless for once in her life.

Alex clapped his hand to his mouth, hissed into Meg's ear, 'Serve you right, Gypsy,' and for good measure gave a tiny bark and sniffed the food on her plate.

Meg grew redder than ever. Nothing maddened her more than to be called 'Gypsy' by her big brother because she knew he was referring more to her untidy ways than to her curly black hair and olive skin.

'Marble Eyes! Marble Eyes!' she taunted, forgetting Uncle Col in her anger. 'Tells lies, tells lies, steals pennies from the Chap-el and buys mince pies!'

The grown-up chatter ceased, Col was watching the children with the utmost interest, a grin spread over his face, then he began to chuckle, a chuckle which progressed to a rich, deep, hearty laugh, the like of which had been uniquely his from infancy. Meg, Rachel, Alex all gaped in unison. Col glanced at their faces and then he was off again, his red head thrown back, his hands clutching his stomach, his Adam's apple wobbling inside its delicate covering of skin.

It was a very contagious laugh and had never failed to infect others. The children began to giggle, Rachel's coming out in swift spurts, Meg's a continuous high-pitched cackle, Alex's deep rumble almost as catching as that of his uncle.

Infant James banged his spoon on his plate and gave a spluttery chuckle; the adults looked at the children and before long the kitchen was echoing with happy laughter such as it hadn't known for many a long day.

*

Later, when all was quiet and the children were in bed, Nellie, Evelyn and Col donned outerwear and bade good-night to the others. Nellie had already left her things at Grace's house as she and Col were staying there for the duration of their visit.

'Don't be in late,' Davie told Evelyn before she left. 'You and I have a small matter to settle and I have to be up earlier than usual tomorrow. That bugger Stashie heaps on the work but the wages never get any bigger.'

He looked tired, Evelyn thought, his eyes were weary and the wide, sensual mouth that she loved was pinched a little – and no wonder! He had been out late the night before and she had smelled that sickly perfume off him – again. The bitter thoughts piled in on her and in a burst of defiance she tossed her head and said, 'I dinna often go out, Davie, and seeing my sister along the road is a rare treat for me as you never take me anywhere, so – if I want to be late I will be. You haven't yet told me why you were in so late last night.'

'Oh, for Christ's sake,' he swore, 'not that old whine again. I told you before, Evie, I will not bide in every night under the same roof as Maggie Grant. If we had the place to ourselves things might be . . .'

'And don't you come that same old whine again!' she spat at him furiously. 'I will not turn my own parents into the street and if you were a man at all you would stop harping on about it.'

A tiny muscle in his jaw was working angrily. He put up his hand as if to strike her and only by a supreme effort did he refrain from doing so. 'Bitch!' he ground out. 'Bloody little spitfire! I'll prove myself, right now if you like. To hell with Nellie, she's able enough to see herself home, you're my wife and I want you – now!'

He made to drag her into the room but she shook him off and said disdainfully, 'There are other ways of proving your manhood, Davie Grainger, only you've never dis-covered them and never will now. Dinna bother to wait

27

up for me, I might be very late, me and my sisters have a lot o' catching up to do.'

She left him there in the dimly lit lobby, his breath coming swift and harsh and she knew that the minute her back was turned he would either go into The Room to work his temper out on the little gramophone cabinet he was making or he too would don his coat to pursue the pleasures of forbidden fruit that he never had denied himself, nor ever would.

CHAPTER 4

Grace lived in a single apartment, better known in Glasgow as a single-end, across the road from the Park. Most houses in Glasgow, whether they were solo, double or treble rooms, were usually stuffed full of children and adults, but Grace lived alone and as a result her little abode was uncluttered, tastefully decorated, and cosy. The kitchen range gleamed like black satin; on its surface and hanging above it was a shining array of copper pans and kettles; yet for all its spotlessness it was a homely room. The inevitable double bed recess, which was very much part of the tenement way of life, had been carefully curtained off, but even so it was still there. The mantelpiece held photographs of all the family. In a faded, sepia impression of King's Croft Maggie stood at the door with Nellie at her skirts and baby Murn in her arms. In pride of place was a picture of a great bear of a man with keen eyes, a full, sensitive mouth, and a mop of dark hair that looked as if he had just run his hand through it. This was Gordon Chisholm, Grace's husband. They had met in an Aberdeen hospital where she had been a nurse, he a surgeon. Grace had loved him from the start and he had worshipped her with all the power of the big, gentle heart of him. They had only been married for a few brief, wonderful months before he was killed in a field hospital in France. Grace had never accepted his death. 'He'll come back,' she confided to her sisters, 'someday he'll come back to me. His was too strong a spirit to be snuffed out so easily.'

The years passed and still Grace held onto her convictions, without rancour or bitterness, and her family worried over this gentle, lonely young woman, and hoped someday that she would accept her husband's death.

But there was a deep contentment in Grace that was a shining thing. It was there in the face she turned to her sisters and brother as they came piling into her kitchen, bringing the fog and the cold of the November night with them.

'Come you into the fire.' She took Nellie's hands and led her to a deep, cosy armchair. 'Your hands are like ice, Nellie, you ought to wear gloves.'

'Listen to the girl,' said Nellie. 'We've been apart too long, I'm thinking. I'm the one who used to tell you these things.'

'We were country girls then,' smiled Grace, 'and there was a certain order about everything. Here, in the town, it's the survival of the fittest. I learned that lesson fairly quickly.'

Nellie sat down and studied Grace as she set about making tea. There was nothing about this darling sister of hers that suggested great strength or fitness. She was an exquisite creature with her smooth, unblemished skin and her haunting black eyes. Of them all she was the one who had changed the least and looked ten years younger than her thirty-four. In fact – Nellie caught her breath – she seemed ageless. Her rich chestnut hair showed no traces of grey, her face was as unlined as that of a school-girl, and straightforward Nellie, who rarely believed in anything that she couldn't see or touch for herself, found herself thinking that it was as if time had passed her sister by, suspending her in a vacuum in which she waited for Gordon to come home to her and nothing would be changed – nothing and no one . . .

Then Nellie saw with a great sense of sadness that Grace had changed. She had always been delicately made but now that fragility of form had honed itself to a terrible thinness that made her look as if she could easily break without much effort.

'Grace,' she spoke imperatively and impulsively, 'don't you find the work at the hospital a wee bittie heavy for you? You're much too thin. I aye told you, you were never cut out for all that lifting and laying and doing all those gruesome things you do to people.'

Grace's pale skin was diffused with colour, a combination of elation and heat from the fire. 'Och, Nell,' she laughed, 'you make me sound like some horrible ogre wi' great fangs and sharpened claws on me! What else could I do, tell me that? Nursing is what I ken the best and like the best. Of course I get tired now and then but so does everybody. Dinna worry about me any more, I'm fine and all the better for seeing you again.'

Col was absolutely fascinated by the kitchen range. He had already amused himself with the black iron hob-top that hinged up and down from the nearby wall, now he gaped in slack-mouthed amazement when Evelyn filled the kettle from a little brass tap in the water compartment.

Nellie relaxed and joined in the carefree chatter. It was good, so good to be with her sisters again, to hear their voices and their laughter, to watch them as they went about just as they had done in those far off days in the kitchen of King's Croft. She was glad she had made the effort to come and visit them yet she was sad also. She knew that Evelyn wasn't always happy with Davie, she had heard their raised voices in the lobby, arguing with one another while she waited on the landing.

She had known from the beginning that he wasn't the man for her little sister, he was too fond of women to ever be able to remain faithful to one and she wondered if that was what the disagreement had been about. Gillan Forbes now — he had loved Evie, deeply and completely; if only it had been him instead of Davie, how different everything would be, but Evelyn's heart had always ruled her head. Nellie knew she was still devoted to her husband and would remain so for the rest of their life together.

At that moment Grace went to answer the door and a young girl of about twenty came into the room, all fresh and bouncy and full of chatter, her dimples coming and going in her attractive, lively face. She lived in the back close single-end and Grace introduced her as Penny McFarlane.

'But just call me Penny Farthing,' she giggled, 'everybody does, I got it at school though nobody dares to call me anything other than Miss McFarlane at the office.'

Five minutes later everyone knew Penny's life story. Her mother was dead, she had lost her father and her brother in the war and had been brought up by a maiden aunt who had ensured she got a good education and whose demise a year previously had made her the richer by three hundred pounds.

'I'm going to save and save,' she confided in her bubbly voice. 'The wages aren't all that good at Daly's where I work but I put away as much as I can after food and rent, and one day I'm going to travel round the world and see all the places I used to read about at school . . .'

Pausing only long enough to sip her tea, she was off again, quite oblivious to Col's fascinated eyes upon her and to Nellie's ill-concealed annoyance at the interruption of what had been a sisterly reunion.

'Aunt Alice was very strict, of course, and might not approve of her money being spent on foreign travel but I want to broaden my mind and learn of different cultures. I won't get married for years and years yet and I might never have children. They're such snottery, noisy wee horrors I hate the idea o' them pawing and whining round my skirts. Mind you, though, if I met a man I really and truly loved I suppose I would want to have his bairns

32

but I would keep it to just two, any more would be a trachle and . . .'

Nellie's face had been growing redder and redder, now she couldn't refrain from bursting out, 'And what makes a silly quine like you suppose she could have bairns at all? Just like that! To order or no' to order just when the notion pops into that daft, empty head that sits so vainly on your shoulders. Bairns aren't toys, you know, to play with and toss aside whenever the mood takes you, they're human beings like you and me and deserve the very best that life has to offer them!'

Penny stared at the other woman, genuinely shocked at such a reaction to her careless words. 'Oh, I'm sorry,' she gasped, her round eyes coming to rest on Col as if she was seeing him properly for the first time, 'I didn't know he was yours, I can see why you're so upset, but surely there's still time to have another . . .'

'You havena understood a word I've said, have you?' flared Nellie. 'I told you bairns canna be made to order but it just went in and out o' that space inside your skull. As for Col, he's my brother, no' my son, but he might just as well be mine for all the love and trust he's given me over the years. As for time, it's running out for me, I'm thirty-nine years old but even supposing I was twenty again there still wouldna be enough time for all the bairns I wanted in my life and never had!'

'Nella.' Col said her name with trembling lips and she spoke a few words of comfort to him, already ashamed of her outburst and to a mere girl who up until a few minutes ago she hadn't known existed.

Penny rose to go, no anger in her, only regret that she had been the cause of such a scene in the home of her dearly loved friend.

'Och, Nellie,' Grace shook her head at her sister the minute the door closed on Penny, 'she blethers on, I know, but she never means to annoy anybody wi' her

33

chatter. She's a highly strung lass and has been living on hope and nerves since her old aunty died.'

'Ach, I'm sorry.' Nellie was exceedingly shamefaced. 'I didna mean to rant on at the girl and though she did say some daft things I should have kent better than to shout at her.' She grinned, her beautiful amber eyes begging forgiveness. 'I havena really changed, have I? Still the same old Nellie, finding fault and letting my spicy tongue run away with me.'

'Look at the time!' Evelyn's eyes alighted on the clock. 'I've got to go or I'll never get up in the morning.'

'Will you be all right, out there in the streets on your own?' Nellie asked anxiously.

Evelyn laughed. 'I used to wonder that too, it all seemed so threatening after the countryside; the dark alleys, the odd drunk staggering home, the midgie men wi' their torches raking the bins late at night; the shadows and the footsteps and the backcourt spooks waiting to catch you if you dared step out o' the back close after dark . . .'

Grace shivered and Nellie said drily, 'You havena lost your knack for storytelling, Evie, you aye did give us the jitters wi' your tales – and you still havena answered my question.'

'This is Govan, Nellie. The Govanites see themselves as a separate community from Glasgow, they still see their wee town as a village and everyone kens everyone else, even the drunks and the midgie men. As for Glasgow, the corner boys only ever fight wi' one another and if you ask a drunk man for your fare home he would give you his last penny and bless you wi' his last breath.'

'Evie!' Nellie was shocked. 'You never have, have you?'

'Ay, once, coming home from Mary's. I lost my tram fare and a bonny wee man, reeking o' whisky, called me "hen" and gave me the last few coppers he had in his pocket.'

'Talking o' Mary,' Grace intervened hastily since Nellie

34

looked as if she was getting ready to give Evelyn a tongue lashing for what she saw as shamelessness, 'she's looking forward to seeing you, Nell, and wants you to visit her and Greg right away.'

'Ay, Mary would say that.' Nellie was diverted, much to Evelyn's relief because she was learning all over again that in Nellie's eyes she was still very much a child to be watched and scolded if it seemed she was getting out of hand. 'But I must confess I'm fair looking forward to seeing my posh sister and I had thought to go over there tomorrow night and have you two for company. I dinna ken Glasgow at all and I'm aye feart o' getting Col and myself lost in the city.'

Grace said she would be delighted to come but Evelyn hesitated as she wondered what Davie would have to say about her going out two nights running. She gave herself a mental shake. Of course it was all right! She seldom went anywhere these days while he had his golf in the summer and his clandestine outings in the winter. Besides, it wasn't often that she saw Nellie and it would be wonderful for them all to meet at Mary's.

'Ay, that's fine by me,' she conceded firmly. 'I'll come over here tomorrow evening around seven.'

She hurried away, with Nellie's warnings about speaking to strange men ringing in her ears. But the dark streets were almost empty and it was but a short walk from Grace's to 198. Despite the flickering light from the gas mantles, it was eerie and shadowy in the close and she jumped when a door on her left opened and a man's voice said, 'Evie, is that you? I thought I saw you coming along the road.'

'Ay, Douglas, it's me,' she answered in relieved tones.

'I was wondering, I know it's late but do you think you could help me with Winnie? She'll no go to her bed for me and I'm frightened to leave her up for fear she wanders off again.'

Without ado Evelyn went into the house of Davie's

parents. Both she and Maggie often helped Douglas with Winnie who had lost her reason when her youngest son, Danny, had got killed at Le Cateau when he was just sixteen.

Winnie's hair had turned white after that and she had taken to sitting at the window, watching and waiting for her boy to come home, singing over and over a tragic little song about a soldier laddie.

Over the years her mental condition had deteriorated and now, as well as waiting at the window, she let herself out of the house at any time of the day or night, very often dressed only in nightgown and slippers. She was possessed of great cunning and always seemed to know where her husband had hidden the key of the door. In desperation he had taken to hiding it under his pillow but while he slept his exhausted sleep she would stealthily slide her hand under his head and find the key. He had once been a strong handsome man but the years of looking after a mentally sick wife had taken their toll till he was now just a shadow of the man he had once been. As she grew worse he had been forced to leave his job in the shipyards and he and his wife subsisted on the pittance they received from the Assistance Board.

The Grants and the young Graingers found other ways to make his life tolerable. Maggie sent down trays of baking; Evelyn made soup and ashet pies which she got him to accept by telling him they were leftovers from the kitchen.

When Evelyn followed Douglas inside she found the room cold and neglected. A miserable fire smouldered in the grate, the dinnertime dishes were piled in the sink where a greasy scum had formed on the cold water that covered them; heaps of clothes lay everywhere, on the chairs, the floor, even on the table. Winnie was crouched on a hard wooden chair by the smoky fire, her calm, sad face distorted by years of phantom visions and unfulfilled yearnings, her thin, white hair straggled over the dirty collar of her shapeless blouse, her skirt was half loosened at the waist so that a portion of grey underskirt showed, and her blue-veined legs, stockingless and shoeless, looked cold and lifeless.

Evelyn glanced at Douglas Grainger. He was ill and haggard, his eyes were bloodshot with weariness, his iron-grey hair was tousled and unkempt. Yet this was a man who had once taken a great pride in his appearance and Evelyn's heart turned over at the realization he was losing a long, long battle to keep his own mind and body together, never mind those of his wife.

'Sit down, Douglas,' she ordered gently. 'I'm going to make you a cup o' tea before I do another thing.'

Brave words! There wasn't enough heat in the fire to warm a cupful of water, never mind a kettleful, so going to the gas meter in the tiny lobby she inserted a coin. She knew by the sound it made as it dropped that the box was almost empty and rashly she put all the small change she had into the slot before going back to the kitchen.

'There was no need to do that, lass,' Douglas greeted her harshly, vestiges of his old pride showing in his eyes. 'I haven't bothered with gas this whilie back. The fire does fine for all we need.'

She said nothing. Instead she made tea on the neglected-looking stove which obviously hadn't been used for some time as she had quite a job to turn the stiff keys in order to get the gas through. But at last the kettle boiled and thrusting a steaming cup at Douglas she then turned her attention to Winnie.

'Come on now, Winnie,' she murmured into the woman's ear. 'You ken fine that you have to get ready for bed. Danny might be here in the morning and you want to be nice and fresh when he sees you.'

It was a ruse she had used often and it never failed to draw a favourable response. Douglas had never approved of it, telling her it was wrong to raise hope in such an unpredictable mind, but she knew she was saying the things that Winnie wanted to hear; when morning came she would never remember anyway since her memory could never hold anything longer than a few minutes at a time.

On this occasion, Douglas Grainger was too lethargic with exhaustion to care how his wife was persuaded to her bed, just as long as she got there and allowed him to go to his.

In minutes Evelyn had undressed the old woman, holding her breath a little as stale odours of sweat were released from her clothing. Attired in a grubby pink nightdress Winnie allowed herself to be led to the bed recess but just as it seemed she was settled under the bedclothes she said in a whining, childish wail, 'Po! I need to pee. Po! I need to pee!'

Over and over she repeated the request till Evelyn went to fetch the chamberpot and placed it beside the bed. Few tenement flats boasted inside lavatories, most were outside on the lower landings, in this case a small, dark enclosure was situated in the back close, under the stairs.

Most families therefore owned a large chamberpot, sometimes two if the household was big, for no one in their senses would venture out to the stairhead 'cludgie' on freezing cold winter nights.

Patiently Evelyn helped Winnie back out of bed to sit her on the pot and wait there with her till she was finished and had clambered into bed once more. She was turning away when her hand was seized in a vice-like grip. 'Danny!' hissed the thin, querulous voice. 'See Danny in the morning.'

'Ay, in the morning,' Evelyn repeated a trifle wearily.

Douglas had already brought out the 'wheelie bed' from under the big bed. He was pale with fatigue and looked as if he might fall asleep, clothes and all, the second Evelyn's back was turned.

Brushing aside his thanks she left him to make her way upstairs. The house was quiet and dark when she let herself in and she stood for a minute in the lobby, savouring such rare tranquillity and also the mouthwatering smells filtering through from the kitchen. In winter there was always a big pan of soup simmering away on the hob and she guessed that Maggie had prepared a fresh pot before retiring and had left it cooking gently and safely beside the dross-damped fire.

The tempting aroma made Evelyn feel hungry but she didn't dare go ben the kitchen at this time of night, Maggie and Jamie slept in there in a double bed recess, so too did the children, all of them together in an enormous brass bed to the right of the door. She had wanted the girls at least to sleep in the recess bed in The Room but Davie wouldn't hear of it, he liked his privacy, he told her, but the day was coming when his family would be too big to sleep together and some of them would have to sleep in The Room whether he liked it or no.

But for now The Room – parlour, playroom, bedroom, and always spoken with and spelt with a capital 'R' in every tenement home, was Father's sacrosanct sleeping quarters and he wasn't too keen on the children playing in there either.

He was fast asleep when Evelyn finally crept in beside him. 'I die when I hit the pillow,' he often told her, and right enough his was a heavy, deep slumber from which there seemed no awakening. Yet he could waken for work without the aid of an alarm clock and was often up and away before Evelyn or any of the family were astir.

He hadn't gone out after all, she could smell the faint but pleasing tang of newly-worked wood, and she was pleased to think he hadn't gone storming out of the house after she had left.

It had been a long day and she had thought sleep would

come easily to her but to her annoyance she felt wide awake and lay for a long time going over the events of the day.

Once upon a time she had kept a regular diary of her life but months could now pass without a single word being jotted down. But that night she was seized with an urgent need to record her thoughts and hanging half out of bed she felt around for the battered old tin box she kept hidden under there.

A strange little thrill ran through her as she retrieved the box and unlocked it with the rusty key that was kept in the threaded brass knob on her side of the bedhead.

With the aid of a torch she began going through the small pile of things nestling in the musty depths of the box. In minutes she was transported back in time as her searching fingers caressed one treasure after another. Here was the corn dolly and the silk stockings given to her by her childhood sweetheart, Johnny Burns, who had died tragically young in a drowning accident; wrapped in tissue paper was the exquisite little pearl drop that Gillan had presented to her one unforgettable Christmas; a knobbly package contained a garnet necklace from Lord Lindsay Ogilvie, Gillan's uncle – old Oggie. She sighed and wondered – where was he now? Was he still alive? He hadn't been that old. What a character, eccentric, generous, lively, a non-conformist: like herself – he had told her that more than once. He wouldn't think that if he could see her now, every day the same, no escape from the reality of poverty and pain – not her pain but the sufferings endured by those she loved.

Quickly she pushed such thoughts away; her fingers touched on a scrap of material lying at the bottom of the box. It was a sampler given to her by Florrie O'Neil for her fifteenth birthday; worked in cross stitch it bore the legend: 'Evelyn and Florrie – Best Friends. 1913 and beyond.'

Even after all these years it pained Evelyn's heart to

read it, for lovely fair-haired Florrie, who had dreamed and hoped for a better life beyond the realms of her cluttered, noisy home, had died of tuberculosis when she was just sixteen years old. Evelyn had never forgotten Florrie, they had shared so many childhood joys and sorrows – Florrie, Johnny, Alan Keith, gone, all gone, their young bones resting in the little kirkyard by the cold blue waters of Loch Bree . . . all except Alan whose unmarked grave was somewhere in the wastes of France where he had fallen so bravely whilst fighting for his country . . . She had grown up with them, now only she was left – but no! Gillan had been part of it, he had shared those growing, searching years.

Gillan! She searched for and found a tiny tissue-wrapped package that contained a thin gold band. She slipped it onto her finger and it all came back to her: New Year 1918, Gillie going back to the war, saying goodbye to her in one of the empty attic rooms at Dunmarnock. He had given her this ring and had told her his heart would always be hers.

'This ring will bind us together for all time,' his voice spoke clearly inside her head. 'Look on it as a marriage of our hearts . . .'

It was the last time she ever saw him, she only knew he had emerged safely from the war, she knew it before even his own mother did for on the morning of 11 November 1918 she had dreamed of him lying cold and afraid in the trenches, the great guns of the Western Front booming, booming, before the Armistice was declared and they fell silent for the last time.

A little sob escaped her, it was too poignant to go back and remember and tearing off the ring she placed it with the other things inside the box. In her diary she wrote:

November 1926, Nellie came today, she brought Wee Col who is little no longer but a bonny tall boy with eyes on him like a summer sky. But

41

growing has made him more fragile, his bones stand out too harshly and I'm afraid of what the passing years will do to him. But it was so lovely to see him and Nellie again. I used to hate it when she treated me like a bairn but now, in some strange way I don't mind any more. Maybe it's because she makes me feel like the child I once was and can never be again.

She brought a breath of the old days with her and later, when we went over to Grace's place and all got talking about Rothiedrum, we all seemed to become more alive, more happy than we have been for ages.

If only Nellie had a baby of her own, her longing for one has grown into a kind of canker that eats away at her heart. If it was possible, I would have one for her because having bairns seems to be all I'm good for . . . and to think that once I imagined myself as a writer and hoped that I would write lots and lots of wonderful books.

Beside me Davie sleeps, never knowing that I lie awake many a night, cold and lonely and afraid of things that are yet to be . . .

Alex still looks at me as if I was a stranger. He frightens me sometimes. I never know what he is thinking, how he feels, yet he is never too proud to show Nellie that he loves her and I can tell he would go and bide with her tomorrow if he could. I wish I could stop thinking about the Devil's Door, it's only a heap of old stones after all and can never harm me or mine now . . .

She shivered and felt afraid. Tucking the diary in beside a pile of others she locked the box and pushed it under the bed. Lying down she cooried into her husband. He stirred and, turning, he buried his sleeping face into her neck. She suddenly felt warm and safe, the shadowy spectres of night fled away, sleep came like a comforting blanket, wrapping her round and round in its deathless, timeless embrace.

CHAPTER 5

It was odd, Nellie reflected, as she sipped her tea and nibbled a wafer-thin sandwich in Mary's pretentious, over-furnished parlour, how things and people could change over the years — and not always for the better. When they were young, all the Grant girls at some time or another in their lives had considered Mary to be the beauty of the family though Mary had never seen herself in such a light. She had been an honest, cheerful, bonny girl, steeped in country ways, with no greater ambition in her life than to 'marry a good man and have lots and lots o' bairns by him'.

When she grew a little older her outlook soon changed when she saw the mess some women could make of their lives by having too many children. Betsy O'Neil had been a prime example of that. In Betsy's muddled, dirty house it was difficult to make sense of anything very much for the jumble of plump little limbs and bare bottoms that had crawled and toddled and walked their neglected way through life. Every year had introduced another hungry mouth into the Cragbogie household and the young and impressionable Mary had decided that that sort of life was the last thing she wanted.

Far better to enjoy herself before deciding on any set plan for the future and with great energy she set about driving half the lads in Rothiedrum crazy to have a bit of what they were sure the others were getting for nothing.

Her figure had burgeoned into glorious flower by the time she was fourteen and that, combined with her rosy good looks and vivacious nature, had seen to it that she had an ardent and jealous following for the duration of that fun-filled and enjoyable period in her life.

Her 'flauntings and flirtings' had often shocked and disgusted the straight-laced Nellie who, seeing it her duty to uphold the 'good family name', had repeatedly warned her carefree younger sister against the error of her ways.

But Nellie needn't have worried on that score for, while Mary took a great delight in teasing Nellie about her own spinsterish lifestyle, and tormenting her with tit-bits and hints of what she herself was doing with boys, she was, in one sense and perhaps the most important of all, just as chaste and virginal as any virtuous elder sister could want her to be.

The reason for that was simple. By the time she was sixteen Mary had decided that the crofting life was not for her. She had had a glimpse of what the good life was all about whilst she was in service, and while she was sensible enough to know she could never aspire to the heights of the landed gentry she saw no harm in steering for a middle course.

When Doctor Gregor McGregor came to take over the practice at Rothiedrum she knew she had found what she was looking for. He had soon capitulated to her charms and it wasn't long before she had become the wife of a man who had, in a very short space of time, become a much-loved and respected figure in the community.

Marriage to Greg, with a maid to bring her tea in the mornings and tidy up after her, brought out the lady in Mary. She soon acquired an expensive taste in clothes and stretched her husband's salary to the limit with her whims and fads for the latest fashions. She cultivated 'suitable' acquaintances and held little tea parties for country gentlemen and their wives and in no time at all she learned to prattle on about nothing and to look with a mildly critical eye on those people of the farmtouns that she had once described in a school essay as being 'the salt of the earth'.

As things stood, Mary might have remained content

enough with her lot had not the war intervened, and in 'doing her bit for the war effort' she had reason to mix more and more with the gentry who were having great fun doing their bit also.

And now here she was, in with the elite of Glasgow's west end, not caring very much to be reminded of the struggle Greg had had to get there, never voluntarily mentioning the poverty they had endured when they had first come to Glasgow five years ago and their clientele had sprung from the worst hovels the Gorbals had to offer. In those days Greg's services had been paid for by the barter system and he had become so overworked and run down, both mentally and physically, he had suffered a breakdown and had been unable to run his practice for several months.

Mary had not been idle during that time. Desperate and on the verge of a breakdown herself she had turned to her family for help and, regaining her strength through them, she had then set her sights on other, and rather dubious horizons.

Greg never really knew how the miracle of their financial recovery came about, Mary simply told him she had been lucky enough to ingratiate herself with the right people, introductions led to more and better prospects so that it wasn't long before the Gorbals became just an unhappy memory and the luxury mansions and flats of the west end a breathless reality.

Greg's clientele was now composed of hypochondriac old ladies only too anxious to spend money on themselves, lawyers, businessmen, judges, baillies, the well-heeled, the well-to-do. All of them frequented his surgery and very often his home as well for there was no more popular man on that side of the Clyde. And the beauty of Greg was that they loved him for what he was and not for what he had and his advice on many matters outside of doctoring was greatly valued, even though he was blunt and honest and never put on any airs and graces for anyone.

Not so Mary; she had lost much of her country charm and was full of the little affectations she had once abhorred in the idle rich. She lived well and she looked it, her hand was never away from the plates of home-made macaroons and chocolate creams that the maid laid out for the visitors.

Her once curvaceous figure had swollen to matronly proportions that made her look far older than her thirty-six years; Rabbie Burns might have described her looks as 'sonsie' since her attractive features were becoming less noticeable in the plump flesh that enfolded them. But her hair was as glossily black as ever and her skin was as dewily fresh as it had been when she was twenty. Also, she had never lost her generosity of nature that had been and still was one of her greatest assets.

She showered her sisters with affection and smothered them with a great show of interest in their affairs, but the way she handled Nellie was wary in the extreme for she knew she could never get away with anything that wasn't open and above board in that formidable lady's presence.

But she couldn't hide her shame and her revulsion of her brother Col. When the parlour-maid fussed in with this that and the other adjunct for the comfort of the guests, Mary behaved in a most peculiar fashion by standing in front of Col as if trying to hide him while at the same time talking rapidly to the maid in a too-obvious attempt at distracting her attention. But Col himself, in his own inimitable fashion, soon sorted out his snobbish sister. Thinking she was playing some sort of game with him he suddenly popped his head out from her skirts and shouted 'Boo!' at the maid, who almost dropped the coal scuttle in her surprise.

Nellie, who saw only too well what Mary was up to, threw herself back in her chair and gave vent to high-

47

pitched and most enjoyable laughter which coincided with the merriment of both Grace and Evelyn.

Their joyous peals filled Mary's elegant parlour and Col, thus encouraged to carry the 'game' a step further, lumbered out from hiding to grin engagingly at the maid and say 'Boo! Boo! Boo!' into her red and startled face.

With a hurried bob and an 'Excuse me, ma'am' the poor girl made good her exit from the room leaving her mistress aghast and looking not quite sure where to put herself.

'Ach, it serves you right,' Nellie told her, wiping her streaming eyes. 'Col will be the talk o' the place now whereas if you had behaved in a normal fashion the poor quine would most likely never have given him a second glance. You've climbed too far above your station, Mary. If you were a real lady you would accept Col for what he is and make the best o' it. Dinna tempt providence, my girl, it has a habit o' dealing wi' the High and Mighties o' this world and you're just about ripe for a good skelping.'

After that Mary was most discomfited and subdued and all at once Nellie was sorry for her. Poor Mary, poor Murn; so different from their sisters, both of them trying too hard to be something they weren't, thinking they had attained their individual, ultimate goals and in their efforts to stay at the top never having the clarity of vision to realize that they had achieved nothing in the way of true happiness.

Murn was so busy chasing ambition she had no time to spare for anything or anybody else; Mary's life was empty of the things that mattered, leaving her too much time for the things that didn't. Her young son had been packed off to boarding school and to fill her days she had her empty-headed friends in for lavish afternoon teas; she dawdled away her time in the elegant surrounds of Charles Rennie Mackintosh's Willow Tearoom or at

Copland and Lye's where Palm Court musicians played music that soothed the perceptive ear; she made a con- vincingly knowledgeable show in front of her cronies when they went to Reid and Lefevre, the art dealers, to look at the pictures; she made a big show of dressing up for the concerts in the St Andrew's Halls even though she understood bothy ballads best and the only pictures she really knew anything about were the sepia prints of her family she kept hidden away in her bureau drawer.

She had forgotten how to behave naturally – even with her own sisters – and looked very crestfallen as she sat playing with her thumbs, her dissatisfied mouth trem- bling a little because she knew she had made a fool of herself and didn't know how to go about rectifying matters.

Grace got up and ran her hand over the glossy black head she had once brushed when they were girls. 'Mary, Mary,' she said in her soothing, musical voice, 'dinna take on so, you have so much to be thankful for in your life, a good man who loves you and a fine healthy son who has aye been a credit to you. We're your sisters and we're here to enjoy ourselves tonight, no' to mope around looking as if one o' us has just stepped out o' the dung midden and the rest no' knowing where to put ourselves for the smell.'

Mary burst out laughing. 'Och, you're right, you're so right, Grace, and I'm a bitch for behaving as I did.' Her eyes sparkled suddenly. 'I know, let's make toast like we used to when we were children round the fire at King's Croft.'

'A grand idea,' enthused Evelyn, and without more ado Mary rang for the maid and demanded a loaf of bread, butter, and a toasting fork.

'Oh, and see that the fire is kept high, Betty, and bring another pot of tea. Mr McGregor will be home soon and

I'm sure he will like nothing better than hot tea and toast to warm him up on a night like this.'

'Oh yes, ma'am.'

Betty hurried away to relate the latest fad to Cook who snorted and was of the opinion that 'some folk didn't know their place in this world. What am I to do with the master's dinner, I'd like to know? He'll no' be fit for it if he goes filling himself wi' the stodgy food she would have him eat. A man needs a good dinner in his belly after a hard day's work.'

'We'll eat it,' Betty decided as she flounced about looking for a toasting fork, wondering aloud as she did so just who was the 'poor sowel wi' the slobbering mouth' that the mistress had been 'gey anxious to hide'.

The sisters had a wonderful time round the fire, chattering and giggling over old times. They took turns at making and buttering the toast, winding a teacloth round their hands when the heat from the flames became too unbearable. Not to be outdone, Col took his turn as well, his eyes shining with enjoyment, his golden red hair gleaming in the firelight.

Mary looked at his happy young face and shame, raw and painful, seared her being. How could she have behaved as she had towards her very own brother? His was a simple, uncomplicated world and never, never would he even begin to think that his own sister could reject him. He had known so much love in his life, to him it was a natural thing, Nellie and Kenneth Mor had seen to that. Croft Donald was full of love for Colin. Wee Col — he would always be that, somehow, an innocent boy who had never knowingly hurt anyone in the whole of his life. Wee Col, till the end of his days. A sob caught in Mary's throat, she remembered suddenly that the days and years of his life were ebbing away and that his tomorrows were as uncertain as the flickering flame of a candle . . .

She looked at him properly for the first time. He was so thin, frail almost, his skin had that transparent quality that one might expect in a delicate child, yet he was so happy – a smile was never far from his face. He exuded trust, he exuded a millionfold the love that had never been denied him from the day of his birth – Nellie's love. She of them all had taken his poor, sick little soul to her heart and she had never let go.

'He loves making toast.' Nellie spoke quietly. 'At Croft Donald he and Calum between them make great mountains of toast for the supper and often's the time the pair o' them bring me up breakfast on a Sunday. There was a time I never could abide such palaver and fuss but I ken now that anyone can change if they have to. When my two lads come in my door wi' a breakfast tray set wi' tea and toast and a wee bunch o' harebells in a jug, they make me feel as good as royalty any day. There was a time I worried about bringin' up other folks' bairns but Dyod! it's been worth it. I wouldn't change them for anything and the best thing of all is the knowing that they wouldn't change me either.'

She smiled at Col, that radiant smile that never failed to transform her face to one of rare beauty, and simultaneously they cried, 'Not for all the tea in China!'

'He kens that off by heart,' she laughed. 'I've said it to him often enough and it's about the one thing he can say that other folk understand.'

'You have a rare and wonderful gift, Nellie,' Mary said in a low voice. 'You have the ability to get into the hearts and minds of children. Of us all you are able to fully understand them, yet, if you won't jump down my throat for saying so, you were such a dour, unhappy creature

51

when you were young it seemed as if you could never love anything or anybody.'

'Och, Mary,' chided Grace, with a quick look at Nellie's face, 'surely you haven't forgotten the reasons for that . . .'

Her words trailed off, and it was Mary's turn to glance quickly at her elder sister.

But Nellie just shook her head. 'I haven't forgotten any o' that and I never will, but time has a habit o' healing old wounds and Whisky Jake is just a bad memory to me now, one that seldom bothers me.'

Whisky Jake. The very mention of the name seemed to bring a breath of evil into the room. Nellie had been a vulnerable and innocent child of ten years old when, in a drunken stupor, he had crept up to her room one terrible night to viciously rape her and leave her bathed in her own blood. During the dreadful years that followed she had hated and mistrusted all men and would have grown more and more bitter if Kenneth Mor hadn't come into her life when he did.

'But he bothers me.' Evelyn spoke quietly. She hadn't said very much at all that evening, she had been thinking about Winnie and about Douglas Grainger and of how worried Davie had looked when she'd told him of last night's happenings. He and his father were extremely close and he had confided to Evelyn that he didn't know how long his father could go on the way he was doing without falling ill himself.

The name Whisky Jake had brought Evelyn out of her reverie. Many years after Nellie's dreadful experience he had come back into their lives again and had tried to rape Evelyn in a house in the Aulton. Jamie had half-killed him for that and had ended up serving a jail sentence for attempted murder, one that had been greatly reduced owing to Nellie telling her story to the newspapers after the trial.

Whisky Jake, on the other hand, had been given a

sentence of twelve years' penal servitude which had safely seen him out of the way but the scars of that terrible time had never healed for either Evelyn or Jamie.

'Not so much for what he did to me, though that was bad enough,' continued Evelyn, 'but Father never really picked up afterwards and now his only solace is in the bottle.'

'Ach! Father aye did drink too much!' said Nellie impatiently. 'He was aye a weak man where alcohol was concerned and never supported Mam the way he should.'

She shrugged her strong shoulders in an unsympathetic gesture which goaded her youngest sister to spring to her father's defence.

'You never did try to understand Father!' Evelyn accused hotly. 'You were aye ready to spring at his throat and worry away like a dog with a rat. You used to hurt him so much with your nagging and – worse than that – your silent, dour, Miss High and Mighty glances. I've seen him looking at you, wondering when the next attack was coming, feart to speak in case he said the wrong thing, feart not to speak in case you thought he was guilty o' something and trying his best to hide it!'

'Better that than condoning his drinking! You were aye far too soft wi' him, my girl!' Nellie spat back, her old talons showing in the heat of the moment. 'Too much alike for your own good, that was why he turned to you the way he did, he kent the rest o' us wouldna let him get away wi' the things that you did!'

It was Mary's turn to oil the troubled waters. 'For heaven's sake, you two, you haven't seen one another in years and after all the niceties are over with you behave like a couple of immature schoolgirls, raking up old grievances that ought to be over and done with. Besides,' she added firmly and briskly, her dark eyes dancing with life because just one evening with her sisters had invigorated

53

her again, 'Nellie, more than any of us, proved her love for Father when she told her story to the newspapers in order to try and save him. None of us knew what she had suffered all those years ago and she never tried to make herself appear any better in our eyes by blabbing it all out in an effort to gain our sympathy. I thought – we all thought – she was just being a bitch for the sake of it and oh, how I used to enjoy teasing and tormenting her about boys. I could never have stood it the way she did but she was Nellie and she was strong, even though she must have suffered hell inside herself. What it must have cost her to bare her soul to the world no one will ever know, but the day she did I seemed to see and understand my sister for the first time and by Dyod! I was proud o' her, and I was glad, glad, that she was my sister. She's still a bit o' a tartar, she wouldna be Nellie if she wasn't, but it would be a gey strange state o' affairs if she was to turn into a milk and water cratur, simpering and smiling and agreeing with everyone.'

She paused for breath, the generous swell of her silk-clad bosom was rising and falling rapidly; her smooth, plump cheeks were pink and glowing and in her enthusiasm she had lapsed into the north-east dialect so that, all in all, she was the Mary of old; uninhibited, natural, charming.

A silence followed her outburst. Nellie looked positively uncomfortable; Evelyn was crimson faced and utterly stunned with embarrassment; Grace had gone on calmly making toast but simply couldn't help smiling a little to herself at the variety of expressions on her sisters' faces and at the pleasure of hearing Mary lapse back into her native tongue.

Evelyn wriggled like a naughty child and opening her mouth said, 'Ach, I'm sorry, Nell, I shouldn't have spoken the way I did . . .' just as Nellie opened her mouth and uttered almost the self-same words.

They eyed one another and burst out laughing and when Gregor came in he found them having a wonderful time round the fire, all enmity gone as quickly as the heap of hot buttered toast had disappeared from the plates. The years had been kind to Doctor McGregor, at forty-seven his handsome face was not so much lined as stamped with the strength of character that had carried him through the war and from there to the difficult years of practising medicine in the Gorbals; the dusting of grey hair at his temples and sideburns made him look more distinguished than ageing, and his eyes still had that same warm smile in them that had attracted Mary to him in the beginning.

Although he mingled so much with the upper classes of the area he had never lost his forthright Glasgow manner nor the rich burr of the Glaswegian tongue; these, mixed with the quiet country reserve he had acquired from his years spent in Rothiedrum, together with his natural kindness and consideration, made for a charming and thoroughly likeable man who never wanted for friends no matter from which walk of life they came.

He had never taken for granted his new-found financial status and had wanted to share it with Mary's parents. His wife had whole-heartedly agreed with him in this but Maggie being Maggie wouldn't hear of it and Jamie, conditioned to Maggie's pride, wouldn't hear of it either.

Gregor had then suggested to Mary that her parents come and live with them – the house was big enough – but Mary was having none of that and had been horrified at the very idea. Her drunken father! Her outspoken mother! And all her friends meeting them and talking about her behind her back. She and Greg had had a blazing row over the affair and in the end he had to give in for the sake of peace though every so often the old argument arose and Mary knew he would never let go of it as long as her parents were alive and living as they were doing.

Much of the old, spontaneous affection had withered and died between Gregor and Mary but when he came in that night and she got up to throw herself at him and kiss him without restraint, a small glow touched his heart and he remembered with sudden poignancy that that was how it had been in the Rothiedrum days when money and position hadn't mattered to Mary as much as love and contentment.

'Hey,' he laughed and kissed her back and held her at arm's length to gaze for a moment into her eyes before he turned his attention on her sisters, especially Nellie, whom he hadn't seen for years.

'Nellie! You look marvellous!' he cried warmly, hugging her and kissing her on the cheek. 'You used to be a skinny, anxious, wee bird of a lass, but now there's a bit more meat on your bones. That big Highlander of yours isn't fattening you up for the Christmas table, is he?'

'And you're looking a fair treat yourself, Greg,' Nellie returned, her face pink with the pleasure of the moment. 'Your years sit well on your shoulders.'

'You make me sound like a well-preserved laboratory specimen,' he chuckled, 'but there's life in the old dog yet, Nellie quine, and who knows what damage I'll do before I'm through.' He glanced over her head to Col, sitting silent and smiling at all the excitement.

'Col! Col, lad!' He took the boy to his breast, then held him back to look at him. 'Bigger than me now, yet when I brought you into the world, let me see, sixteen – no – eighteen years ago, you were such a tiny wee tadpole of a thing I was frightened you would slither right out of my hands onto the floor.'

'Tadpole!' Col thought that was very funny and he

was still laughing when Betty answered her mistress's summons on the bell.

'Bring another pot of tea, Betty,' ordered Mary. 'Oh, and another loaf of bread, more butter, scones, and some pancakes –' She looked at Col. 'I'm sure my brother would enjoy toasting scones and pancakes at the fire.'

'Your – brother – ma'am?'

'Yes, you heard me, my brother.'

Betty fairly hurtled from the room to tell Cook and the kitchen-maid the latest tit-bit of news while Mary looked at Nellie as if hopeful of that lady's approval.

Instead Nellie said grimly, 'You have forgotten your manners, Mary, you were brought up to say "please" when you made a request, yet you speak to that poor bit quine as if she was a piece o' dung somebody brought in to your house on their boots.'

Mary stared at her, then throwing herself back in her chair she let out a squeal of laughter and gasped, 'By Dyod! I was right about you, Nellie lass, you've never changed and never will, and if it pleases you I'll bob and curtsy to the servants and say please and thank you for every blessed thing they do for me in future.'

'There's no need to go that far,' Nellie replied sourly and as Greg's deep laugh boomed in her ears she was glad, so glad, that for one night at least Mary had reverted to the Mary that everyone had once delighted in for her generosity of heart, soul and spirit.

CHAPTER 6

Before Nellie left for home she pressed some money into Evelyn's hand. 'Use this to buy a good piece o' meat for the Sunday table and some fruit for the bairns,' she instructed and when her sister opened her mouth to protest she put up her hand. 'Wheesht, I can manage, dinna worry.' Her wide mouth widened into a wry smile. 'I wouldna give it to you if it meant depriving my own family so take it and spend it wisely. If I gave it to Mam she would just shove it back in my face but I ken you have more sense in your head so no' another word.'

She was silent for a long moment, regarding her sister, a mist of tears in her amber green eyes. Putting out a hand she gently stroked Evelyn's head. 'Such bonny hair, you've grown into a beautiful woman, my girl, you could have had everything – any man you wanted . . . But that wilful heart o' yours was aye your ruler. Romance and love were everything to you and look where it's got you.'

'When all's said and done, romance and love were everything to you too, in the end, so you can't use these cryptic judgements on me any more, Nellie.'

Nellie sighed, she drew her hand away. 'Ay, but there's love and love, Evie quine, it should be a selfless thing, giving and sharing. Kenneth gives me more o' himself than any human being has ever given me and he's as faithful to me now as he was when we wed. Marriage has to be built on faith and trust, Evie, otherwise it can bring more pain than happiness and love itself can become more o' a burden than a pleasure.'

She sensed Evelyn's withdrawal from her, both mentally and spiritually, and she knew there was nothing more she could say. She had tried but it had been in vain, and she realized that Evelyn's love for Davie was a blind and destructive thing that might one day break her spirit with its selfish demands on a heart that had given more than enough already.

There was a clamour from the kitchen, everyone wanted to say goodbye; her moment with Evelyn was over and God knew when she would get a chance to talk to her again.

The children piled through, tearful, clinging, all of them wanting to prolong the moment of parting, only Alex was missing and she knew he would be alone somewhere nursing his hurt and his grievances. He had begged her to take him home with her to Croft Donald and she had knelt down to him and put her arms around him while she tried to explain why he must stay here with his own mother.

'She doesn't want me,' he had growled, 'she never wanted me, she would never miss me if I left. I would be a good help to you, Nellie, I like the country, I like Kenneth Mor, he could teach me how to become a farmer, big and strong like him.'

'You are big and strong, Alex, nobody needs to teach you how to be that, but there are other kinds o' strength besides big muscles and hard bodies. You have to be strong o' heart and mind too, Alex, and one day I hope you will understand what I mean. Anyway, you're much too clever a lad to fritter yourself away on a croft, one day you'll be more than any o' us could have dreamed, but in the meantime I want you to bide here and look after your brother and your sisters. I canna just whisk you away from your own family but I want you to remember I love you and hope you'll be a wee man for Nellie. Promise me that, Alex, promise me, if no' I'll go from here wi' a sore and heavy heart and I'll be no use to anybody.'

He had promised, his face white and tearstreaked, the words surly and grudging, then he had demanded, 'When will you be back? Will you be away for years and years again?'

'I dinna ken that, Alex, I have my own family to see to and nobody has the money these days to go traipsing about the countryside. But I'll try to come as often as I can though I make no promises. I was never one to say things I didna mean, as well you ken, so just you keep writing me these grand letters o' yours and let me know how you are getting on.'

With that he had to be content though he had kept well out of her way as the time of parting drew closer. The younger children, however, had no such inhibitions and they kissed and clung and wept and waved at the window till she and Col were lost to sight round a corner of the road.

'Bye bye, Wee Col,' lisped little James.

'Goodbye, big, sniffly, barking boy,' cried Meg.

'Bye bye, gentle gee-up cuddy,' whispered Rachel Grace quietly, tears in her eyes for the loss of such a happy and loving companion as Col had been.

He had been a great success with all the children. He had played games with them in The Room, he had laughed and sung with them and he had given them coalie backs and cuddie rides till he was pale and exhausted and had to be stopped in his tracks by Nellie or he would have driven himself till he dropped.

Maggie turned away from the window. 'Ach, it was so good to see our Nell again, eh, Jamie? She's no' one to mince her words nor ever will be but a lot o' the anger has gone out o' her and that steely strength o' hers is more a thing to be depended on now rather than feared.'

'Ay, it was good,' agreed Jamie, whose hands were shaking a little. It had taken most of his own strength, not to mention all of his willpower, to abstain from the bottle for the duration of his daughter's visit, for never

never could he have borne the accusing glances in those keen eyes of hers if by any indication he had shown that he had been drinking any more than she considered 'a decent dram'.

So he hadn't touched one drop, for he was only too aware of his own weaknesses and knew that for him to take 'a decent dram' meant following it up with many that were indecent in Nellie's eyes. The effect of such temperance was telling on him, however, and much as he had enjoyed seeing both Col and Nellie again, he was relieved that soon his life would revert back to normal, though he was immediately ashamed of himself for thinking such a thing.

When at last the first few drops of alcohol burned his throat he cried for Nellie and for all the things and people in his life that had become less to him than the anaesthetizing effect of hard liquor on his senses, but it was too late, much too late for him to turn back now. Everything that had been precious in his life had become dull in his mind. Once he had known raw longing for so many things: a long, long time ago he had cried and he had laughed and he had loved with a passion that had known no boundaries. The earth and the seas and the lands of Aberdeenshire had once mattered very much to him, they were in his blood, he had been born with the purling of hill burns in his ears, his first breath had been laden with the scents of clover, and wild thyme, purple heather, and rich, dark loamy earth and dung; his first impressions of the world around him had been of the Clydesdales and the soil falling away in waves from the blade of the plough and all around had been the great skies and the wide plains reaching to distant hills of blue and gold; he had watched the peesies birling and dipping above the green fields of his childhood and their haunting, lonely cries, together with the wind in the trees, had been the music that had beat and pulsed in his head all through the days and years of his growing.

Wherever he went these well-remembered sounds had followed him and he had never thought to forget their call and their pull on his emotions. Now it was all just a half-forgotten dream, diluted almost beyond the recall of his drink-sodden mind; only when he was sober did he recollect any of it and it was then he turned to the bottle to deaden his memories and rob his heart of its pain.

Dark closes, grey streets, noisy pubs, these were his sights and his sounds now and he had to smile and talk and laugh with the rest or there would be no life left for him any more – but through it all there was Maggie, a tower, a support, compassion and affection still there in her eyes for him when other women would have denied a man such as he existed.

And Evelyn, always his lass, forever his ally, God knew why, he was no more a father to her now than he was a husband to Maggie, better for him if he was dead and gone and they no longer had to look after a creature of so little worth.

He drank, he forgot, who were Maggie and Evelyn anyway? And why did the bairns come to him when he could hardly see them or talk to them for the numbness that saturated his being? He wasn't Jamie King Grant any more, that laughing, happy entity belonged to another dimension that had no claim on his life now.

Viciously, Alex kicked the toes of his shoes against the wall of the playground shed, the dark, bitter thoughts that had beset him since Nellie's departure festering away in his head till he felt that the world, and everyone in it, was against him.

She should have taken me, she should! he told himself in a familiar burst of self-pity. Mother doesn't want me, only Father and Grandpa like me and they're too drunk and too busy to be bothered half the time.

It was cold in the boys' playground, a bitter wind

whistled round the fine old red sandstone school and came skelping over the concreted play area, swirling up dust and paper debris that eddied into every available nook and cranny.

The headmaster's large ginger tom came into the shed to wind itself ingratiatingly round the little boy's legs. He smiled and picked it up, it purred and clung to his jersey. His mouth twisted and seizing the animal's tail he gave it an almighty tug. The cat snarled, more surprised than hurt, its claws raked the flesh of the boy's face and it was his turn to let out a startled cry.

The cat twisted out of his grasp and tried to make good its escape but the enraged Alex wasn't going to let it get away so easily. Seizing its tail once more he dragged the frightened creature back towards him and bending down he wound the long waving tail round and round like a rope till Ginger's screams of pain and terror filled the shed.

'Hey!' A skinny, undernourished looking boy with a runny nose and holes in his jersey came bounding in. 'That's Mr Patterson's cat! You're hurting it! I'm telling, I'm telling on you, Alex Grainger!'

Alex forgot the cat. He advanced towards Snotters Monroe, his fists bunched in front of him, and in minutes he had reduced the newcomer to a snivelling, cowering, sobbing bundle.

'Need any help?' Another boy entered the scene, a big boy with flame-red hair and a perpetually belligerent expression on his primitive features. This was 'Mad Monkey Morrison', otherwise John Ian Morrison, Alex's best friend and his confederate in crime.

'Na.' Alex slapped the dust from his clothes. 'Snotters knows when he's beaten, zat right, snottery nose?'

Robert Monroe didn't answer but remained crouched on the stone floor, his head between his knees, shaking it every so often as if to ascertain if it was still attached to his body – 'snotters and all' to quote John.

'Och, c'mon.' Alex grabbed the boy's arms and helped him scramble to his feet. 'At least you're no' a coward . . .'

'Na,' smirked John, 'cowards aren't daft enough to tackle old Marble Eyes when he's in a bad mood.'

'Take that back.' Alex's fists were up again, he was glaring at John from gathered dark brows.

'Keys!' John made the thumbs-up sign that stood for submission. A whistle sounded in the playground and the boys scrambled to take their places in the chalked-off white lines.

Mr Patterson was a tall, well-built man with piercing grey eyes and a head of thick iron-grey hair. He had handled boys all of his working life and he knew how to handle them well. 'Firmness and discipline' was his motto and there was never a day passed that he didn't put it to use.

A boy only needed to look into his magnetic eyes to immediately obey orders, knowing if he didn't a visit to the Head's room was inevitable and it was seldom a social call, either. Three of the best, a doubler if the offender merited it, all delivered from the thonged end of a leather tawse. If the belt was the end of the punishment, the pupils of Wheatfield School, be they boys or girls, felt they had got off lightly, but if it was followed up by a note home from the Head, another hiding could follow from the trouser belt or the shaving strop of an irate father who was all for firmness and discipline also.

All things considered it was in everybody's best interests to stay on the right side of 'Rat Pat' and it was a very orderly line of boys who filed out of the playground and up the steps into the assembly hall where Miss Jemima Mutten was playing a lively rendering of 'Step We Gaily' on the ancient school piano. Unkindly if appropriately known as The Lamb because her name lent itself so beautifully to her habit of dressing in clothes that would have suited a girl half her age, she was just about leaping off her stool with enthusiasm for the lively tune that was rippling out from under her stubby fingers. Her bobbed brown hair was almost hidden under the confines of her pink cloche hat whose colour matched that of her fashionably cut suit which boasted a big bunch of artificial daisies in the lapel.

Miss Mutten was a spinster lady of fifty-seven, as innocent of the wiles of the world as she was ignorant of them. She was aware that she was known as The Lamb behind her back but in her guileless way she imagined that the label referred to her placid nature, and she was most gratified that her pupils cared to view her in such a light.

The boys poured into the hall from one door, the girls came in from the opposite side. The two crocodiles marched upstairs, much reduced in volume since the infants had disappeared into their downstairs classrooms while the older children turned off into their respective rooms along the way. In the short progression from playground to classroom, Alex and John had hatched out a programme for another of the little diversions that had made them top dogs of the school. Down below, Miss Mutten played on, sublimely unaware that two of her pupils were about to add some more grey hairs to those she kept so well hidden under the crown of her blessed cloche hat.

After school the two boys put the first stages of their plan into operation. The word was passed around Wheatfield. There was to be a battle with the Catholic school in nearby Lewis Street. Fights between the two factions were anything but uncommon but this was to be a Big Battle and nobody was to say anything to anyone in authority or woe betide them. Everyone, with the exception of the girls whose place it was to stand on the sidelines and cheer, was to join in and they were to come armed with sticks and stones and anything else they could think of. The place was the piece of open waste ground at the top of Lewis Street, the time was the following Friday after school.

The word went around like wildfire. By dinnertime next day all the pupils of the Catholic school knew about the Big Battle and were greatly looking forward to it.

To prove their superiority, or to tempt providence, or perhaps a mixture of both, Alex and John made one of their little trips to the Catholic Church which was right next door to the Catholic school. There they tiptoed inside to sit in a pew and clasp their hands to their lips and bow their heads in homage to the beautiful statue of the Virgin Mary up there on the wall above the altar. They looked the vision of boyish piety with their hair shining in the chaste light from the stained glass windows, and when they went to kneel in front of the altar, the picture was complete if one didn't look too closely and catch the glances of challenge they were throwing at the angelic-looking Catholic boys who were lighting candles and saying prayers as they did so.

'We'll get ye, Marble Eyes,' mouthed one blue-eyed, baby-faced sprite.

'Ay,' whispered another, 'we'll make a real monkey out o' you, Morrison, ye deserve everything that's comin' tae ye.'

For answer the intruders stuck out their tongues and made their way to the entrance porch. There they helped themselves to some scraps from a pile on a table that were for sale, they took some coppers from a collection plate on the same table and on the way out they crossed themselves and sprinkled themselves with holy water from a font near the door.

It was an easy enough matter to sell the scraps to a group of small girls who were huddled together in a doorway exchanging their own scraps from prized collections in albums. Those that the boys proffered temptingly in front

66

of the girls' noses were Angels, the most coveted pictures of all, fat cherubs with little wings, leaning pensively on fluffy white clouds, eyes turned upwards as if they were viewing heaven and couldn't quite decide whether to fly there or get there by means of their own peacefully floating cloud. Both John and Alex had a whole sheet each of those valued Angels and, what's more, they were offering them for an extremely reasonable price.

Deals were struck, apron pockets willingly gave up sticky hot pennies and the boys hurried into a nearby close to count their ill-gotten gains and plan out what they could buy with them.

'Have ye been robbin' gas meters?' teased Mr Winkie, the newsagent at the bottom of Lewis Street.

'Naw, jist the Chapel,' said John daringly, but with a sweet smile that belied his words.

The newsagent raised his eyes as he put a copy each of *Playbox* and *Jingles* on the counter. The boys gathered up the comics, Mr Winkie turned to put the money into the till and quick as a flash John helped himself to a couple of liquorice sticks from a box at the side of the counter.

'Oh no you don't, Monkey.' The newsagent caught the boy's hand in a none too gentle grip. 'Get off wi' you or I'll tell yer faither you've been stealing again. I hear tell he's a dab hand wi' the belt.'

'You shouldn't have done that!' Alex said furiously as soon as they were out of the shop.

'Ha! Listen to Angel Lugs!' smirked John. 'I suppose the money and the scraps just fell into your hands in the Chapel . . .' his grin broadened, 'sort of like manna frae heaven.'

'That was different, nobody saw us! Old Willie Winkie in there's a gasbag and wouldn't think twice about telling on us.'

'Ach, I'm away hame for my tea.' John slouched off just as Meg came along swinging her school satchel.

'Where have you been?' demanded Alex. 'I saw you

leaving school at four and that was a half hour ago. Jinking the work again, eh, Gypsy? Leaving it all to Rachel as usual.'

'And what about you, Marble Eyes? You're late too, have you been stealing out the Chapel again? If no', where did you get the money for the comic? You'd better give me some or I'll tell Mother about the Big Battle you and that Mad Monkey are planning.'

'Ya! Tell all you like, Gypsy-Wets-Her-Knickers, there's a lot I can tell about you.'

Meg looked at him aghast. 'I don't do that, I don't, you're telling fibs.' Her face was red, her words ended in a half-sob.

'Ay, you do, I've seen you coming home, bursting to pee and holding it in, all the boys talk about the way you hold yourself, and I've seen you pretending to fall in a puddle so's you can say you got yourself wet that way when all the time I know you did it in your knickers.'

'I hate you, Alex Grainger,' she said, with tears of rage dancing in her eyes.

As she rushed away, he called after her, 'And I'll come home when I like, I'm a boy, remember!'

She wouldn't tell, of that he was sure. He began walking the short distance to Stashie Dunbar's carpenter's shop. He would go and see his father; after all, Nellie had said he had to be a man and men didn't go rushing home to do cissies' work when there were girls to do that sort of thing. He puffed out his chest. It had started out being a horrible day but it had turned out to be a good one after all. His eyes gleamed. A week to go to the Big Battle, he didn't know how he was going to contain himself till then.

CHAPTER 7

Stashie Dunbar's workshop was a poky little place, more a hut really, crammed into a row of half-derelict outbuildings behind a smiddy situated at the top of a cul-de-sac. It was a quiet place and rather pleasant, with trees and a field on one side and a row of douce, grey council houses with gardens on the opposite side. Since these were mostly tenanted by old people who were seldom to be seen outside their front door, 'The Sac' as it was known seemed far removed from the mainstream of Govan and Alex liked it here. Dunky the smith was a most amenable and interesting man and never seemed to mind the boys of the neighbourhood gathering in his premises to watch the horses being shod. Usually there were a few horses waiting in the field to have their shoes changed and when Alex wanted to be quiet he would come here and talk to the horses and perhaps feed them a carrot that he had pinched from somebody's garden, though it was easier to go to the plots of land on the outskirts of Govan when the owners were either absent or intent on doing something else that did not involve the vegetable patches.

Those who knew Alex would have been surprised at a side of his nature which demanded respite from activity and noise. He told nobody of his little trips to the 'horse fields', not even his father, though occasionally Davie found him wandering there alone and Alex would quickly make up some excuse about waiting for Davie to come out of Stashie's place.

Tonight, however, Alex had neither the time nor the inclination to speak to the horses, it was too dark and too cold for such pastimes, and he made straight for the carpenter's shop, feeling he had to justify his words to

Meg about not coming straight home and thinking it was better to while away the minutes in the men's company since he enjoyed the smell and the feel of wood almost as much as his father did.

The interior of the workshop was dim and dusty, cobwebs festooned every corner, piles of sawdust and bits of wood lay in heaps everywhere, a pair of moleskin trousers that had been dipped in tar were nailed over a chink in the roof cladding in an effort to keep out the rain; ancient jackets and overalls hung from rusty nails in the timber uprights; a few ramshackle cupboards were arranged along one wall, some sagging shelves contained an assortment of chipped and cracked Delft crockery together with one or two smoke-blackened pans; an assortment of packets held tea and sugar and the dubious remains of perishable food; potatoes, with shaws on them over two inches long, spilled from a split cardboard box reposing beside a grease-stained gas cooker. In the darkest and dustiest corner of all was an iron bedstead with a sagging mattress and an array of filthy blankets and coats half-hiding slipless pillows from which feathers were escaping and scattering themselves over the bedding.

In this redoubtable and unhealthy atmosphere Stashie both lived and worked, bothering no one and in turn expecting that no one should bother him. When, on one memorable occasion, a sanitary inspector had called to examine the place, Stashie had denied sleeping there, telling the man that the cooker had been installed so that he could cook himself a mid-day meal in order to keep his strength up and that the bed was there for him to rest in as required since his health had never been the same since he had been mustard-gassed in the war.

His story was so convincingly earnest the inspector had gone on his way thoroughly ashamed of his snooping, and as not one resident of The Sac could claim that

Stashie's way of life was an annoyance to them, he continued to live and work in a state of dereliction and squalor, coughing and spluttering his weary way through life.

For he hadn't lied to the inspector on one account. He *had* been gassed in the war, his gasping lungs were proof enough of that, he had also received a spray of shrapnel in one leg with the result that he had a peculiar limping gait, his good leg stepping eagerly out, the other, unable to keep up, getting there in a series of stiff little hops so that he appeared to half-run, half-drag himself about.

Added to all this was a distinctly humped back that had come about from continual racking and coughing and so bad had it become that he never seemed to be able to draw enough air into his labouring lungs and went about wheezing and rasping.

To the uninitiated it was a frightening experience to be in Stashie's company and to listen to the rattling of his lungs as he laboured to get air into them; some folk thought he was going to die there on the spot because he not only sounded like a dying man, he looked like one with his stunted body and his deathly white stoorie face peeping out behind his huge, black, handlebar moustaches.

But Davie was only too well used to him and his appearance. They had worked together in the carpenter's shop at Fairfield's Shipyards and when Davie, restless and dissatisfied with his lot, had declared his intention of looking for another job, Stashie had voiced his plan for setting up shop on his own. He had never married, women and children in his opinion being the worst burdens that any man could take upon himself.

At the time, Davie was in a mood to agree with this opinion, and when Stashie told him he had some money put by and knew of a good place to start a woodworking business, Davie jumped at the chance to go and work for him and had regretted the decision ever since. He soon discovered that the older man was close-fisted and mean, the two had continual arguments over the question of wages but by then it wasn't so easy for Davie to move to another job, they were few and far between these days, and so he stayed on and grew to despise the twisted little man with his filthy habits and his scrooge-like ways.

But one thing and one thing alone kept the pair from each other's throats, their mutual love of working with wood. Hardly a word would pass between them as they sawed and hammered, planed and polished, and the results were like jewels in the midst of ashes; the warm reds of mahogany; the golds of pine; the ochres and the ambers of walnut and maple; the exquisite inlays and ornate carvings that put the finishing touches to the work. The business had been slow to get off the ground but the word had spread till now there weren't enough hours in the day to get the things finished in time and very often Davie worked late, or went home for his tea before going back to The Sac to put in his extra hours.

Stashie did not welcome visitors into his domain, he only put up with Alex because the boy showed an interest in wood and displayed a natural aptitude for whittling little carvings out of any old scraps that Stashie could be coaxed to part with. When the boy put a wary face inside the door Stashie growled at him to 'shut the buggering draughts out', making Alex duck hastily inside to stand beside his father and watch as he added another layer of polish to a writing desk.

'What brings you here?' asked Davie, so engrossed in what he was doing he had barely looked up at his son's entry.

'Och, nothing much, I just wanted to walk you home from work and maybe help carry your tools for you.'

At that Stashie glanced up from a scratched and battered table whose surface was covered in cup marks, cigarette burns, and blobs of grease from the candles he burned to 'save gas' when he was eating his solitary meals.

'Don't you be taking any o' my tools hame wi' you, Grainger,' he warned. 'They see enough wear and tear in here wi'out you making use o' them as well. I know fine you make bits and bobs o' furniture and maybe sell them too for all I know or care, but any siller gained from the use o' my tools has more right in my pooch than it has in yours.'

Davie's jaw tightened. 'Don't foul your breeks, Stashie. When I came to slave for you I brought with me the tools I've been gathering all of my life so you mind your business and let me mind mine.'

'Can I make a cup o' tea?' Alex was holding a match to a gas ring as he spoke but Stashie stayed him with a hacked and callused hand.

'Naw, don't light the gas, son, there's tea in the pot there, just sit it on top o' the fire and it'll be steamin' in no time.'

The boy placed the battered pot on top of the smouldering cinders that Stashie had referred to as a fire. Under his breath Davie muttered, 'Bloody old miser,' which Stashie pretended not to hear.

Alex noticed that he was struggling with an untidy straggle of sums that he had written down on a grubby jotter and, going over, the boy stood at his elbow and watched.

'Here!' Stashie looked up. 'You're a nosy wee bugger! Go and pour the tea and make yourself useful.'

'Are these your books?' Alex ignored the order. 'Can I do them? I like sums.'

The carpenter was astonished, he pulled deeply on the cigarette that was never far from his lips and was immediately seized with a violent fit of coughing that rendered him speechless and breathless for several minutes. When he recovered it was to the sight of the boy poring over the jotter, his pencil thoughtfully held to his cheek, his tongue sticking out in concentration. He had rewritten the sums, neatly and cleanly, and now he put pencil to paper and began writing rapidly. Stashie was too fascinated to interfere further. Ten minutes later the boy threw down the pencil and gave the man a triumphant grin.

'There, finished, have you got any more?'

'How do I know they're right?' asked Stashie suspiciously.

'They're correct, they're easy, I was doing worse in the infants' class when the others were still learning to write numbers. I'll do your books for you if you like, they're in an awful mess. I could make them so's a baby could understand them. A shilling a week, half an hour every night after school.'

'Sixpence,' haggled Stashie craftily.

'A shilling – and cheap at the price. You'll save yourself a lot o' time that could go into your work. Take it or leave it, I'm away home for my tea.'

'Here, come back, lad,' cried Stashie hastily, 'you've got your bob, though you'd better earn it or never show your nose inside this door again.'

'It's a deal,' Alex said calmly, his strange eyes glinting in the lamplight. Turning to his father he said laconically, 'C'mon, Father, another minute and you'll be doing overtime, eh, Stashie?' With a cheeky wink at the carpenter he made good his escape with Davie hot on his heels.

Outside in The Sac father and son looked at one another and erupted into peals of laughter. When he had recovered Davie slapped the boy on the back and gasped, 'I never thought I'd see the day, old Stashie lost for words and so shocked he forgot even to cough. Good on you, Alex, that was the best bloody piece of financial engineering I've ever seen in my life. But I didn't know you were good at sums, according to your reports you're lazy in your school work forbye being a disruptive influence in

74

class; there was never anything about you being a mathematical genius.'

'Oh no, Father, I'm no' a genius – yet,' giggled the boy, 'I *am* good at sums but . . .'

'You just won't apply yourself in the classroom, eh, lad? Well, never mind, I was a bit like that myself at school though that doesn't mean you have to be the same. I didn't have the brains for sums, only the hands for creating things. It would be nice if there was one in the family with a head on their shoulders.'

'There's nothing wrong with working in wood,' said Alex stoutly.

'There is if you don't get paid for it,' Davie returned meaningfully and determined to himself that he would ask Stashie for a rise the very next day.

Over the next few days Alex was in a suppressed state of excitement. The day of the Big Battle was coming nearer and each night he came home, bubbling over with impudence and impatience. He fought with Meg and publicly disgraced her by referring to her as Gypsy-Wets-Her-Knickers; he made his grannie furious by getting another hole in the jersey she had darned only the previous evening; he ran full tilt into Rachel on the stairs, making her drop the ash can she had been carrying down to the midden for emptying; he refused to help her clear up the mess, saying he didn't do cissies' work; when he found a half-full bottle of whisky hidden behind the cistern in the stairhead cludgie he brought it upstairs and pretended a great show of innocence by holding it up and wondering whose it was.

He behaved out of character, and was talkative about his first 'job', looking meaningfully at Jamie in a silent challenge that said all too plainly if he could get paid work at his age there wasn't any reason for Jamie not to get work at his, however menial and low paid.

When his mother took him aside and gave him a good shaking he merely smiled into her crimson face and asked her if she thought the bottle he had found belonged to his grandfather.

She and Davie argued over him, they always had, but lately the rows were getting more heated. Davie had always been tolerant with his eldest son and had never lifted a finger to him. Torn jerseys, ripped pants, gashed knees, they were all part of a boy's growing up, he told her, he had done the same things himself and he wasn't going to hit the boy for behaving true to nature.

'You wouldn't have him a jessie, would you now?' he would say and leave the subject at that.

But this time even Davie had to admit that the boy was getting out of hand and father and son disappeared into The Room for a full hour. When Alex finally emerged he was flushed but in no way downcast and in bed that night Evelyn asked Davie what had taken place.

'We had a man to man talk, that's all.' Davie sounded tired of the subject. 'He has a head on his shoulders, that lad, it was a treat to talk to him and listen to his views on various matters. What if he isn't brilliant at school? He'll make up for it later, he's taking it all in even though it seems he isn't.'

'And that was all?'

'Ay, that was all. What did you expect? For me to take him over my knee and give him a good thrashing? That sort o' treatment never did anyone any good.'

'It did you no harm. You've told me how your own father took the belt to you when you were young.'

'Maybe I needed it. Alex doesn't, he and I get on well together and I'm no' going to jeopardize that for anyone.'

'So you'll allow him to go on behaving like a devil! Tormenting Father, being cheeky to Mam, behaving horribly to his sisters and brother. He treats Meg no better

76

than a dog and if you dinna ken that then you must go around deaf and blind half the time.'

'Ach, she deserves it, she's a lazy whittrock and it's time you took her in hand. I'll never chastise the lassies in the family. As for the lad behaving badly towards your parents, maybe he feels shut in by them, surrounded by grown-ups telling him to do this, that and the other. They'll have to learn this is our house and our bairns and if they don't like it they know what they can do.'

'Oh, we're getting round to that again, are we? You just dinna ken how to give up, do you, Davie?'

'And you never learn when to keep a hold o' that sharp tongue o' yours. You're beginning to sound like your sister, Nellie.'

'It might be better if I started behaving like her as well. You've got more respect for Nellie than you have for me – you even show more consideration and respect to Alex than you do to me.'

'That lad will go far.' He spoke as if he hadn't heard a word she had said and his voice was filled with admiration as the scene in Stashie's workshop came into his head again.

'Ay, but in what direction?' Evelyn said bitterly, but knew it was useless to argue further. When Davie made up his mind about a thing there was nothing that she could say or do to make him change it.

CHAPTER 8

Fanny was being difficult. She had taken to her bed with a bad dose of influenza and she would neither take the medicine that the doctor had left for her nor would she sup the bowl of beef tea that Evelyn had made. She was good at making such invalid fare. At King's Croft, whenever any of the family were off their food, Maggie had hastened to concoct a jug of tasty thin broth made from the best meat juices available. The very smell alone was enough to tempt the most delicate appetite and as they grew up the Grant girls learned the recipe from their mother and many's the time each and every one of them had had reason to be thankful for the knowledge.

Fanny had specifically requested the beverage, her voice holding an even more querulous note than usual as she lay amongst her pillows, wizened, yellow, her stained molars showing as she wheezed and grumbled, her grey hair spread over a lilac shawl in straggly spikes.

'I don't feel like anything solid, Evie,' she intoned with a pitiful little sigh, 'so be a good lass and make me something that will go down easy. Lizzie is no use at that sort o' thing. She's always been as strong as a horse and doesn't understand what it's like to be of a delicate disposition.

'The last time I was ill she brought through a great platter o' mince and tatties that would have choked a cuddy and there she stood, proud as punch and right pleased with herself, expecting me to eat it in the state I was in. My stomach it was that time, a bilious attack, the very smell o' food was enough to put me off, but Lizzie . . .'

'I'll see what I can do, Miss Gillespie,' Evelyn hastened to assure, knowing that the old lady would regale her for hours with Lizzie's so-called faults if she was allowed. Fanny liked everyone to know that 'the other member of the household' was no more to her than a paid companion and 'very fortunate to have gained herself such a respectable position'. In truth she depended very heavily on Lizzie for everything pertaining to her own well-being and that of the running of the house, and though she would never admit it to Lizzie herself she liked to boast proudly to her friends: 'the woman is worth her weight in gold' and, 'treasures like that are rare indeed this side o' heaven'.

This morning, however, her 'treasure' was wearing a thunderous expression on her countenance and when, for the umpteenth time, Fanny thumped her stick on the floor and at the same time rang the little silver bell she kept at her bedside, Lizzie exploded, 'There she goes again, Evie! As regular as a dose o' the skitters! I don't know how I put up wi' her, that I don't. If I hadny lost my Albert in the war I wouldny even have known that a wee fart like Fanny Jean Gillespie existed. Her and her airs and graces, her fads and her fancies! It's too much, Evie, too much for a sensitive body like myself to put up with.'

'The war?' Evelyn questioned in soothing tones, wondering how on earth anyone of Lizzie's age could possibly have had a man young enough to fight for his country.

'Ay.' Lizzie took out a large, manly handkerchief and dabbed at her eyes. 'Och, no' the last war, you understand, the Boer War, it was. We were engaged just before he went off and – oh, my – we were that in love and used to talk about what it would be like when we were wed and of all the bairns we would have. We both wanted at least four and were like a couple o' bairns ourselves we were that young and in love. And then he went away from me and I never saw him again and now look at me, no more than a skivvy to that – that spoiled wee witch ben the room there.'

Evelyn looked at the mourning brooch pinned to the neck of Lizzie's blouse. So that was it. Once upon a time this large cheery-faced woman with her unattractive figure and her dinner plates of hair had known a great love in her life and now she pined for her man and would likely do so till the end of her days ... How sad, how terribly sad and lonely she must often feel, yet no one looking at her now could possibly guess at such a thing or think to give her the sympathy she deserved ...

Lizzie saw her look and her hands went up to the ornament at her throat. 'Och, no, Evie,' she explained gently. 'This isny just for Albert, no, this bonny brooch is for them all, all three o' them, I know they won't mind sharing in it because, after all, they each had a share o' me when they were alive and it's only right I should remember them all together.'

'All – three o' them?'

'Ay, Albert, Edward and George.'

A small suspicion entered Evelyn's mind. 'But these are . . .'

'Ay.' Lizzie had forgotten Fanny, she was beaming from ear to ear. 'A Prince Consort and two monarchs, one after the other, I aye thought it gey strange that I should know men wi' names like that, in that order; first Albert, then Edward, then George. It was just a great pity they all went and died on me without me ever getting the wedding ring o' one on my finger.'

Wildly Evelyn wondered just how much of the story was true but she had no time to question Lizzie further since Fanny was not only thumping her stick and ringing her bell but was also shouting at the top of her high-pitched, demanding voice.

By dinnertime both Evelyn and Lizzie were exhausted. Fanny had kept them running at her beck and call the entire morning and then she had fallen out of bed and had demanded to see the doctor again. He had just departed, having given her a sedative to calm her down. His instructions to Lizzie had been sharp and succinct: Miss Gillespie was resting, and as he had a dozen other patients to see who were suffering from the same complaint as herself, he wasn't to be called again unless it was an emergency.

'Just see that she doesn't get out of bed,' was his parting shot and Lizzie, in a state near to tears, gazed into her plate of steaming broth and sighed, 'I don't know how I'm going to manage her, that I don't. She'll sleep all day and expect me to see to her every whim all through the night, and I'm that wabbit as it is I could fair be doing wi' just dropping into my own bed this very minute.'

'Och, Evie,' she put a large, red hand on the girl's arm, 'would you be a good lass and consider staying the night? I know this is Friday and you have the weekend off but this is an emergency – no' hers but mine.'

Evelyn opened her mouth to protest, the very idea of spending even one night in the gloomy old house filling her with dread, but a look at the woman's strained, woebegone face changed her mind.

'All right, Lizzie, but just one night, mind. I'll have to run home and ask my mother if she'll look after the children and God knows what my husband will say when he finds out, but as it's the first time this has happened I'm sure he won't mind.'

She knew only too well that he *would* mind but Lizzie was so overwhelmed with gratitude she couldn't very well go back on her word and so she went home and told Maggie what had happened.

Maggie sighed, she had been looking forward to getting her feet up and listening to her favourite radio programmes that evening. There would be no hope of that with four children to feed and get ready for bed but she had met Lizzie and liked her very much. She reminded her of Big Mattie who had lived in the Aulton with

81

Grandmother, both of them belonging to Jamie's travelling days and therefore great friends of the family.

'But see and be back the morn's morn,' Maggie told her daughter. 'I have things to see to myself this Saturday, I promised Mrs Boyle I'd do the close for her as she's away seeing her sister this weekend.'

'I'll be back in time, Mam,' Evelyn said, and hurried away.

Winnie Grainger was at her window, singing her tragic little song. At sight of Evelyn she held out her hand and cried, 'Have you seen Danny? Have you seen my boy? Tell him I'm waiting — tell him.'

'I'll tell him,' shouted back Evelyn, and wondered why an impression came to her of a pale ghost sitting in a window aperture, watching for another ghost who couldn't reach through the invisible, impenetrable barrier of living death.

It was like a scene from an olden day battlefield. The troops had gathered, purposefully, bravely, some eagerly, others afraid but determined not to show that they were anything but delighted to join in the coming fray. Their ages ranged from five to twelve years old, the big ones at the front, the little ones at the back, more a reserve team than anything but there just the same in case the 'real' soldiers should falter and fall when the charge came.

The two factions were arranged on either side of the big piece of waste ground at the top of the backcourts which joined Lewis Street and Younger Park Street; a row of brick-built middens and wash-houses were like the walls of a fortress in the young imaginative minds of the children who had gathered on The Waste outside the safety of 'The Walls'.

The residents at the top end of Lewis Street were used to the fights that took place between the Protestant school and the Catholic school, both of which were near enough to The Waste to incite fresh ire in the respective minds of 'soldiers' who were beginning to quake a little in their boots at the thought of what was in front of them, not so much the kind of scars that might be inflicted during the Big Battle, but the more certain bruises that a trouser belt or a shaving strop could apply when another batch of torn breeks and holey jerseys came marching not-so-bravely home.

The lines were in place; an odd, rather eerie silence fell over The Waste. The onlookers, who had stayed back after school, glanced at one another, and, since they were composed mainly of girls who viewed the battles of 'silly boys' with contempt, began to giggle and comment on Billy Boyle's dirty knees, Harry MacMaster's filthy socks.

A freezing wind skelped across The Waste, a drizzle of sooty rain began to fall, the dark tenements loomed up on either side. 'Wullie, yer tea's nearly ready' came from one open window on the other side of The Wall.

'Ay, in a minute, Jean,' came the reply. 'I'm jist waitin' to see what they weans are hatchin' oot. By the look o' it, this is a big one.'

'Ach, yer worse than a wean yersel',' came Jean's tired answer. 'See and no' be long, the chips will spile – and there's an awful draught frae that window, it's causing the fire tae smeek.'

The battle cries went up as the lines charged towards one another.

'Proddy Dogs!'

'Catholic Pigs!'

The onlookers began to shout and to cheer on their favourite side.

'Proddies! Proddies! Proddies!'

'Catholics! Catholics! Catholics!'

In some cases it was individual 'soldiers' who were personally favoured by the watching mob and the names went up, over and over.

'Billy, Billy, Billy!'

'Jimmy, Jimmy, Jimmy!'

The lines had met, the Big Battle had begun, good-natured brawling, shouting, pushing. Somebody produced a stick, then another; pocketsful of ammunition in the shape of small stones began whizzing about. There were cries and grunts as the weapons found their mark. Cuts, bruises, grazes appeared thick and fast. The air of camaraderie was dissipating rapidly, the Big Battle was turning serious and one or two of the smaller children began to cry.

The watchers on the sidelines began to grow excited.

'Get into him, John!'

'Batter the life out o' him, Ian!'

'Mad Monkey's a cissy! Mad Monkey's a cissy!'

'Marble Eyes! Marble Eyes! Steals Catholic pennies and buys mince pies!'

The fighters were becoming more inflamed with battle fire. Small stones were dismissed as being useless, bigger 'weapons' in the shape of bits of rubble were pounced upon eagerly.

Blood started to run. The watching crowd was silent for a few moments, then somebody began to chant, 'Fight, fight, fight! Kill, kill, kill!'

In seconds the cry swept through the crowd like a tide. It was an oddly primitive sound. The veneer of civilized behaviour fell away like a veil. Even those children who had dismissed the whole thing as being 'daft' were caught up in the hysteria.

'Fight! Fight! Fight!'

'Kill! Kill! Kill!'

The chant went on and on, monotonous, dangerous. Some of the smaller boys were losing their footing and they were falling, under boots that stamped and scuffled and paid no heed to human obstacles.

Windows beyond The Wall were being thrown open, heads were popping out, necks craning to get a better look at the battle scene.

'Here! That's no ordinary fight!' Wullie cried in consternation. 'Some o' they weans are getting hurt. Jean, come here and look at this!'

'Send for the polis! These weans are killing one another! The last time I saw anything like that was in the war!'

'Send for the polis!'

'Send for the polis!'

Alex was enjoying himself. This was some battle, not like these other silly little fights with everyone shouting 'keys' or 'chapsies' when the going got too rough and the scrimmage ended with everyone shaking hands in light-hearted acknowledgement that neither side had won.

A big tackity boot caught him in the shin, he went down, a dozen pairs of boots trampled him into the mud and the dirt of The Waste. A heartily wielded stick, studded with projecting nails, missed its mark and crashed down on the back of his head. For a few seconds he was aware of the cold rain on his face before everything went black and the Big Battle was over for him.

CHAPTER 9

The door went just as Evelyn was sitting down to her tea. It had been a quieter afternoon than she or Lizzie had anticipated. Fanny had slept her way through it, the blissful silence in the house had brought back the smile to Lizzie's face and she had even been moved to sing 'Rock of Ages' as she set about making a cheese omelette for the meal.

Despite Fanny's grumbles, the 'other member of the household' was an excellent cook, the savoury smell of her omelette seeped into every corner of the old house, and when she and Evelyn finally sat down at a table set with buttery toast that had been made at the fire, and home-made scones still hot from the oven, they smiled at one another in pleasurable anticipation of the coming treat.

Lizzie brought the plates to the table and onto them she turned out the omelette, piping hot, little rivulets of melted cheese running over the edges to settle in golden pools on the fingers of toast that were arranged on the plates.

'I never made any for her ladyship,' Lizzie said with a touch of defiance. 'Wi' her being in the delicate state she's in she'll no be feeling in the mood for anything solid. A bowl o' beef tea will suffice her when she wakes up – if she ever does,' she ended with a fat chuckle.

Evelyn pushed back her hair from her fire-flushed face and picked up her knife and fork. 'Lizzie,' she said softly, 'you're no' going to hear a word out o' me for at least ten minutes. Food like this deserves complete and utter concentration and I'm going to give it my best.'

Lizzie poured piping hot tea into the cups, Evelyn

raised her fork to her mouth — and at that crucial moment the doorbell rang and kept on ringing.

'Mercy!' Lizzie held one thick coil of hair away from one large lug. 'Was that the bell, Evie? Or has that damt scunner ben the room started her tricks again?'

The 'damt scunner ben the room' had indeed started her tricks again. The ringing of the doorbell had roused her from a deep slumber. She was stiff and sore, her head ached, her mouth was like tinder, all she wanted was a cup of tea, and — what was that delicious smell that pervaded the house? Lizzie had made one of her wonderful cheese omelettes and the spiteful besom hadn't even bothered to waken her to see if she wanted any.

Seizing both her bell and her stick she alternately rang one and thumped the other: thump! brr! thump, thump! clang, rringg! thump, clump!

The house, which had a bare five minutes ago been drowsing and dreaming in peaceful contentment, was all at once a bedlam of noise.

Throwing down her fork Evelyn rushed to answer the door while Lizzie, marking a much more sedate path, went to see what her ladyship wanted this time.

'I'm hungry.' Fanny Jean wasted no time on preliminaries. 'I'll have tea and toast and some o' that omelette you thought you would sneakily eat behind my back. A fine way to treat an invalid, I must say.'

Lizzie said nothing, instead she drew herself up to her full height and pushed out her considerable bosom, an action which could intimidate the most persistent door-to-door salesman or bring silence to the cheekiest grocer boy.

But Fanny was of sterner stuff, ill or no, she was in full possession of her own intimidating faculties and without so much as the flicker of an eyelid she repeated her order, her voice rising a little with barely suppressed impatience.

'I never made you any omelette.' Lizzie sounded triumphant. 'A bowl o' broth and a bit bread will lie better on that queasy stomach o' yours – and you'll get it when Evie and I have had our own tea . . .'

Just then Evelyn came into the room. All the colour had drained from her face, leaving it so white Lizzie was moved to cry out, 'Lassie, lassie, what's wrong? You look as though you've seen a ghost.'

'No ghost, Lizzie, a policeman. My son Alex has had an accident and I've to go to the hospital at once.'

Both Fanny and Lizzie were immediately filled with concern, the latter rushing to fetch the girl's coat from the hallstand and help her into it while the other, her voice suddenly firm and decisive, offered all sorts of comforting words and sensible advice.

The door closed, Lizzie looked at Fanny, the old witch would get her omelette after all and it would be no fault of hers if it choked her on the way down.

Evelyn hurried away, her mind filled with every sort of fear for this eldest child of hers who not only seemed to court trouble wherever he went but who seemed to revel in it and to positively gloat over the varying emotions he could rouse in the people around him.

She was used to the rough and tumble of his life but never before had he injured himself badly enough to warrant being taken to hospital. Her heart beat so swiftly in her throat as the policeman escorted her to the sprawling grey building some streets away that she could hardly breathe by the time she got there and was ordered by a stern-faced nurse to compose herself or she would be 'no use to anybody'.

Davie was at his son's bedside. He reached out to take her hand and squeeze it tightly and she was glad of his strength in those first moments of dreadful uncertainty.

Alex lay very still. His head was swathed in bandages, his deathly pale face was a mass of lacerations and bruises. His hands lay outside the bedclothes, still and peaceful looking; he looked small and defenceless and very, very innocent and if Evelyn hadn't been so upset she would have laughed at such a description being applied to a child who often seemed to belong more to the Devil than to God.

Oh, how could she? How could such a thing have entered her head at such a time? She shivered and held on to Davie's hand and everything she wanted to know came tumbling out so fast he smiled a little and told her to 'steady on', it wasn't as bad as it looked.

'A fractured skull, concussion, enough cuts and bruises to satisfy the warrior in him for a lifetime. But the doctor said he'll be fine, he's a strong, healthy lad.'

'But how did he do it? It can't have happened in school, surely?'

'One of these so-called battles between the two schools. I don't know everything but it turned nasty and developed into a sort of riot. Three other boys were brought in along with Alex, all of them younger than him.'

For the first time Evelyn became aware of her surroundings and sure enough, several parents that she knew by sight were standing by bedsides on the other side of the ward.

'I wonder how it started?' she said quietly, refraining to add the next thing that sprung to her mind, namely, who had started it. Something had been brewing this past week, Alex had been keyed up and excited . . .

The boy groaned and opened his eyes. 'Father.' His hand reached out, Davie took it and held it firmly.

All the old uncertainties boiled in Evelyn's breast, she felt sick and ill with sadness and hurt. He would never stop rejecting her, even now, when he was badly injured and afraid; it wasn't his mother he turned to but his father, always his father . . .

'Mother.' Her name came out in a long, drawn-out sigh, his other hand came out to her and gently she took it, feeling as she did so a sense of wonder at the feel of that small hand in hers. Sometimes she put more years on his shoulders than was realistic, he often behaved so strangely, he said things that were more suited to a much older child, his eyes watched you and you felt that you were being scrutinized by a being that had known other worlds beyond, or before, this one . . . And now this young and trusting hand, normal, soft, a little boy of eight years old seeking to hold on to something familiar in an alien, frightening place.

He fell asleep, still holding on to their hands.

A nurse came and told them it was time to go. 'He'll be fine,' she assured them with a smile she must surely keep in reserve for all the anxious parents who passed through her life. 'He isn't in any danger so you can sleep easy tonight. Come back and see him in the morning if you like.'

She had a nice face and a comely figure. Evelyn saw the look Davie threw at her and she went on ahead: more hurt, more uncertainty. God, was there no end to it? Davie and Alex. Alex and Davie, if it wasn't one it was the other, devouring her strength, sapping her emotions.

Once outside Davie took her arm. 'You were right about Alex, I *have* been too soft with him and this is the result. I'll be firmer in future, I promise you that, sweetheart.'

He was being his nicest, his voice held that velvety, intimate nuance that had once turned her knees to jelly and had dissolved all her resistance. His fingers brushed her breast, he pulled her in closer. 'Come home now, Evie, it's been a long day for us both. After we've eaten we'll go straight to bed. I need you tonight, darling, it's been a long time since I held you in my arms and felt that silken body o' yours next to mine.'

'No, Davie.' She pulled herself away from him with an effort — it was always difficult to resist him when he spoke like this and looked at her with eyes that were black pools of desire in his handsome, intense face. 'I told Lizzie I would spend the night and I can't let her down. She needs me more than you do, you can have me any time, but only when it suits you.'

'This is Nellie's doing!' His mood changed with startling suddenness. 'Ever since her visit you've been acting as if I was something the cat brought in.' His fingers dug into her flesh. 'I won't have it, Evie, you're my wife and I have a right to know what's making you behave as if you've nettles in your breeks!'

'It isna Nellie,' she said, and left him standing there, under the lamplight, his eyes boring into her retreating back, she could feel them on her, compelling her to turn back and submit to him as she had always done in the past.

But this time she walked on, resolutely, her head held high on her proud young shoulders, and she didn't look back once but made her determined way back to Drumoyne and Lizzie who was so glad to see her she hastened to put on the kettle and switch eggs in a bowl in order that Evelyn should get her sadly belated tea.

Alex spent Christmas in hospital. He beguiled the nurses, mistrusted and disliked the doctors, and terrorized the other children with gory tales of his misdeeds and adventures. He was so proud of his bandaged head that, when the day came to have the dressings removed, he armed himself with a syringe he had coaxed one of the other young patients to remove from the sterilizer, and brandishing it like a sword he threatened to jab anyone who came within three feet of him.

The same thing happened when the nurses approached to remove three stitches from a neck wound, this time it wasn't pride that prompted his action but stark fear of the pain he knew might be involved in such an operation. Instead of a syringe he was forced to use a menial bedpan as a potential weapon, simply because the lad who had been daring enough to raid the sterilizer had gone home and no one else could be bullied into providing him with anything more sophisticated.

When his fear of the nurses and their little surgical trolley became apparent to the rest of the ward, the chant went up, 'Cowardy, cowardy custard, eats his Mammy's mustard!'

No one said these things to Alex David Grainger and got away with it. An hour later the stitches were removed and as soon as authority turned its back he was up and out of bed and beasting in to his antagonists with all the might of his new-found strength.

But then he fainted and had to be carried back to bed and the nurses sighed and wished that Christmas might be as still and holy as the carol singers were proclaiming though there was scant hope of that with the likes of young Grainger in their keeping.

CHAPTER 10

Though no one said as much, Christmas at 198 was a much more peaceful affair than usual that year. Maggie had been saving baking ingredients for months and she stirred fruit dumplings and rolled pastry till her arms ached and the sweat broke on her brow from the fire's heat.

She had acquired certain little habits since coming to Govan, some would have called them indulgences, others might go as far as to say they were addictions, but whatever they were Maggie felt she needed them in an existence that was in the main humdrum and predictable.

One of her weaknesses was 'black strippit balls', a confection which could be had easily enough from Miss Cunningham's shop at the corner. Rachel liked nothing better than to run errands for her grannie, her reward being two of the round, striped, mint balls which she was allowed to pick straight out of the crumpled paper bag Grannie held out to her. Some of the sweets were smaller and not so rounded as the others but Grannie always made sure she got the biggest and plumpest of all and the little girl knew that they had been put at the top especially for her. But she wasn't allowed to see what was in those little packets that Grannie got from Dark Dan who owned the cramped and dingy little tobacconist's in further-away Skerries Road. Dark Dan looked just as his name implied, he was stooped, and mean, and old, his wrinkled skin was black with age and age-old dirt. His claw-like hands with veins on them like purple rope would streak out and scrabble the money from the counter and Rachel always made sure her own hands were well out of the way of those frightening talons.

Dark Dan always wore a dirty red nightcap on his bald head. It had a bedraggled tassel hanging from a few precarious threads on the pointed end and Rachel knew that one day the tassel would fall onto the counter just as she was putting the money there for 'Grannie's sherbet'.

Dark Dan snuffled and sneezed just like an ancient dog, he wasn't too fussy about using a hanky either but simply drew one of his greasy sleeves across his nose, whereupon he would sniff and snort, crinkling up first one nostril and then another. After that, with watering eyes, he would say to no one in particular, 'That was good, ay, ye canny beat a good snort and a sneeze anyday, good, good, ay, good.'

Rachel wondered about those sniffles and snorts because Grannie sometimes had them too and though her eyes watered a bit like Dark Dan's she never looked any the worse for it and laughed when Rachel asked if she had a cold.

It was strange too that she wasn't allowed to have even a 'wee taste' of Grannie's sherbet but she always got a penny instead and then she could run down to 'the Tallies' at the corner of Younger Park Street and buy whatever she wanted.

So Maggie 'snorted' her snuff and thoroughly enjoyed an extra two ounces that Yuletide with no Alex to observe her every move and ask her rude questions concerning her habit of locking herself in the scullery every so often, this being about the only private place in the house where one could have a wash in peace and indulge in a bit of snuff-sniffing.

Jamie too was more relaxed these days, instead of hiding his bottle he drank from it openly and somehow managed to do so in moderation. He had a night out with Big Aggie's Man and Joe Liddel from 196 and they came back happy but reasonably sober to gather round the fire to sing a few songs while Jamie played his fiddle.

Meg openly declared that she hoped her big brother

would never come home again and she did her share of the chores with only scant complaint. The brasses on the front door gleamed, the elegant companion set that sat on the red and green tiled hearth in The Room had never known such loving care; she washed and pipe-clayed the front step; the week before Christmas she helped Rachel to blacklead the range. Both little girls were happed in long peenies that reached to their ankles and their hair was tied back with bits of narrow ribbon. Sleeves rolled to elbows they scoured away the sooty dirt and rubbed the steel rims of the grate with emery paper, then the whole range was polished till it looked and felt like black-grey satin. After the cleaning of the house the cleaning of the people came next. Friday night was bath night for the whole family, the preparation for which began on Thursday. The fire was cleared of cinders, large ones being kept aside, the rest riddled into the ash can for the midden. Cinders, sticks and coal were layered into the grate and the fire started up again till it was red hot and glowing, then it was banked up with dross and left to simmer away all night and into the next day to heat an assortment of kettles and pots.

On Friday night the paraffin and the bone-combs came out, hair was unpleated and searched for head-lice and nits and one after the other the children went into the zinc tub in front of the fire. Meg usually elbowed her way in first in order to escape the scum and rinsings off the rest, but this time she allowed baby James to wallow in the steaming clean water and was altogether very motherly towards him, soaping his curly brown hair and being very careful not to get suds in his eyes, sponging his little body with tender concern while he joyfully played with a yellow rubber duck Jamie had bought off a door hawker for tuppence.

'Our Meg is after something,' Maggie told Evelyn. 'She brushed my hair twice last night and ran to Dark Dan's for Jamie's tobacco without having to be told more than once.'

Meg, being Meg, *did* want something. During the days preceding Christmas she spoke long and loudly about Maisie Thomson's beautiful hair ribbons; she harped on about Morag McFarlane's wonderful doll with its china face and jointed arms and legs till the entire family were driven to distraction and Rachel actually asked to go to bed early one night because she said she couldn't get to sleep for her sister talking about dolls.

Not that Meg was particularly fond of dolls, to her they were too pertinent to the domestic scene to be truly desirable but they were possessions and Meg had always craved the things that somebody else possessed.

On Christmas morning she got her ribbons but had to make do with a gentle-looking little rag doll that Evelyn had made from scraps of material. The first disappointment over with she positively gloated over her rag doll; Morag McFarlane had nothing like it, *her* mother couldn't make anything and just wait till Morag saw a doll like Raggie Aggie that nobody else in the world owned except Margaret Mary Grainger.

Everyone got some little thing they wanted that Christmas; Rachel received a brand new pencil case, it smelled of new wood and had a sliding lid with her initials carved on it. Her father told her it was from Santa Claus but in the note she had sent up the lum she hadn't said anything to Santa about starting school soon and she knew that the tangerine and the threepenny bit were from him but the beautiful pencil case had come from her father's hands.

Little James was delighted with his pull-along cart which had also been made by Davie; in his hospital bed Alex fairly bounced with joy when he saw his wooden horse and cart.

Jamie was pleased with a new tobacco box, Maggie smiled when Davie said he hoped she wouldn't hit him with the new rolling pin he had made her. For once they were at peace with one another and on Christmas night Douglas came upstairs and everyone went ben The Room and danced with one another to the tunes from the exquisitely fashioned gramophone Davie had given to Evelyn for her Christmas.

Everyone had received something from the labour of his skilled fingers. He had been quieter and kinder since his son's accident. Every evening after tea he had gone ben The Room to saw and hammer and polish. His life was a round of work, sleep and work, and very often he dropped into bed pale with exhaustion.

Evelyn knew it was his way of trying to make up for all the hurt he had caused her and she danced in his arms on Christmas night, the tears of her love for him misting her eyes. He smelled of shaving soap and new-washed hair, the arms that held her close felt strong and warm and safe. She felt the beating of his heart next to her breast and she wanted to be with him like this forever, lost, lost, in this sweet joy of music and of a love that seemed to have been born again this holy, beautiful night.

Even Winnie seemed to have found a certain sort of peace as she sat there by the fire, the flickering light dancing over a face that was childlike and serene in its composure. Douglas had dressed her in a blue wool frock and had somehow managed to get her to exchange her slippers for a pair of shoes. She wore no stockings but that didn't matter, she was warm by the blaze, the eyes that gazed into the flames saw nothing but the thoughts that went on inside her head but at least she didn't mention Danny's name and her husband began to relax and even to enjoy himself.

Evelyn danced with him, she danced with her father, but most of all she danced with Davie and wanted it only to be him and her in this room with the music and the love all around them.

And the time for that came, when the rest of the household was asleep and it was just she and he sitting together by the glowing embers. He glanced at her: her young face was lovely in the soft light, she looked sweet and innocent yet this was no inexperienced girl but a woman who had given birth to his four children. She was no longer eighteen but there in the firelight she looked it and suddenly he remembered the days when passion had consumed them both in flames of desire that never seemed to be quenched; he thought of the times he had held her warm to his breast, in nights of cold dark that shivered the skin but couldn't penetrate the cocoon of warmth inside the blankets.

It had been a long time since he had held her and touched her like that and reaching out he unpinned her hair so that it cascaded down to her waist in a tumble of fiery tresses.

'Davie, oh, Davie,' she whispered. 'It's been a beautiful Christmas and you were so good to everyone.'

'Wheesht, don't talk.' He held a finger to his lips. She made no protest when his mouth gently sought hers; he kissed her nose, her neck, his lips moved to her ears and she groaned a little as the shivers of longing tingled the base of her spine.

In minutes they were lost in that lovely world of love they so seldom entered these days. They undressed, their naked limbs stirring, responding to one another; his body was hard with desire, sweat broke on his brow; she moulded herself to him, the pain, the hurt, the loneliness forgotten in those wonderful moments with her Davie. He would always be hers – always . . . They didn't go to bed for hours but lay there at the fire, awash with a passion that seemed never-ending. Sleep assuaged them for a little while, but in the early hours they woke cold and cramped and crept between the sheets to hold one another till they were warm again. His mouth against her ear said things that made her giggle, his hands moved over her silken flesh and for the rest of the night they knew nothing but ecstasy and warmth and love.

Mr Patterson and Father Brennen arrived at the door at almost the same moment. They knew one another quite well and each respected the other's authority in their different fields.

Father Brennen was a fine figure of a man with twinkling blue eyes and a craggy face imprinted with laughter lines. He gazed into the piercing grey eyes of Wheatfield's headmaster and gave a knowing nod. 'We've come about the same thing, I'm thinking.'

Mr Patterson nodded rather grimly and made a succinct reply before turning his attention to the gleaming brass bell at the side of the door.

It was a fortnight into the New Year and Evelyn was at home that day.

She tried not to look too surprised at the sight of the callers and ushering them inside she bade them sit down and politely offered them a glass of sherry.

They glanced at one another. Hogmanay wasn't too far in the past for its happy memories to have dissipated. Both men smiled and gave a murmur of assent.

Maggie came through from the scullery, wiping her hands on a towel which she hastily tucked under her arm as it was the kitchen towel and not fit for gentlemen's eyes to look upon.

'Mr Patterson, Father Brennen,' she acknowledged in some confusion. 'If I had kent you were coming I would have cleaned and tidied the house.'

The north-east reserve was very strong in Maggie. She hated to be caught with her apron on and she was very conscious of the streamers of washing hanging from the pulley. Maybe Davie was right about that after all, though of course, she excused herself quickly, she wasn't to blame if visitors like these arrived at the door unexpectedly.

'It's all right, Mam,' Evelyn said quietly.

'Maybe The Room would be better,' Maggie pursued stubbornly. 'The kitchen is no place for anyone other than family.'

'There's no fire in The Room, Mam, it's warmer in here.'

Mr Patterson took a sip of his sherry and cleared his throat. 'Don't worry yourself, Mrs Grant, I won't stay long. It's about Alex, I was very relieved to hear he's on the mend and will be home from hospital shortly. No doubt we will soon see him back at school and I would like, Mrs Grainger, if you and your husband could bring him along personally. I think it would be a good idea if I spoke to all three of you in my office since what I have to say to Alex might carry more weight if his parents were there too. Nothing to worry about really, so don't upset yourselves about it. I just feel the time has come for Alex to start heeding the rules a bit more. He really is a very disruptive influence in school and will have to be made to see that he can't go on as he's doing.'

He paused and thought of Miss Mutten. The poor soul had almost suffered a nervous breakdown when he had spoken to her regarding keeping a more watchful eye on Alex Grainger and to report to him if she thought there was any sign of trouble brewing in that quarter.

'I do try, Mr Patterson, I really do try, but you know, I've always believed in the maxim "boys will be boys" and in my experience they do grow out of their rough and tumble ways, given time.'

'This isn't an innocent boy we're dealing with here, Miss Mutten, this is a calculating troublemaker. He laughs at authority and flaunts himself at trouble. I know he's a clever lad, he thinks beyond his eight years, and it's up to us to see that that kind of intelligence is guided into the proper channels. It's up to you as his form mistress to give the boy a bit more of your attention. I can't have this sort of thing happening again. Someone could have been killed, Miss Mutten!'

At that Miss Mutten had broken down and sobbed all over his desk and it had taken him a good ten minutes, together with a tot of brandy, to calm her down again.

Father Brennen laid down his glass and gave Evelyn an apologetic look. 'I too would like to have a word with the young rascal. He and I have a few scores to settle. I don't mind visitors coming into the church, indeed, I welcome them, but I have a suspicion that Alex has been thinking more of his physical welfare than of his spiritual well-being, when he takes it into his head to enter the House of God, so perhaps, Mrs Grainger, when he's fit and well again, you might bring him along to me for a little heart to heart talk.'

'Ay, Father, we'll do as you ask.' Evelyn felt hot with embarrassment and shame and was very glad that the visitors only stayed for a few more minutes before taking their leave.

Alex returned home a week later, full of bounce, brimming over with renewed health. After an initial spell of politeness he soon returned to his old self: he tormented Meg unmercifully, he made Rachel fetch and carry for him, telling her that he was used to having everything done for him by the nurses.

When Jamie took him aside and told him that he wasn't in hospital now and not to bully his little sister any more, he retaliated by taunting his grandfather about his drinking. Raising his eyes to the ceiling, he said with a calculating air that he might go on a bottle hunt to pass the time, and with a chuckle of pure fiendishness he rushed off to rummage about in the lobby while he wondered aloud if that was a glint of glass winking at him from behind the gas meter.

Maggie, unable to bear his insinuations a minute longer, landed him a hearty smack on the face, then worried about it for the rest of the afternoon for he had gone very pale, not with hurt as she imagined but with suppressed rage that she should dare to do such a thing when he was just fresh out of hospital. To worry her further he feigned a headache and frightened everyone by rushing to the scullery and pretending to be sick.

Davie was fully taken in by his wiles and was about to get on to Maggie for hitting the boy in the first place, but instead he went through to the scullery to assess the situation for himself. There he found Alex, standing by the sink, the tap on at full blast and not a sign of vomit anywhere.

The boy was sent to bed forthwith and peace reigned in the house for the rest of the night but next morning it was little James's turn to be singled out. His big brother accused him of wetting the bed and complained that he hadn't had a wink of sleep all night because his nightwear had been soaked and the bed had smelled.

To add fuel to his tongue it was discovered that he was telling the truth. His small brother was prone to bedwetting but never before had it been brought to the light more openly. For the rest of the day James was fretful and sulky and threw such a violent fit of temper at dinner time that even Alex was moved to stare at him in awe.

After that he appeared to have a turn of heart and settled down to play soldiers with James in front of the fire. Later on in the day he smiled bewitchingly at Maggie and said if she gave him a few pennies he would take his little brother to the Tallies at the corner to buy him ice cream.

Her first reaction was to refuse but Alex turned his not inconsiderable charm on her and she relented, mainly because she was so exhausted with the bothers of the last day or so she was only too glad to get both children out of the house for a while.

It was Big Aggie's Man who found James, hanging from a lamp post by his braces in the darkening street. The little boy was so terrified he could neither speak nor cry and curling into the wiry arms that had rescued him he whimpered like a frightened puppy and was sick the minute he was carried over the threshold.

'The wean could have been killed.' Big Aggie's Man was white with rage. 'A fall from the top o' a lamp post would have been a long way for a wee lad like that. It was a good job I came along when I did, it's freezing out there and you'll be lucky if he doesny catch pneumonia.'

When Davie came home he took his eldest son ben The Room, put him over his knee, and thrashed him on the bare backside with one of his own slippers till the boy's skin was red and bruised.

Alex made not a sound but when his father was done with him he threw himself on the floor and fell into a passion of weeping. He ached, he burned, but more than that he was humiliated beyond measure. In the depths of his rebellious young heart he knew he would never again do anything to incur such wrath in the father he worshipped with every fibre of his being and whose approval meant more to him than anything else in the whole of his world.

PART 2

Spring/Summer 1928

CHAPTER 11

Mary was pacing up and down, up and down, her feet making little sound on the luxurious Persian rug that was spread out in front of a blazing fire. It was cold for March with snow flurrying down in the street outside and rasping against the window panes.

Mary stopped her pacing to go over and look out for the umpteenth time in the last ten minutes. A familar figure, wearing a somewhat shabby green wool coat but with no hat to hide her flaming red hair, was coming along, bent into a wind that was whipping up the snow eddies and plastering them against the tall trees that lined Cleveden Mansions.

With ill-concealed impatience Mary waited by the fire. A few minutes later Betty opened the door to usher Evelyn into the room whereupon Mary ran forward to take her sister's cold hands and lead her to the fire.

'Bring tea, Betty,' she ordered, then, as if Evelyn's presence had reminded her of someone else she added, 'Oh, scones and jam too, Betty – if you please.'

Betty threw her a surprised look before closing the door. Mary turned to her young sister, 'There, now and then I do remember my manners. Oh, Evelyn, it's so good to see you. How is everyone? I wanted Grace to come as well but she tells me her shifts are very awkward at the moment.'

Evelyn held her hands to the blaze. It was on the tip of her tongue to tell Mary that she could see all of her family together if she would only deign to make the journey to Govan but she hadn't visited for years and never showed any inclination to do so.

She was, if anything, more 'above her station' than

107

ever, having moved from her flat to the refined elegance of Cleveden Mansions. It was Evelyn's first visit and she glanced around at the expensive furniture and the rich drapes and wondered if this sister of hers would ever curtail her spending of Gregor's money.

Mary herself looked like a cat who lived on the cream of the land. She was plumper than ever, her glossy dark hair had been arranged in the latest fashion, the cream blouse she wore must have cost more than all of Evelyn's wardrobe put together, but the fine material was straining at the seams even though the flesh underneath was restrained by heavily boned corsets.

'Well! Do you like it?' Mary was watching her sister's face.

Something made Evelyn deliberately misunderstand. 'Ay, your clothes are beautiful, Mary, a far cry from the days when it was wincey blouses and hopsack peenies.'

'No, silly, the house, what do you think of the house? Isn't it just too elegant for words? Greg thinks it's too big, he says he used to feel much more comfortable when we lived in Rowanlea Cottage in Rothiedrum, but then, he's getting to be a stuffed shirt these days. I adore it and of course our neighbours aren't your usual run-of-the-mill. The Honourable John Carmichael is a big name in the City and Mr Alistair Kerr-Campbell is an artist of very high standard. He does stained glass windows for churches and cathedrals and his work has been recognized by Royalty.

'His wife has the most exquisite taste in clothes and has invited me to join her on a trip to some of the big fashion houses in London. Lord Quigley-Jameson is an advocate of great reputation, he and his wife have a holiday home in Maidens and I put the idea to Greg that we should have one too, though I thought Innellan near Dunoon might be better for us. Sir Harry Lauder hides out there – Laudervale you know . . .'

She paused for two reasons, one to catch her breath,

the other to gaze with surprise at her young sister who was staring at her as if she was seeing a stranger.

'Evelyn, what on earth's wrong?' she laughed, somewhat self-consciously to be true. 'Have I said something . . . ?'

Her question hung unanswered. Betty heralded her arrival with a discreet clearing of her throat and put a laden tray on a table near the fire. Betty knew her mistress very well – as, indeed, did Cook. As well as scones there was a plateful of cream cakes and another piled high with hot pancakes straight off the girdle. All were arranged on heavy silver plates on top of a fluted silver tray.

'Betty!' Mary's voice was sharp. 'I didn't ask for all this.'

Betty, who was standing with her hands meekly folded on top of her stomach, feigned great surprise. 'Sorry, ma'am, I'll take it back . . .'

'No, no, Betty, you might as well leave it now, I'm sure my sister will enjoy the pancakes.'

'Yes'm.'

Betty went out, her lips curving into a smile. Sister indeed! That had been a good idea of Cook's, she had lost count of the times she had been summoned to fetch an extra plate of this and that after the bare minimum had been asked for in the first place. It was as if Mrs McGregor was trying to pretend to herself that her requirements were of a spartan nature and never never must she appear to look greedy.

'Sugar, dear?' Mary, playing the perfect hostess, stood poised with the sugar tongs.

Evelyn felt so numb she could barely answer. She was appalled. This wasn't Mary, bonnie Mary who had once romped and laughed and who hadn't cared if she got dung on her shoes from the yard and who had talked and behaved in the most natural way possible. This well-upholstered woman with her perfect clothes and her affected speech was a stranger. She had been bad enough when Nellie was here that last time but now – she was impossible!

'Mary.' Evelyn looked directly into the other's eyes. 'I didna come all this way to talk about clothes and houses and rich people who live off the fat o' the land! You wrote me a letter asking me to come here to see you and I had the notion that it was for a specific reason. I have a job and a family and a husband to see to and I havena the time nor the inclination to spend precious money on tram fares on a freezing cold day just to listen to prattle!'

'Oh, Evelyn.' Mary straightened, a strange look coming into her eyes. 'Of course I didn't ask you here just to waste your time.' She put down the tongs and began to walk up and down, her hands clasped to her bosom in a most dramatic gesture. 'I asked you because I felt I needed someone – someone of my own kin to talk to.' She spun round. 'You might not think so but I do miss my sisters, I miss the confidences, how it used to be when we told one another our worries and problems.'

'But you don't have problems now, do you, Mary? Life is so cosy for you, you lack for nothing, yet . . .'

'Why, Evelyn, surely you aren't jealous?'

A spiteful tone had crept into her voice and Evelyn stood up, her green eyes sparking dangerously. 'Oh, no, Mary, none o' us are jealous o' you and your protected way of life. If you had let me finish I was going to say you lack for nothing yet you've got nothing, none o' the things that really matter, that is. Oh, you have a wonderful husband and a fine son but I doubt if you ever really see or hear either of them in the true sense. When did you last ask Greg what he would like to do, where he would like to go, what kind o' people he would like to see? As for Donald, do you really know him? What do you talk about when he comes home? Mr so-and-so's fancy house in Maidens? Mrs what's-her-name gabbling on about her silly frocks and whether she should wear kid shoes or suede to the merchant ball? Does Donald really care if your curtains are velvet or your fireplace real marble? Or have you turned him into a conniving little money grubber like yourself so that he canna think beyond the glitter and the gilt . . . !'

'Evelyn!' Mary was shocked and not a little unnerved. Evelyn McKenzie Grant in a fury had always been a force to be reckoned with but the child had grown into a woman and it seemed that her temper had grown with her.

'And that's another thing!' Evelyn stamped her foot, something that she hadn't done since far off childhood. 'Why have I suddenly became "Evelyn"? Isn't Evie good enough any more? Who is this Evelyn that you talk of in a voice that would sound better in a hundred-year-old hag? Whoever she is she can stay and eat those ghastly cream cakes along with her fat sister! She can simper and look pleased to be called Evelyn and she can grow old and stout before her time but the person that I ken as Evie is going! Goodbye, Mary!'

'Wait, Evie, oh, please wait! I really didn't ask you here to waste your time. I really do have something important to tell you if you will just come back here and stop looking as if you would like to kill me.'

'Well, what is it?' Evelyn turned slowly from the door.

Mary had begun her pacing again, her clasped hands held to her mouth, one thumbnail inserted between her small, white teeth.

All at once she swung round to face her sister. 'Evelyn – Evie – oh, Evie,' she exclaimed in a most tragic voice. 'I'm going to have another baby! I'm pregnant and I don't know what I'm going to do about it.'

'Do about it? Why should you want to do anything about it? Anyone would think you were dying the way you behave.'

Mary sunk heavily onto a red velvet chaise longue and sighed. 'Oh, Evie, you simply don't understand. I don't want another baby, not at my age. I'm very happy with my life as it is, I just don't see how a new baby could possibly fit into it . . .'

'Fit into it!' Evelyn had quite a struggle to control herself. 'Well, *you* will just have to fit into *its* life and put yourself out for somebody else for a change! A baby will give you something real to hold on to and even if you aren't pleased, I haven't a doubt that Greg will be over the moon about it.'

'He doesn't know!' Mary wailed, screwing a scrap of lace into a tight ball and holding it to her eyes. 'I – well, to be quite honest, I thought I needn't tell him at all, I thought when I was in London with Mrs Kerr-Campbell I could stay behind for a few extra days and – and . . .'

'So,' Evelyn's fists curled at her sides, 'the reason you really wanted me here was to find out if I approved of you murdering your own baby, and Greg never knowing a thing about it. You thought you could go off to gawp at clothes with your vain friend and while you were about it just pop into the nearest clinic and hey presto! No bairn to complicate your cosy existence.' Twin spots of crimson burned on Evelyn's cheekbones, she wanted to take her sister and shake and shake her and try and knock some sense into her empty head but she was sensible enough to know that that sort of treatment would do no good at all. Mary needed a strict lesson, something really drastic to make her see the error of her ways or she might go on as she was doing till it was too late for everyone concerned.

'When I think o' Nellie,' Evelyn kept her voice low in an effort to control her fury, 'all her life yearning for a bairn and the passing years bringing her nothing but crushed hopes and here's you, girning and fretting because you *are* having one. You dinna deserve another baby but you're having it and if I hear another word about you planning to get rid o' it I'll – I'll come over here and personally rip every hair from your head and when I've done that I'll make damned sure that all your posh pals get to know about the *real* Mary McGregor . . .'

The door opened, Gregor came in. He looked tired, Evelyn thought, his eyes lacked their usual smiling warmth though when he saw the visitor he dropped his bag and putting his arms round her treated her to a hearty bear hug. Evelyn straightened, she smiled at him, she would tell him something that ought to bring the life back into his face.

'Och, Greg,' she said breathlessly, 'it's so good to see you again and doubly so at a time like this. Congratulations. Another bairn is just what you and Mary need,' she laughed. 'The pair o' you are getting too stale and lazy for words but a new baby will soon change all that.'

She ignored Mary's frantic signals and she was rewarded with the look of pure astonishment on Greg's face.

'A new baby? Evie, what are you blethering on about?' He turned to his wife and spread his hands in dumbfounded appeal. 'Is this true, Mary? You never said anything to me . . .'

'She was going to tell you this very afternoon,' Evelyn got in there first. 'In fact, just before you came through the door we were picturing your face on hearing the news. I'm sorry I was the first to let it slip as I ken how anxious Mary was to tell you herself.'

She said no more, Gregor had gone over to his wife to stare at her in disbelief before putting his arms around her to laugh and kiss her and tell her it was the best news he'd had in years.

Evelyn didn't wait for tea but stole quietly away, a deep sense of satisfaction making her giggle to herself and smile at Betty who was hovering outside the sitting room door, ostensibly dusting a small table which she had already polished and dusted only that morning.

She walked along the tree-lined avenue, the wind at her back now, the snow whirling in great feathery flakes around her head. Her mind was filled with the events of the last hour and she wasn't fully aware of anyone that might be coming or going in Cleveden Mansions. Not that there were many people about anyway. This was a quiet residential area, the solid grey stone houses sat well back, separated from the street by elevated gardens and tall hedges which effectively shuttered the buildings from curious eyes.

Lights were beginning to wink in one or two windows, warm, amber lights that gave the impression of luxury and intimacy behind the heavy drapes. In front of her a man came down a flight of worn steps and hurried along towards Great Western Road, his coat collar pulled well up about his ears. Something about his walk was vaguely familiar and Evelyn was brought out of her reverie with a start.

That tall, dark figure, the sureness of his stride, reminded her so much of . . .

Her heart began to pound, then it missed several beats and she leaned against a wall for support as she struggled to get back her breath. Flakes of snow brushed her cheeks, adhered to her eyelashes, she peered through the white swirls at the receding figure.

It *couldn't* be . . . oh, dear God! It wasn't Gillan! This stranger who was walking rapidly away from her just moved and carried himself in the same manner as someone she had known and lost a long, long time ago . . .

But she had to know, had to make sure that it wasn't all just a figment of her imagination.

*

Still feeling strange and breathless, her feet somehow carried her towards busy Great Western Road then she began to panic in case she should lose sight of the man amidst other pedestrians and she started to run towards the corner.

He was gone! Frantically she glanced up and down the road but there was no one, no one who looked and moved and walked like Gillan Forbes of Rothiedrum House, Aberdeenshire.

A taxi-cab came along, gathering speed as it neared the spot where she was standing. A face looked from the window, Gillan's face! His eyes gazed out at nothing in particular. The snow whirled, blotting out the street but the impression of that face, that dear, handsome dark face, was imprinted in her mind as clearly as if it was still there in front of her before he was whisked out of her life as swiftly and as briefly as he had come into it.

She stood where she was for a long time, fighting to regain a sense of normality. People walked past, traffic trundled noisily by, but she neither saw nor heard any of it.

Her clothes and her hair became plastered with snow and it was only the leaden cold of her hands and feet that eventually stirred her to move away from the spot where she had been transfixed for the last half hour. As one in a dream she walked the length of Byres Road to Argyle Street where she boarded a tram.

Nothing was real to her, she sat in a daze, deeply shaken by the strange interlude, unable to think of anything beyond that time, that moment, that now, when she had glimpsed Gillie's face. Gillie, oh, Gillie, her heart cried, if only we could have talked, just for a little while, somehow I could have carried on with my life feeling more contented than I do now . . . But even while her heart told her these things her head warned her that she was just clutching at straws that had drifted briefly into her life from the mists of the past . . .

115

'Fares, please.'

The conductor stood in front of her, solid and real. She resented him, she resented everything that was loud and mundane and insensitive. She didn't want to go home, not yet, the children would clamour, her father might be drunk again, the kitchen would be full of wet washing, Davie's eyes would watch her and wonder what was going on inside her head, and Winnie Grainger would be at her window, singing that monotonous song that went on and on without end.

She decided to go and visit Grace. That calm, un-demanding presence was what she needed just now. But Grace wasn't alone, Penny Farthing was there, a very smug Penny Farthing these days. Her ambitions to travel had been readily pushed aside when she had fallen in love with the under-manager of Daly's whom she had married six months ago. She was now three months preg-nant and full of it – in every sense. She had wanted someone to talk to and had made the journey from Garrowhill, where she now lived, to visit Grace.

Marriage and pending motherhood dominated her conversation. Evelyn stirred her tea and heard none of it. Grace saw her sister's face and tried everything to get the talk away from domestic matters but Penny was as thick-skinned as she was boring and when she finally took her leave the two sisters just looked at one another and gave heartfelt sighs of relief. Evelyn couldn't help smiling. They had just got rid of one 'baby bore' and here she was, about to heap on more coals.

She told Grace about her visit to Mary and when she was finished Grace shook her head. 'Och, Evie, it's hard to believe she has turned out like that but I'm glad you handled it the way you did. Now that Greg knows, the besom willna dare to get rid o' the baby . . .' Her great dark eyes held her sister's green orbs. 'That's no' all that's ailing you, Evie, you've been strange and faraway ever since you came through my door.'

Evelyn sighed. 'No, that's not all, Grace.'

She disclosed her encounter with Gillan. Grace was silent for a moment or two before saying thoughtfully, 'Life, Evie, is stranger than fiction, you saw Gillie, you lost him, but if it's meant, you and he will meet again. I really believe that if you want something badly enough it will happen and that's why I'm certain that one day Gordon will come back to me.'

She placed her delicate fingers over her sister's. 'But there's some big difference between you and me, Evie. You already have a man who means the world to you, if you had spoken with Gillie it would only have complicated all these passionate emotions in that romantic heart o' yours and in the end it wouldna really have brought you any sort o' contentment or happiness.'

Evelyn knew that Grace was speaking a lot of sense but in her highly emotional state sense was the last thing she wanted to hear. 'Ach, Grace, of course you're right, but it would have been nice – to hear his voice – just for a wee whilie. It was all so strange, the snow, the trees, that tall figure coming down the steps in front o' me. I wonder what he was doing there? When I was able to think more clearly I thought perhaps he might live there but Mary would have mentioned it, she's only been there five minutes but already she's able to rhyme off all the neighbours by heart.'

'She mentioned an advocate, didn't she? Gillie is maybe a friend o' his and was just in visiting –' She paused, her lovely face was troubled. 'Promise me you willna go haunting that place, Evie. He might never go back again and you will only make yourself ill looking for something that was never meant to be.'

'Ay, Grace, I promise.'

Even as she spoke the words she knew that she would never again tread the tree-lined avenue of Cleveden

Mansions without expecting to see the elusive figure
of a tall dark beloved man walking along in front of
her.

CHAPTER 12

Evelyn came home, flushed and excited looking. Davie noticed at once and thought how desirable she looked with her pink cheeks and her beautiful green eyes sparkling. Yet, for all that, she seemed restless and distant and he wondered what had happened to make her start when she was spoken to, as if her thoughts were very far away indeed.

The children too were excited that night but for reasons far removed from those of their mother. They were at the window, watching the flakes of snow swirling down to smother the backcourts in sheets of white.

'I'll make a snowman,' decided Meg, pushing her brother James aside so that she could better see through the frosty panes.

But he was growing bigger, more able to defend himself, and he promptly nipped her arm in retaliation.

Meg knew better than to make any sort of fuss where her little brother was concerned because he was quite capable of creating a scene of such passion she would be sent to bed for being the instigator of the trouble.

He was a gifted child, normally quiet and well behaved, but when riled his temper was something to be feared and respected. He had already let fly at Alex with his soup spoon but had missed him and had chipped a bone in Rachel's nose instead.

He had been devastated by the accident and for a week afterwards had cried himself to sleep for he worshipped this sister of his and always turned to her when he was troubled or afraid.

Although he was barely five he was already a brilliant natural musician. He played the fiddle better than Jamie himself and wasn't slow to point out a wrong or a harsh note; his father had bought him a mouth organ for Christmas and from it he could extract any tune asked of him. His great ambition was to own a piano but that was something that was beyond his father's pocket and he had to make do with the instruments he had.

He had the power of second sight like his mother, who had inherited it from her paternal grandfather, but he was too young to be able to deal with the strange visions that beset him from time to time and he wouldn't go to sleep unless an oil lamp was left burning all night.

For these unusual abilities he paid dearly in that he was introverted and anxious, and misunderstood by other children, who were wont to torment and tease him unmercifully. He went by the nickname of Spooky Jim and not knowing what that meant but hating the sound of it, he disliked going out on his own and clung to Rachel more than ever. His parents were dreading the day when he would start school but the time for that was drawing closer and the grown-ups were bracing themselves for the event as they were only too well aware that he would be entering into an even harder world than anything he had known so far.

'I'll look after him,' Alex would vow, his fists bunching as if in anticipation, but one look from his father soon quelled his fire. He had quietened down since the memorable time of the Big Battle and was doing well at school, much to everyone's relief. He was possessed of a great initiative and flair for making money. As well as his 'accountancy' job with Stashie Dunbar he scrounged or found wood from whatever source, chopped it up, tied the bundles with string, and sold it round the doors for tuppence a bundle. When his 'business' began to take off and he could no longer carry enough wood to satisfy his growing number of customers, he had, with a bit of help from his father, made a wooden barrow out of scraps from Stashie's shop so that he could trundle his wares round the streets.

Davie was tickled pink by his elder son's resourcefulness and gave him every encouragement he could, and while the boy was by no means an angel and would have fought with his shadow if he was goaded enough, he was, all things considered, sufficiently improved to please everyone who had known him in his 'devilish days'.

He still liked to be top dog, however, and when Meg mentioned making a snowman he said his would be bigger and better, and the two squabbled as they had always done until Davie packed them off to bed with many warnings not to kick one another or there would be trouble.

Their sleeping arrangements were different now that they were older. The two boys slept in a wheelie bed which came out from under the big bed at night, the girls shared the double bed in the recess and everything was much more peaceful than previously. It didn't always work out, though: James was often beset by nightmares and would seek comfort in Rachel's arms, disturbing both Alex and Meg, who weren't slow to voice their displeasure. The arrangement also meant that there was less space left in the kitchen for the adults who previously had enjoyed comparative freedom and privacy when the children's recess had been curtained off for the night.

Davie complained about being cramped and restricted and the usual arguments would start between him and Evelyn concerning her parents.

But no matter what, a good hour had to elapse from the time the youngsters were in bed, to when it was judged they were safely asleep so that anything of a personal or private nature could be discussed by the adults. Tonight was no exception. Maggie sat darning a pile of socks, from time to time eyeing Evelyn, who she knew had

121

something on her mind. Jamie fiddled with his pipe, cleaning the stem with a piece of pliable wire which when sufficiently loaded with tar was then scraped clean on the bars of the fire.

Davie tried to read his newspaper but couldn't concentrate. His nerves were on edge, he felt restless and confined. Since his son's accident he had stayed more at home in an attempt to pacify Evelyn, but it was more than that – he had to admit it to himself. He had wanted to ease the guilt of his own conscience. Since his marriage there had been other women, trivial affairs that meant nothing to him except perhaps a boosting of his ego and a need to release some of the resentment he'd felt at having to marry for the sake of giving Alex his name.

He had wanted so much from life, he had wanted to travel and see the world. The war had effectively forced him to postpone his plans but it wouldn't have been forever – if it hadn't been for Evelyn he would have had his freedom instead of being trapped in a life with nothing to look forward to but weary days that were all the same and endless arguments with Stashie about wages and conditions.

Sometimes he felt like running away from it all and lately it was taking him all his time not to resume the old habits which had been so hard to break. He moved in his seat and watched Evelyn from the side of his newspaper. He loved her, that was the trouble, she had captivated him from the start with her vibrant beauty and her quality of spirit. Her own untamed desires had been a match for his and it was thoughts of her that had kept him going throughout the miserable years of the war.

Even now he only had to think of her naked white limbs for the familiar stirrings to start in his loins and then the anger against Jamie and Maggie would begin all over again. If it wasn't for them there wouldn't be all this waiting for bedtime so that he could make love to his wife, it could be spontaneous and free, here by the fire with the children asleep in The Room instead of crowded together in the kitchen . . . Oh God! Evelyn had been lovely as a girl but the passing years had made her even more beautiful and desirable. She was very quiet tonight, her hands were folded serenely in her lap and she was gazing into the fire. The flickering flames did odd things to those wondrous eyes of hers, they looked more amber than green and their expression was dreamy, yet somehow very alive – but pensive, he felt somehow that he was viewing the emotions of her soul and that her feelings were all mixing together, struggling with one another.

What did she think of when her body was still and her mind took over? He realized suddenly that he had never given much heed to what marriage and children had meant for her. She seldom complained even though there were times she looked weary beyond measure. She was so clever – gifted – she had wanted to be a writer – to write books – and instead . . . She had given it all up because she loved him, she had sacrificed so much of herself for love and all he had done was blame her for giving up her own freedom so that she could be his wife. Oh, Evie, darling Evie, his heart cried, so sad, so lost, I never meant to hurt you . . .

He wanted to take her in his arms there and then and crush her to him – her lips were slightly parted, she was wearing a blue cotton blouse that showed the gentle swell of her breasts . . . his trousers were tightening between his legs and he could do nothing to stop the hard pillar rising against his stomach . . . Hastily he lowered his newspaper, then he grinned to himself and thought, why should he? It might do Maggie some good if she was shocked out of her domestic composure: there she sat, darning, her hands never still, rough hands, he could see the dryness of the reddened skin, he would say that for her, she wasn't lazy, she was always working about the house, helping Evelyn, seeing to the children, baking, cooking, sewing. She must have been beautiful once. She was still a fine-looking woman in a rather haughty way, that proud tilt of the head, the arrogant thrust of the chin, her hair silvery-blue in the light of the gas mantle . . .

He moved again, relieved to feel the heat dissipating from his vitals. The scraping of Jamie's pipe was getting on his nerves, he was always buggering around with the damned thing. It was as ancient as he was himself but, despite the fact that he had been given several new pipes, he never failed to declare, 'I'll no' part wi' my Stonehaven pipe, it's been wi' me a long time and will see me fine for the days that are left to me.'

Davie was very fond of Jamie, always had been, there was something about the man that made him popular with everyone who crossed his path, he was open and frank and he could tell a good story, mainly about his days spent travelling the highways and byways. A sudden vision of the youthful Jamie came to him. There had been a man, black haired, dark eyed, filled with life and hope; there wasn't much left of that man now, drink had been his ruination yet Davie didn't hate him for it nor did he attribute it to weakness: he might have turned to it himself if he'd had to wrest a living from the wind-scoured harshness of the north-east soil. That, and the heartache he'd suffered in leaving that same bleak landscape, had reduced the once-strong gypsy Jamie to a man physically old before his time. Spiritually he would never grow frail, nor his sense of fun die, and Davie smiled as he recalled how it was when Jamie and Big Aggie's Man got together, both of them unconscious comedians in their own right, especially after a few warming drams to get them going . . .

'Mary's pregnant.'

Evelyn's pithy statement fell like a stone into the silence of the room. 'And she doesna want the bairn,' Evelyn continued, still in that oddly concise manner.

Maggie showed no surprise. 'She wouldna. Mary being

124

Mary willna want anything that might disturb her fancy existence but Greg being Greg will make certain that she has the bairn and no nonsense about it. It's high time they had a sister or a brother for Donald and I just hope it will bring Mary to her senses at last.' A secretive smile touched the corner of Maggie's mouth and from her apron pocket she extracted a letter. Smoothing it out she gazed from one interested face to another. 'Tis strange, gey strange that Mary should be expecting a baby after all these years and even more of a coincidence that her sister Nellie should write telling me that she too is going to have a bairn.'

This piece of news was received with a stunned silence before everyone clamoured at once to hear more. In her delight Evelyn couldn't wait for her mother to speak but rushed over to take the letter and read it for herself.

Dear Mam, [she read aloud] my hand is shaking so much I can hardly put pen to paper. At last, at last it's happened, I am going to give Kenneth the bairn we have both longed and prayed for. When he heard the news he was so beside himself with happiness he did a Highland Fling with all the children in turn.

I know you will all be as pleased as I am and I wrote this letter as soon as I was certain of my facts. I know also, Mam, that you will be thinking, in that practical way of yours, that I am no longer a spring chicken, and you might start worrying about all the things that most likely will never happen. But I feel in the best of health and you can be assured that even if I don't knuckle down and put my feet up, Kenneth will be fussing over me like a broody chick and indeed has started doing so already.

The baby is due at the end of August and I would like fine if Evie could maybe be here with me nearer my time. I know it is a lot to ask but it would be grand to have some of my own family around me at such a time and I wouldn't have said anything if it wasn't for the fact that I am just a wee bit apprehensive about the birth itself. Evie is a dab hand at bringing bairns into the world and could maybe give me a few hints. It's funny, Nellie the eldest, wanting the wee sister who is still, to me, just a bairn herself.

But life is never consistent and I would of course pay Evie's fare if she said yes.

I wish you could all come, I want to see you, Mam, and Father, the bairns, Grace, even Davie for all he thinks I'm a targe, but we understand one another, Davie and me.

I have written to my darling Grace with the news, and I also dropped Mary and Murn a line though I don't suppose it will make any difference to them.

Give the little ones a cuddle from me and a special big one to my bonnie Alex.

Love and affection from your daughter, Nell.

Evelyn threw down the letter and did a war dance round the kitchen, so beside herself with delight she forgot all about the slumbering children till Meg's voice came sleepily, asking what was wrong.

'Nothing's wrong, Megsie,' laughed Evie. 'Your Aunt Nell is going to have a baby and everything's right.'

'Is that all?' Alex's voice came scornfully. 'I wouldn't mind if she was having a horse – but a baby!'

Jamie was quietly overjoyed for Nell, his eldest child. At long last she was going to be completely fulfilled and no one deserved it more. In his exuberance he half thought of celebrating with a good dram, but no! One would only lead to another and he wasn't going to spoil this moment for everyone.

'Your Aunt Mary's having one as well.' Davie sounded bemused. Thank God it wasn't Evie in the family way. All that had stopped with James's birth. He couldn't have fed another mouth and he had been careful when making love to his wife. Even so he often found it difficult to come out of her at the crucial moment and there were times when his burning need to release himself properly almost made him throw caution to the winds and allow his passions full rein . . .

'Lord preserve us! Aunt Mary too!'

Alex's precocious words made everyone laugh and retire to bed in the best of good spirits.

As soon as they were under the blankets Evelyn realized that Davie was in a highly aroused state. He hadn't yet touched her and the hardness of his penis digging into her thigh came as something of a shock, immersed as her mind was with Nellie's news and that fleeting glimpse of Gillie's face from a speeding taxi. She had looked forward to bedtime so that she could be free to think about Nellie, but more than that, she couldn't lie to herself, she had wanted to recall every little detail of those oddly unreal moments in Cleveden Mansions with the snow swirling all around her and a tall, dark man walking along in front of her – oh, Gillie, Gillie. She wanted to imagine what he would have done if he had turned and saw her, how he would have looked, what he would have said . . .

And now here was Davie, pushing up her nightdress, winding his arms around her body, drawing her in closer and closer to his demanding hardness till she felt she would suffocate beneath him . . .

'Davie, don't.' She pushed him away and he rolled on his back, cursing her, asking her what the hell was wrong.

'I dinna ken, Davie, I – I just want to think, there's little enough time for that in this house with everyone demanding my attention every minute o' the day.'

'Christ! Surely as your husband I'm entitled to some o' your time as well? Maybe you would like it if I . . .' He was about to say if he began going out again to seek more amenable company but he let the words hang in mid-air.

127

She wasn't listening anyway. She had got out of bed and had padded over to the window. It was bitterly cold, the chill seeped through her nightclothes and made her shiver and cross her arms over her breasts.

A movement in the white street below caught her eye. There was Winnie Grainger, flitting along like a ghost in the lamplight, her nightgown billowing out behind her in the raw March wind.

Evelyn watched, feeling strangely detached from it all: Davie, the children, Winnie Grainger down below, in her madness leaving her warm bed to wander wintry nights in an endless search for a son whose bones lay rotting in some nameless grave in France. Would it always be like this? The misery, the poverty, the despair that engulfed her so often of late whenever she tried desperately to think of some way out?

And now, she had seen Gillie again, she hadn't touched him, or talked with him, but just that brief sighting of him had brought it all flooding back, the laughter, the sweetness of the Rothiedrum days. It had been good – so good.

Wearily she turned back to the bed and touched her husband's moodily hunched shoulder. 'Davie, your mother, she's out there in the street again.'

'Hell!' Angrily he sprang up. 'That bloody woman will be the death o' us all! Can't Father watch her? Surely he must have heard her going out.'

'Your father is exhausted, Davie, he has to look after her every minute o' the day, he's a human being and needs his rest like everyone else.'

'He should lock her in – or tie her in!' He was throwing on his long woolly drawers and vest as he spoke, gritting his teeth at the touch of the cold material against his warm flesh. With another oath he let himself noisily out of the house, banging the door behind him.

He had wakened James, she heard the little boy's sobs filtering through from the kitchen, then all was quiet again and she knew that Rachel had taken him into bed with her and was soothing him back to sleep.

Her teeth chittering with cold, Evelyn watched Davie running along the snow-dusted road, his hair tousled, his braces dangling at his hips; she heard the dull thud of his shoes on the pavement and hoped he wouldn't trip for he hadn't taken time to tie his laces.

Winnie had made good headway, she was thin, spry for her age, and she could scuttle along quickly when she wanted to.

But ten minutes later Davie was back, leading his mother along, talking soothingly to her, all his anger gone.

Poor Davie, she didn't blame him for losing his temper, it was all so futile, so sad.

She climbed back into bed, the cold sheets embraced her and she shivered. Sometimes she hated Davie, some of the things he said and did were heartless and cruel. He had never been honest about his earnings, the children sorely needed new clothes, she had forgotten when last she had a new dress – yet he was always smartly turned out and he made sure he had his golf in summer and his nights out in winter. She lay back and shut her eyes. At least, he used to go out quite regularly during the long dark nights, but lately, for over a year in fact, he had curbed his wanderlust and she had sensed that he was trying hard, oh so very hard, to keep himself on a tighter rein. For that she was more than thankful. How she had hated the thought of those other women, she had smelt their perfume on his clothes and sometimes he hadn't been able to look her in the face.

She could never forgive him for that secret life of his and no matter how hard he tried to make it up to her she would never forget and she would never trust him . . . but, God help her! She still loved him, she always would until his dying day. He would die young . . . Her heart grew cold within her. Why had she thought that?

Why had the same dreadful thought tormented her for years?

Then she remembered, Twiggy May, the old speywife of Renfrewshire who had collected old clothes and who had read cups in Seal McWhirter's kitchen at Dunmarnock.

But there was more to Twiggy May than that, she was possessed of the second sight and could see into the future. She had told Evelyn that there would be many men in her life, one of whom had always loved her — Gillie, that had to be Gillie — the other would bring her trouble and strife but despite all that she would love and care for him to the end.

'He'll no' live long.'

The echo of those words came ringing over the years, so plain and stark it was as if Twiggy May was standing in the room speaking to her.

'No, oh, dear God, no.'

Evelyn whispered the protest into the cold, dark room. She couldn't imagine life without her Davie, it was too terrible to contemplate.

Her pillow was wet with tears and she hadn't been aware that she was crying. She felt cold, so cold, as if the fingers of death had touched her, and when Davie finally came back she reached out to hold him close to her breast. He was frozen, his nose against her cheek was an icy blob.

'Oh, Davie,' she murmured, 'forgive me for being such a bitch, it's just — well, sometimes I feel trapped in this life we've made for ourselves and then I begin to feel afraid because I canna seem to see any way out for us.'

'That's exactly how I feel,' his voice held a note of surprise, 'but I never imagined you felt that way too, I thought it was all enough for you.'

'Ach no, it just seems pointless talking about it, that's all. Oh, Davie, I love you so and I wish I could do something to make your life better than it is.' She murmured the words against his neck, his pulse was beating, warmly and strongly.

He kissed her, his lips were cool and sweet, his tongue curled into her ear and she shivered.

'It was always you, Evie,' he sounded strange, sad for a moment, 'from the beginning it was always you I loved.'

'Are you sorry?' She spoke quietly, fearfully.

'Never for loving you, never for that, only for some things that never should have happened — but did.'

'But that's life, Davie, it does that to all o' us.'

'And in the end it carries us off.' He laughed a trifle bitterly.

'What made you say that?' Her voice was sharp with apprehension.

'Och, just things that people say for the sake o' talk.'

His mouth nuzzled her ear again, then it moved to her breasts to suck and kiss them till her nipples were hard, aching points of fire and great surges of desire swept down into her belly. He played with her and teased her till she could stand it no longer and with a groan she moved her legs to allow him in between them. She no longer wanted him to be gentle with her, she was burning with her need for him and arched her body against his, all the while urging him to drive himself into her with the sort of passion they had denied themselves since James's birth.

His brutal thrusts made them both gasp, deeper and deeper he pushed till it seemed he must surely be inside her very womb and she lay back, bathed in sweat, wanting only that final release from her agonizing ecstasy.

'Together, Evie,' he panted, 'the way it used to be, I'm ready — oh, my darling girl, I can't hold back, not this time.'

His words echoed inside her head, somehow bringing her back from the edge of no return. His seed was potent and she was very fertile, it would be madness to have another child when they could barely clothe and feed the four they had now . . . and in the cold light of day he would blame her . . .

But it was too late, he was beyond the brink, he kept on moving inside her till his release came and then he collapsed against her, unmoving except for a spasmodic twitching of his lower limbs.

'Evie, my own little girl.' Tenderly he stroked her hair. 'It was so wonderful, like how it used to be.'

Gently she kissed his hot face and murmured her words of love into his ear. In minutes he was asleep beside her but she found herself unable to relax, her mind was in a ferment, so much to think about, so many beloved people claiming her thoughts but above all, she wished that she could do something that would help Davie to feel master of himself again.

If only he didn't have to work for Stashie Dunbar, if only there was enough money to enable him to set up in his own joinery business . . . If only . . .

She sat up suddenly, her pulses racing. There was something, the garnet necklace given to her by Lord Lindsay Ogilvie all those years ago. She had always vowed that she would never sell it unless it was really imperative, that she would keep it and save it for a rainy day.

Well, that day had come and she could hardly wait for tomorrow so that she could start to put her plan into action.

CHAPTER 13

Maggie stared at the garnet-encrusted gold necklace Evelyn had placed in her hands. She had seen the self-same piece of jewellery several times and she hesitated for a long time before she spoke.

'Evie, do you remember you showed me this once, a long time ago? I laughed when you said Lord Lindsay Ogilvie had given it to you and promised that one day I would tell you about him – and about me.'

'Ay, Mam, I do remember, but I never thought the day would come, you were aye so strange about the Forbeses and in particular about Gillie's great uncle. We all wondered why you seemed to hold such a grudge against that family but when we asked you aye got so angry and wouldna speak.'

Maggie's green eyes were very pensive. 'It wasna easy for me, Evie, I could never think o' them without getting into a rage –' She sighed. 'Och, it's an old, old story, lassie, and it had its beginnings long before you were even a glint in your father's een. Megsie Cameron, your grandmother, was a young servant lassie at Balmoral, there she became entangled wi' one o' the young gentle-men who used to visit there and for her sins she was cast out to fend for herself. You ken the next part o' the story for I never hid the fact that my father was a nobleman though there was nothing noble in the way he treated your grannie.

'What neither you, nor Jamie, nor any o' the rest o' my family kens is that Lord Lindsay Ogilvie was the heartless rogue who bedded Megsie Cameron, then left her wi' a bairn and precious little else she could call her own.'

Evelyn was staring round-eyed at her mother. 'You

mean that Oggie – darling old Oggie – is your father?'

'Ay, none other, which makes Lady Marjorie and Gillan cousins to us all.'

'Cousins.' Evelyn sat down suddenly. She had decided to ask her mother's advice about the garnet necklace but never, never did she expect that the sight of it would bring about such a string of earth-shattering revelations.

'Then – Oggie is my grandfather,' she whispered.

'Indeed he is.' Maggie's eyes grew misty and faraway. 'He came to see me after you and he met one day up at the Big House. He had taken a real liking to you, lassie, and wanted to try and make up for his neglect of my mother and of me by seeing that you had a decent start in life. Oh, like a fool I refused and I've regretted it ever since. Blood is thicker than water when all's said and done and ever since that day I've hankered to see him again. But it's too late, much too late for that now, I sent him away wi' his tail between his legs and from that day to this I've never seen him again.'

'I kent he was special.' Evelyn spoke as if to herself. 'When at first I refused to accept the necklace he said some strange things – about me having as much right to be at Rothiedrum House as he had himself and that the necklace belonged – in the family. I didna understand any o' that at the time but I do now – oh, darling old Oggie – I do now.'

Putting her head in her hands she burst into a passion of weeping. Maggie stayed quiet while her daughter rid her heart of its pain, then she gave her a hanky and made her blow her nose and with tears in her own eyes she said, 'There, there, lassie, best to get it all out o' your system.' She held up the gold necklace and the blood-red stones seemed to catch fire in the flickering flames from the grate. 'This piece o' jewellery has known a wheen o' adventures and if it could speak it would have some gey peculiar tales to tell. Lord Lindsay, my father, gave it to his niece, Lady Marjorie, my cousin. When your father was taken to prison for what he did to Whisky Jake I swallowed my pride and went to ask her ladyship for help. She didn't give me money, instead she gave me the necklace. I sold it and used the money to get the best lawyer in the land for your father.

'Years later you showed me the self-same necklace and told me how you had come by it. Dyod! How I laughed. That rascal Lord Lindsay! I guessed he had spotted it in a shop window, recognized it, and, having bought it back and put two and two together, he presented it to you, knowing fine well you would show it to me and I couldna very well make you give it back. Ach, I wish things had been different between him and me, it would have been fine knowing a man wi' the same sense o' humour as myself.'

'Oh, yes, Oggie's such an individual,' Evelyn said eagerly, her eyes red and puffy but shining just the same. 'I loved him so, if I had kent he was my grandfather I wouldna have let go o' him so easily, but it wasn't to be, he's so far away, probably in Africa, he might even be dead, I lost them both, Oggie and Gillie . . .' She paused and looked at her mother, then in a rush she told of her strange experience in Cleveden Mansions the day before.

'If it's meant, you'll meet him again, Evie.' Maggie seemed to echo Grace's words, then she sighed. 'Such a fine lad, if only you and he . . .' Giving herself a mental shake she grew brisk. 'Sell the necklace, Evie, it's what your grandfather would have wanted, he couldna give you money but was determined to help in some way and the time has come for you to put his gift to good use. It willna do anything for anyone lying mouldering in a dark corner. Tell Davie about it but dinna mention a thing about Gillan being your cousin, he might be jealous, Davie was aye jealous o' Gillan.'

*

135

Davie made no fuss as to how she had come by the precious piece of jewellery, rather he was only too delighted to learn of it and Evelyn realized then just how desperate he was to get out of the bit. In the old days he would have needled and pried and would have driven her to distraction with his suspicious questions.

As it was he could hardly wait for the weekend so that they could both have the time to go round the various jewellers to see which one would offer the best price for the necklace. As it happened, they suffered the same depressing search that Maggie had once experienced when she had tramped the length and breadth of Aberdeen looking for a generously minded jeweller. And in the end they were forced to do as Maggie had done all those years ago, accept a poor offer and a 'think yourselves lucky, times are hard' lecture when a little man with seedy eyes and a skull cap on his shiny bald head, finally – and most unwillingly – counted the notes into Davie's palm.

'Will it be enough for you to set up in your own business?' Evelyn wondered when they stood in a close, counting the money all over again.

'Hardly, but it doesn't matter, I could go into partnership with Stashie, the bugger has a good thing going for him. If he agrees it would mean the end o' all the degrading squabbles I've endured for so long, he would have to toe the line if we were partners.'

Evelyn experienced a great sense of disappointment, she had wanted more, much more for Davie than this, but the sight of her husband's shining eyes made her hold her counsel and there, in a draughty close in the middle of Glasgow, she hugged him and they both laughed as they hadn't done for a long time.

To celebrate they had tea at Miss Cranston's and that night they queued for an hour outside a picture-house in the town but didn't mind, there were buskers to entertain them and an old man to dance and sing for them, and all of it worth the few pennies they threw into the soiled caps on the pavement.

In the warm dark inside the cinema Davie put his arm around her shoulders, she snuggled against him and felt seventeen and it was oh, so good, to get away from the house and to feel young and carefree again . . . and Gillie was her cousin. She couldn't quite take that in yet, she needed time to be by herself so that she could get used to the idea. For as long as she could remember he had been Gillie, a young man who seemed always to have been in her life, now he was Gillie, her second cousin, they shared the same blood, ties that inextricably bound them together for all time. Happy as she was that one thought kept creeping back into her mind and the wonder and the sadness of it brought tears to her eyes even while she looked and laughed at the larger-than-life film stars acting their part up there on the silver screen.

Stashie Dunbar put up very little objection to Davie's suggestion of becoming his partner, in fact he was altogether amenable to the whole idea and sat down there and then to discuss terms and conditions. Certainly he grumbled and argued over the amount Davie mentioned to secure the deal but all in all he was quite pleased about everything and was most anxious to show the young man that he intended to be a fair and honest partner.

'I know o' a good lawyer who will have the necessary papers ready in no time,' he nodded, gasping a bit as he gulped the dram of whisky he had insisted they both have to celebrate.

'I know o' a better one,' Davie returned firmly, anxious that the older man should see he could be business-like when he wanted.

'Makes no buggering difference to me, son,' Stashie maintained, pulling deeply on the soggy remains of his cigarette. He then fell into a fit of coughing that prevented further exchanges. His fragile lungs were worse than ever these days and his fits of coughing sometimes worried even Davie who had been used to them for years. Some said he had 'the galloping consumption', the dread disease that made people discuss it in whispers lest more boisterous ponderings might invite fate to bestow similar terrors on themselves.

Glasgow was full of it, the tuberculosis, it spawned and flourished everywhere, from the meanest hovel to the most respectable home, though it proliferated most where living conditions were insanitary and over-crowded.

But Davie was so used to the sounds from Stashie's labouring lungs he never attributed them to anything more serious than the combined results of mustard gas and nicotine poisoning, and, because he saw the man almost every day of his life, he never noticed that his eyes were growing more sunken or that his pocked unhealthy pallor had become whiter and more waxen-like than ever.

And forbye, once the legalities of the partnership were finalized, with Stashie's signature safely scrawled on the documents, Davie was so full of his new-found status he had little time to spare for the sufferings of a man who had made him suffer enough with his mean, penny-pinching ways. After that, things changed for the better as far as Davie was concerned. He no longer picked up a weekly wage but saw to it that he got a fair share of the profits. He made Stashie take in more commitments than he would hitherto consider and to balance out the extra work he hired a young lad fresh out of school to do the more menial tasks connected with the trade.

'We canny afford an apprentice,' Stashie had growled, 'we'll never make any profit wi' that young bugger mooning around the place, getting under our feet.'

'He's a good worker and he doesn't moon, he's keen

to learn and we need someone like him to do the sort o' footery things that used to take up a lot o' my precious time. Now I can get on with the real carpentry and if we all pull together we'll make a real go o' this business.'

Davie had the last word; young Joss Coburn stayed. He enjoyed the work and learned quickly. The industrious sounds in the ramshackle hut at the top of The Sac were so satisfyingly intense they almost drowned out the fearful hackings and raspings from Stashie's sick lungs.

CHAPTER 14

Midsummer was just a week away and the weather was hot and sultry. Evelyn woke to a loud squeaking from the street outside. It was a familiar sound; if there were no extra hands to help them carry their load of washing to the steamie, the women of Govan heaped their bundles onto home-made bogies or into ancient prams, and set off for the communal wash-house.

This one was early, anxious no doubt to secure a favourite stall for the sum of a shilling an hour. Each enclosure had its own boiler, sink and small iron, and on cold winter days the steamie was a warm and congenial place to be.

In summer it was rather too warm for comfort but a necessary evil for busy housewives trachled with the never-ending task of keeping their bairns clean. Summer or winter, it was considered something of an outing for lonely old ladies who were provided with cheerful company for the duration of their time spent there.

Evelyn had gone only once, when she was new and fresh from the country, and she had been awed at the noise of the machines, and of the bustle of children tramping blankets for their mothers. Women with turbans covering dangerous looking steel curlers had scurried about, looking most intent and business-like and all of them seemed to know just what they were about and what they had to do next.

As well as everything else there was an iron drying rack called a horse which, when pulled out and hung with clothes, was then pushed back into a quick-drying chamber. Evelyn had heard the women shouting, asking one another if there were any spare horses, and in her naïveté she had imagined the steamie to be attached to a stable of some sort.

She had felt strange and out of place and hadn't realized she was meant to have her stall for only an hour till a large, red-faced woman had burst in to tell her in plain terms that her time was up.

Hot and bothered, she had bundled her wet washing into a sheet, tied it up as best she could, and had run from the place, red-faced, humiliated, feeling she wanted to leave Govan there and then. To make matters worse her bundle had burst in the middle of the street, much to the amusement of passers-by who nonetheless, seeing her anguish, had hurried to help, all the while offering kindly words of sympathy.

'I'll never go back there, Mam!' she had exploded the minute she got home and Maggie had taken the sodden washing into the scullery to immerse it in soap suds and hang it on the window ropes to dry.

After that Evelyn had made do with the backcourt wash-house and today was her turn, the squeaky pram wheels had reminded her as soon as she opened her eyes.

But for a few moments she lay, watching the sun slanting over the red sandstone walls of the building opposite, in her mind's eye picturing it dappling the cool earth beneath the little grove of trees surrounding King's Croft.

A familiar feeling of nausea seized her but she fought it down, she wouldn't allow herself to dwell on it, she didn't want to acknowledge to herself that she was pregnant again so she forced her mind onto other things. She thought of the long, hot day ahead, the kitchen would become like an oven, with the sashes thrown wide to catch any stray breezes that would bring with them the heavy stale stench of the backcourt middens. It would be oppressive and dusty and her washing would hang limply on the lines but at least it was better than a warm rainy day when nothing ever got dry and bits of black soot adhered to the damp clothes.

She was alone in the bed, Davie was already up and away to The Sac. It had always been his habit to rise early so that he could creep into the kitchen and sup a solitary breakfast before the house was astir. It never entered his head to go down to the wash-house to fill the boiler and kindle the fire beneath it.

That wasn't his place, it was woman's work, he had made that clear from the start, but Jamie didn't mind, summer or winter, providing he hadn't been hitting the bottle too hard: he got up early on his daughter's wash-day to go down and stoke the boiler fires.

He looked tired, she thought, when she went through that morning, his face was blue-veined, his eyes puffy, but as always he greeted her warmly and went to the scullery to pour hot water from the kettle so that she could have her wash.

Maggie was over at the fire, stirring an enormous pan of porridge with a wooden spoon, the three eldest children were up but James was just wakening and Evelyn plucked his hot little body from the sheets, to kiss his sleepy face and ruffle his tousled hair.

'He peed the bed again last night, Mother,' complained Meg in aggrieved tones. 'Rachel took him in beside her for a while and I don't want to sleep beside them any more. Can I have a bed o' my own? In the cupboard recess in The Room? I wouldn't bother you or Father. Betty McIntyre sleeps in The Room with her parents and she says it's great no' to be kicked by her brothers any more.'

'Betty McIntyre's a baby,' sneered Alex. 'She was sent ben The Room to sleep because she grat like a bairn when Bobby showed her his willie one night . . .'

'Eat your porridge,' ordered Maggie firmly, fixing a button here, tying a shoelace there. She was more than a grandmother to the children, she was Head Mother as well, and though Evelyn was grateful for her help, and acknowledged the benefits attached to such a capable pair of hands, she sometimes wished that Maggie wouldn't take so much upon herself.

When first they had come to Govan, Evelyn had insisted on doing everything herself but it had been a useless attempt, her mother had been birthing and rearing bairns for most of her life, her word had been law and she wasn't going to take a back seat when her help was so obviously needed, and Evelyn often had to bite her tongue to stop herself saying things she might later regret.

Maggie had served the porridge, she now tied a bib round little Jimmy's neck and began helping him spoon food into his mouth.

'Mam,' Evelyn said quietly, 'he's five years old, he can well feed himself, you'll have him a baby all his life if you go on treating him like one.'

'Och, he is a baby,' Maggie returned indulgently, kissing the nape of his neck. 'He's such a nervous, shy wee thing and needs help wi' so many things yet.'

The smell of food was making Evelyn feel sick and she pushed her plate away, avoiding her mother's eyes. Meg and Alex were arguing again, Evelyn looked at them and swallowed hard; four children in a room and kitchen were enough, she could cope with that, but five — five young and hungry mouths to feed, five growing bodies to clothe as well as all the other demands . . . Certainly things were a bit better financially since Davie had gone into partnership with Stashie but even so, purse-strings were tight. They didn't have that much more than before because Davie said he was trying to build up the business and didn't want to take any more out of it than was necessary. God alone knew what he would have to say about another baby on the way . . .

'It isna easy for you, lass,' Jamie observed as he helped his daughter downstairs with her washing. 'No privacy, no peace, your parents breathing down your neck at every turn.'

'No, Father, it isna easy,' she agreed, 'but never think I dinna want you or Mam, it's just . . .'

'Ay, I ken fine, it's just you should have a place o' your own, you and Davie. Why don't you go back to Rothiedrum, Evie? You've never been happy since you left.'

'No, I canna do that, Father. Davie would never fit into the country ways, he likes the town and would never settle anywhere else. Besides – even if we wanted to we couldn't afford it, there would be no work for Davie in Rothiedrum, no' the kind o' work he would want, anyway.'

In the busy hours that followed she forgot her worries. In some strange way she enjoyed this washday ritual, it was about the only time she could be alone to dream for a while, to empty her mind of mundanities and just let her thoughts drift.

The interior of the brick-built wash-house was always warm and steamy, no matter the weather. The wooden sinks had sloping fronts which made for a comfortable standing position. Her packet of Co-operative A1 washing powder soon had a good lather going and she swished white windsor soap over the collars before rubbing them on the washing board.

The adjoining backcourt wash-house abutted onto that of 198. Inside it, Mrs Boag from the single-end at the top of the street was doing her washing. Evelyn could hear her emitting a highpitched tuneless dirge that was meant to be a song of some sort.

It was about the only time that Isa Boag made any sounds that could be described as buoyant; in the normal way of things she went about her business with a glum countenance that seldom cracked into a smile.

She and Big Aggie had continual loud altercations that were the talk of the street. They argued about anything for the sake of it; whose turn it was to do the close; whose turn it was for the wash-house, the clothes lines, and so on.

Isa accused Big Aggie's Man of many things, not to his face but through the medium of his large, domineering wife. The most recent allegation had amused the entire neighbourhood.

'Your man peed the close,' Isa had stated aggressively. 'I saw him, wi' my very own een, standin' at the close-back the other night, peein' against the wall like a horse, gettin' rid o' all that beer he knocks back.'

'My man wouldny do that, he *knows* better!' Big Aggie had yelled defensively, not for her man's sake but for her own, since she liked to think she had a reputation for cleanliness that was second to none.

'His buttons were undone and he was peein' against the wall!' persisted Isa Boag. 'He was makin' more steam than a bob's worth at the steamie and when he saw me he turned right round and shook the damned thing *at* me.'

'And how would you know what he was shakin'? I doubt if you've ever even seen one! You didny get these two lassies o' yours in the normal way o' things, you pulled them out the midden when you were rakin' to see what you could get. Oh ay, I know all aboot that, Isa Boag, it's been the talk o' the steamie for years.'

And so it had gone on, the recriminations, the denials. Afterwards, Willie Dick wasn't seen for a week. When he finally emerged into the light of day he was sporting a black eye which he said he had acquired on the brass drying rail above the range.

Evelyn smiled to herself as she rubbed and scrubbed and listened to Isa Boag's 'singing'. The next minute there was a yell, followed by scuffles and bumps. Evelyn guessed what was happening. Isa's eldest daughter, Patsy, round-shouldered and dour like her mother, was the unmarried mother of two unruly toddlers, who, according to Big Aggie's dark mutterings, had come from the midden the same as the rest of the Boags. No matter from whence they had sprung, Isa Boag treated them as she had her own children when they were young.

Renowned for her thrift, which some called meanness, she had never been one to waste anything, far less a boilerful of good hot water, so into the house she had stumped to emerge holding two small boys by the scruff of their collars. Under much duress they were stripped and dumped without ceremony into the suds and weren't backward about voicing their protests. When the bumps and yells had died down, Isa herself appeared in the doorway of 198's wash-house.

'Have ye a bit windsor soap ye could lend me, Evie?' she queried, slitting her eyes against a cloud of smoke from the wet-looking cigarette that was dangling from her lips.

'Come in, Isa,' invited Evelyn hospitably. 'If you'll just wait a wee minute I'll be finished with these collars and you can have the whole bar.'

Isa came in to lean her mottled arms on the draining board, the ash from her cigarette cascading down on top of a white shirt that had just been washed. She had a very distinctive appearance, had Isa Boag, 'a bachle o' a wifie, wi' a face on her like a bashed turnip' being the fond description of her female contemporaries. It was a cruelly accurate description as everything about her was untidy and oddly flat, as if she had been put through a mangle and had never reverted back to a normal human shape.

Her wide nose was crushed into her shapeless face which lent her small eyes an almost oriental slant; her greasy brown hair was perpetually encased in menacing-looking steel curlers which lanced out from a mangy green headscarf; an ample brown cardigan, which had once belonged to her husband, was pinned across her flat, floppy breasts but only partially concealed the dirty, flower-print apron that was never off her back. 'She goes to bed wi' it on,' claimed Big Aggie who, acting the good if nosy neighbour, had once tended Isa when she had 'flu and had witnessed 'wi' her very own een' a corner of the apron sticking out from the blankets.

Beneath a heavy tweed skirt, Isa's thin, white, fire-mottled legs plunged into rolls of stockings while her large, splayed feet were stuck into brown-check slippers with dingy grey 'fur' collars. In these she shuffled every-where, even to Greasy Joe's at the corner to 'fetch fish suppers for the weans' tea'.

She was not above a flutter on the horses and could 'talk nags' with any man in the street. Her own man had long ago departed this earth. 'And far better he'll be up yonder, poor sowel,' was Big Aggie's opinion. Despite Isa Boag's mournful appearance, Evelyn liked her; she enjoyed her quaintness and her equally whimsical manner of speech and, if nothing else, Isa could always be relied upon to take anyone's mind off their worries, she was so busy blethering away about her own.

She chatted away to Evelyn, like an amiable dog who had buried its bone and no longer fretted that it might be stolen, then she remembered the children waiting for her in the clothes boiler, and with an attempt at speed she grabbed the proffered soap from Evelyn's hands and made for the door. There she bumped full tilt into Big Aggie herself. It was like a collision of two enormous ocean liners. Both women went down, with Big Aggie, having put her foot on the wet cake of windsor soap, slithering gracefully if unwillingly the length of the wash-house floor, before coming to rest at Evelyn's feet. Evelyn was helpless with laughter and could do nothing except hold onto the sink and give way to her mirth.

The women ranted at one another but, surprisingly, Big Aggie's ire was short-lived. Red-faced and panting she struggled to her feet and pausing only briefly to catch her breath she gasped, 'Come quickly, there's been an accident in Skerries Road, a tram has run over a woman and there's some who are sayin' it's Winnie Grainger.'

Without another word all three women ran to the scene of the accident, Isa stopping only long enough at her door to deliver two sopping wet boys into her daughter's arms.

CHAPTER 15

A crowd had gathered in the street outside the chemist's shop. Evelyn pushed her way through but stopped short at the sight which met her eyes. Everyone had piled out of the tram, the driver and the conductor were standing close together, white-faced, talking in low voices. Mr Laing, the chemist, was on his knees, bending over the body of a woman lying half under the tram wheels.

Evelyn couldn't see her face, only the lower half of her body. Her mangled limbs were covered in blood, her clothes were in tatters, but Evelyn recognized the cheap, print frock and the remains of a slipper that adhered to one poor white foot. She had helped Douglas Grainger dress his wife many times and she had lost count of how often she had helped Winnie to don her slippers . . . That dress, that thin little dress with its sprinklings of pink and blue roses – only last week Douglas had come upstairs to show it to herself and Maggie, his face both anxious and pleased.

'She needed a new summer frock, it isn't much but it's all I could manage . . .'

His words rang in Evelyn's ears, she shuddered. 'Mr Laing.' She touched the chemist's arm. 'I'm Evelyn Grainger, this – I think – I canna see her face but – I'm certain she's my mother-in-law.'

'I know who you are,' he said kindly, as he spoke peeling off his white coat to gently place it over the crushed body lying on the blood-spattered tram rails. 'She's gone, lassie, there's nothing anyone can do for her now – except perhaps pray.'

Isa Boag put a comforting arm round the girl's shoulders. She smelled of old chip grease and nicotine but even so Evelyn was very glad of her stout support in those dreadful moments.

'Oh, dear God!' The tram driver staggered and would have fallen but for a dozen pairs of hands reaching out to hold him up. 'She just ran out,' he muttered through bloodless lips, 'I couldny stop in time, I couldny!'

The police arrived, followed by an ambulance, just as Douglas Grainger burst onto the scene to absorb it in one swift horrified glance.

'Winnie?' He spoke her name like a question, his voice rising on the last syllable. Wildly he looked around and made a pathetic appeal to the crowd, as if feeling he had to exonerate himself of blame. 'I only left her for a few minutes, I had to get the messages, she wanted biscuits for her tea . . . I only left her for a wee while . . .'

'Sir.' A tall policeman put a steadying hand on his arm and spoke quietly to him. A few minutes later the crowd watched sympathetically as he followed the stretcher into the ambulance, still clutching a packet of tea and a crumpled bag of broken biscuits he had bought at Miss Cunningham's shop on the corner of Younger Park Street. The old lady always kept a large tin of broken biscuits to sell to the neighbourhood youngsters. They had been all that Douglas Grainger could afford – and Winnie had never minded what they looked like, just as long as she had a biscuit of some sort to dip into her late-morning cuppie . . . only this morning she had been too impatient to wait and had gone out looking for Douglas – then she had forgotten all about him and had set out to look for Danny instead . . . perhaps, at last, she had found him.

No matter how much they might disagree in the course of everyday living, when it came to times of tragedy the people of the tenements closed ranks and helped one another all they could. In the days following Winnie's dreadful accident, Douglas Grainger couldn't have had more kindness and sympathy shown to him.

On the day of the funeral, the big black horses in their plumes and gear waited in the street outside 198, champing their bits and tossing their proud heads. It was very hot, the road was sticky with melting tar; all the windows were thrown wide but there was no wisp of a breeze to stir the muslin curtains. One or two solemn-faced children stood at close-mouths to stare in quiet wonder at all the activity. The knot of people outside 198 murmured in subdued tones amongst themselves and fanned their warm faces with newspapers in an effort to keep cool.

Maggie fixed the knot in Jamie's black tie. 'Are you sure you'll be all right?' she whispered, looking anxiously at him. 'It's a fair walk to the cemetery, you look all in as it is and you'll boil in that heavy suit.'

'Ach, I'll be fine, Maggie,' he said gruffly, ashamed of himself as he always was when she showed concern for symptoms that were the results of his own excesses. The blackness of his garb accentuated the whiteness of his face and hair. A lot of whisky had been drunk over the past few days and he hadn't refused a single glass. Winnie Grainger was dead, it was only decent to see her off with a good dram or two, the other men were doing the same thing, it was a funeral after all, everyone drank at a funeral. So he had consoled himself as he anaesthetized his senses with alcohol.

Evelyn stood at the window, wishing that a cool wind might blow in to embrace her hot body. Her head ached, she felt heavy and sick, she had a painful stitch in her side and she was glad that Grace had taken the children over to her house for the day.

Quite unconsciously Evelyn's hands moved to her belly. She hadn't told anyone about the baby yet, far less Davie, and especially not at a time like this. He would have to know sometime, of course, but later, much later. She was only three months gone after all, it wouldn't show yet . . .

She glanced over at Davie and his father. Both men were composed but drawn and tired looking. Although in a sense one had lost a wife, the other a mother, a long time ago, death had struck the final blow and neither man had spoken very much since the accident.

'Poor Mother,' Davie had said to Evelyn when the news had been broken to him, 'she diced with death for so long, going out of the house in those freezing winter nights wearing only her nightclothes, trudging the darkest and meanest alleys and wynds, speaking to drunks and prostitutes and God knows who else, and in the end she is killed almost on her own doorstep, fully clothed and in the broad light o' day. I don't miss what she was, Evie, but who she used to be, my mother, for better or for worse, it makes no difference any more. She's out o' it now, it's my father I worry about, he gave everything he had to her. He gave up everything to be wi' her, it was a life filled wi' emptiness, now it's an emptiness filled wi' life – his life, because as he gets more and more used to being on his own he'll become more and more aware o' himself and his needs and it will be hard for him to pick up the pieces again.'

It was a long and profound speech for Davie but Evelyn knew what he meant and she too worried about Douglas Grainger and wept for him in his loneliness.

The coffin containing Winnie's body had been brought upstairs and placed in The Room. Davie had been grateful to Maggie for suggesting that, since his father's house was really too small for a funeral.

'We can see to things better up here,' Maggie had told him. 'You and Evie could move downstairs till it's all over and we'll squeeze your father into the kitchen somehow

– it wouldna be very nice for him, to be in The Room – or downstairs – wi' the coffin.'

He had taken her hand and had squeezed it, much to her surprise because he seldom, if ever, displayed any warmth towards her. 'Thanks, Maggie, it's good o' you to think o' it.'

'It's your house,' she had returned drily.

He had smiled wryly at that. 'Point taken,' he had nodded and had said nothing more on the subject.

The undertaker came upstairs, the coffin was fetched from The Room, the black-coated procession made its way downstairs. Jamie's feet were a trifle unsteady beneath him but Davie's steadying hand under his elbow helped the moment to pass.

The knot of people at the close-mouth moved aside, a hushed silence descended over the street, the heat beat down over the rooftops, the horses jingled their harness; the echoes of a lusty cry two streets away came stout and brave and cheerful to the ears of the silent groups of people in Camloan Road.

'Ra-ags! Any old ra-ags!'

It was a normal, boisterous sound, welcomed by the children who had been bundled indoors till the mournful business of a funeral was over with. Small faces appeared at windows. 'Mammy, Mammy, the ragman! Can I . . .'

Curtains moved, the young faces disappeared as swiftly as they had come.

The coffin was placed on the hearse, the driver took up the reins, wheels began to rumble, the menfolk in their black suits and bowlers composed themselves for the walk to the cemetery. It was a well turned out procession. No matter how impoverished the circumstances, the folk of the tenements somehow managed to give their departed loved ones a good send-off; from birth to the grave, a few pennies a week life endowment gave peace of mind, and it was as natural to have a visit from 'the insurance man' as it was to pay the milkman when he came on his rounds.

The neighbours had clubbed together to buy a wreath, it, together with other floral arrangements, sat on top of the coffin, and it was altogether a most impressive funeral hearse with the dressed horses arching their plumed heads and the line of soberly attired mourners following behind the carriage.

'Ach, poor, poor soul,' Mrs Boyle sniffed into her hanky. She had made an extra special effort with the pipe clay in order that the close shouldn't get a 'showing up' for the funeral. 'It's maybe a terrible thing to say but she's as well away. Life was nothing to her without her laddie.'

'She had her man and her other boy,' commented Mamie Black from the back close single-end. Mamie had lost her husband and a brother at the Somme and had been left to bring up three children on her own. 'Too bad she didn't make an effort to appreciate them better.'

'Her mind was away, she didny know what she was doin',' came from Mrs Jarvie, top landing. 'Something just snapped in her head when her youngest boy got himself killed.'

A curtain twitched at an upstairs window. Isa Boag glanced up. 'There's Creepin' Jesus at her window, too sleakit to watch openly like the rest o' us.'

'Ach, she's no the full shillin' either,' was Mamie Black's opinion. 'She frightens me to death the way she comes slinkin' past my window at all hours. Why she canny go down to the midden in the daytime, beats me.'

'She's ashamed o' her rubbish,' sniffed Isa Boag disgustedly.

'Ay, an' you should know what you're talkin' about,'

put in Big Aggie meaningfully – but quietly, out of respect for the dead.

'Ashamed o' her rubbish?' queried Mrs Jarvie with raised brows.

'Ay, just that.' Isa Boag's lumpy face squashed into a conspiratorial grimace and the others lowered their heads to hear better. 'Meths.' She spoke the word in a long, drawn-out hiss.

'You canny mean she's a . . . ?'

'Whit else? I've seen and smelt the bottles for myself.'

'Ach, it canny be, no' Creepin' Jesus. She signed the Pledge at the Band o' Hope when she was eight. Her man tells everybody that.'

'To put them off the scent,' persisted Isa Boag. 'And a pledge taken so long ago isny worth the paper it's written on. He'll likely be one himself – her man – a meths drinker. He has that queer, blotchy face on him.'

'But he has the asthma,' said a dainty little Italian woman who had married a Scot and went by the name of Angelina McTavish. 'The sound of it comes up to us in the flat above. That will be why he has the yellow face, no air getting into his lungs.'

'No, it's her cooking that causes that queer colour,' decided Mrs Boyle triumphantly. 'She uses nothing but the frying pan, you can smell it a mile away.'

'Maybe that's why she acts so queer – the meths, I mean,' said Mamie Black thoughtfully.

A concerned ripple ran suddenly through the crowd. One of the funeral horses had stumbled on the sticky tar and had gone down. There was a tense silence while a sacking hood was slipped over the beast's face. One of the men sat on its neck to calm it. Then it was up and after a few moments the procession got going again. The onlookers dispersed; the curtains became still at the windows;

Winnie Grainger had left her single-end at 198 Camloan Road forever.

In days to come, Evelyn could never pass by 'Winnie's window' without expecting to see her white, sad face staring out, singing in her tuneless but oddly sweet voice the song that had become familiar to everyone who had ever passed along Camloan Road. She had disappeared into the mists of time and of memory because those who had never loved her soon forgot her. It was difficult to remember a shadow and that was what Winnie had become in the latter years of her life.

Douglas, too, disappeared along a shadowy unfamiliar road but there was hope at the end of his tunnel because his journeyings were of this life and his goal was Canada, that faraway land where so many Scots pinned their faith in the difficult years after the Great War.

Douglas had always paid life insurance policies, both for himself and his wife, and he had never fallen behind with the premiums, no matter how hard it had been of late. After Winnie's funeral bill was paid there had been some surplus money left, enough for him to pay his fare to Canada where he was to stay with an old workmate till he got on his feet.

The parting of father and son was poignant, filled with the grief and pain of not knowing when, if ever, they would meet again.

'I'll write, son.' Douglas swallowed the lump in his throat. 'I was never one for that sort o' thing but I'll do my best to keep you posted.'

'Ay, Father.' Davie dashed away his tears and took his father to his breast. 'I'll miss you, you've been a good father to me. May all the luck in the world go wi' you, you deserve only the best from now on, you've given so much o' yourself these last years, now you have to take something back.'

Douglas looked deep into his son's eyes. 'You'll be good to Evie and the bairns? I know fine you didn't bargain for another but you canny lay the blame for that at Evie's door.'

Davie didn't answer, simply because he was too ashamed to admit that he had already done just that, and in no uncertain terms either.

He had ranted at his wife when she had broken the news of the forthcoming child. He had told her they couldn't afford another one, that Stashie was acting the mean old man again and making excuses about the customers not paying up.

Then he looked at her and saw something in her face that had never been there before. She was pale and strained, the glorious hair that had always been her pride and joy lacked the rich sheen that gave it so much of its beauty, those eyes that had always sparkled and danced with life were dull and uninterested; but there was more, much more than just physical signs of apathy. She gave the impression of not caring very much about anything any more, she just stood there while he shouted at her and never so much as answered back, whereas in the old days she would have defended herself with spirit and might even have flown at him with tooth and nail, such was the tempestuous nature of her make-up.

He had been afraid then, afraid of what he was doing to his Evie, and after that he had been kinder to her and more considerate than he had been for years. His father's words had brought it all back and with the poignancy of parting so strong in his heart he vowed afresh to try and make a better life for Evie and the children.

'I'll be interested to know how you get on in Canada,' he told Douglas. 'Who knows, if things don't get better here I might follow you out. Once I got a job and a home together I could send for Evie and the bairns.'

'Don't do anything rash, son,' advised Douglas. 'I've only myself to consider now, and never forget, Evie has her parents to think of. Oh, I know fine you've aye resented them in your home but they're her family and never despise the love and loyalty she holds in her heart for them.'

'I'm never likely to forget that,' Davie answered a trifle bitterly, but said no more, his beloved father was going somewhere far away from him and all else paled into insignificance now that the time to say goodbye was here.

So Douglas Grainger left 198 Camloan Road, never looking back at the window where his wife had kept her long, lonely vigil. All that belonged in the past now, his mind was on the journey over the ocean and the life that awaited him in Canada where so many Scots had settled over the years.

It wasn't long before the window was occupied again, this time by Mrs Jenny Jack, wife of Jack Jack. Mrs Jack looked much older than her man. Her extremely large and palsied head continually nodded backwards and forwards on her hunched shoulders, her teeth were reminiscent of great uneven yellow-brown fence posts, jutting out from a bulldog-like lower jaw, grey hair was scraped back into an untidy bun, suspicious looking bloodshot eyes glared out from behind big round glasses, her skin had the appearance of brown-mottled parchment and she sat every day at the window, one massive wrinkled arm resting on a velour cushion on the sill.

The children of the neighbourhood had bestowed witch-like qualities on poor, harmless Winnie, but now their imaginations were stretched to the limit over what to call Jenny because to them she was more than a witch, she was a fearsome gaping creature who glared at them so fiercely as they passed by they were soon afraid of passing her at all. It became a test of nerves to approach 198 and run the risk of Old Evil Eye, as she had quickly become, casting a spell over them.

But oddly enough it was Jack Jack who inspired the most fear in them. Old Evil Eye might look frightening but her swollen rheumaticky legs saw to it that she was mostly imprisoned at the window; Jack on the other hand seemed always to be abroad, both by night and by day, and if his wife didn't get you with her malevolent glares, Jack got you in a more physical way, usually by the scruff of the neck where he held you firmly till he had administered a good hefty cuff or two on the ears.

His strength was phenomenal and oddly disquieting because he was a tiny little man, was Jack Jack, with short stubby legs encased in wide trousers and a round, florid face leering out from under a scone-shaped tweed bonnet.

He was always smartly dressed, sometimes in a navy suit with a watch-chain dangling from the pocket, at other times he stepped out confidently in a light-coloured flannel suit, with a cap of the same shade and material, sitting proudly on top of his 'Monk's haircut'.

At first his appearance invited ridicule from the youngsters, he was made to be laughed at with his pompous struttings and his quiet air of respectability sitting heavily on his narrow shoulders. But a few well aimed cuffs from a surprisingly meaty hand soon changed the minds of would-be tormentors and Jack Jack went on his confident way, enjoying a refreshment now and again at one of the better-class pubs and indulging in an occasional flutter on the nags. When Isa Boag heard of this last 'vice', as Big Aggie was wont to describe it, she tried to ingratiate herself with the little man, but to no avail.

'Just who does he think he is?' she sniffed huffily. 'A bloody wee fart like that wi' legs on him like deformed porridge spurtles. They're no' even high enough for a dog to get a good pee against, and to think a totie wee keelie like him has the cheek to tell me it's no' decent for a woman to gamble. I could teach him things on that score that would make that bloody fancy bunnet o' his rise off his heid a' thegither.'

'Ay, and that's no' all.' Big Aggie nodded self-righteously, for once agreeing with every word Isa said. 'The nags and the booze is no' the only things he's enjoying. That poor wife o' his doesny know the half o' it.' She lowered her voice and rasped confidentially, 'He's been seen, up a close, wi' a hoor, twice his size and paps on her like a feather bolster. Goin' at her he was, his wee legs workin' away at the double and his trouser bottoms raisin' enough stoor in the close to blind an army.'

'How did he reach her?' Isa wanted to know with comic sarcasm. 'Did he bring the stepladders or did she?'

To their new home, Jenny and Jack had brought with them their grandniece, Jessie Jack. Her parents were both dead and rather than put her in a home she had been adopted by her great-aunt and uncle. It had been a brave move on their part and one that showed a noble side to the Jacks that their new neighbours had to appreciate despite all the odds.

Fourteen-year-old Jessie Jack had suffered an attack of meningitis as a baby which had left her mentally retarded for life. She was a big, hefty, lumbering creature with wild ginger hair sprouting out from her abnormally large head. She was belligerent and unruly and appeared to have no idea of what was right or wrong, helpless babies in prams being the main targets for her unpredictable temper. She scratched and nipped them, stole their toys and belted them till they screamed. She stole sweets and money from older children and soon became the neighbourhood terror.

Mothers complained to the older Jacks, and when that didn't work they complained to the police, but Jessie Jack seemed to have an uncanny ability to sniff out the law and was sly enough never to be caught in the act. After that the children of each close took it upon themselves to act as spies and as soon as Jessie was sighted the cry went up 'Clout's about! Clout's about!' whereupon babies were immediately whipped indoors and the children fled before 'Clout' could get at them.

When all was said and done, the new neighbours to the street were reckoned to be a poor exchange for the quiet and respectable Graingers, the children in particular mourning not so much Winnie the woman who was now no more to them than a ghost in their memory, but Witchie Winnie, the amiable soul who had conveniently played the part they wanted her to play and who had never harmed a fly, far less a child. Jenny, Jack, Jessie: all of them were to be feared and respected in their own right. The only way to live with Jessie and Jack was to avoid them whenever possible, the only way to pass Jenny's window was by dares and double dares and woe betide the boy or girl who received the full brunt of Old Evil Eye's glares. For hours afterwards they quaked in their shoes as they waited for the 'spell' to take effect and everything, from a skelped backside to a doubler from the teacher, was attributed to Jenny's malicious scowls. In reality she was just a sick old lady who suffered dreadful pain from rheumatism but to the children she was Ogress personified.

Evelyn wasn't alone in mourning the absence of Winnie's well-kent face from the window, nor was she the only one to pine for the familiar figure of Douglas going along the street for the messages, his worn canvas bag clutched in his hand, his weary face breaking into a smile as he paused to pass the time with a neighbour.

Camloan Road was the poorer for their going, and every resident there, man, woman and child, would have acknowledged it.

CHAPTER 16

It was both strange and wonderful to be back at Croft Donald. Grace had arranged that her fortnight's holiday should coincide with Evelyn's trip to Kenneray in order that she should accompany her. She hadn't said anything to either Nellie or Kenneth about coming and the look of surprise on their faces as she stepped down from the trap was a joy to behold.

'Grace! Evie!' Kenneth boomed, and gathered them both to the great hard wall of his chest while Iain Cameron, who had collected the visitors from the tiny station several miles away, discreetly took the horse's reins to lead him away to the stable.

More than ten years had elapsed since Kenneth had last set eyes on the sisters and his delight on seeing them again was infectious. When he had finished hugging them he took one in each arm and birled them round and round till they were breathless, laughing and dizzy. The years certainly hadn't diminished his legendary strength nor his hearty, booming laugh; he was as tall, if not taller than they remembered him, his barrel-like chest, which housed a set of lungs like enormous bellows, was as deep as an ox and thickly furred with hair that was the same colour as his luxuriant red-gold beard. He had always worn the kilt and when he whirled the women round, it flew up to reveal a fine pair of hairy strong legs.

His cool blue eyes were alight with pleasure and turning to Nellie he roared, 'Would you look at them, Nell lass! Are they no' a sight for sore eyes? Are you no' going to say hallo or are you just going to stand there all day thinking about it?'

162

Nellie came forward awkwardly, the girth of her swollen stomach making her look very un-Nellie-like. All of her life she had been sparsely padded and rather gaunt and though marriage to Kenneth had certainly rounded some contours others had remained the same. Her face had become fuller over the years but her breasts had remained austerely small and rather flat. Now they bulged and strained at the seams of her smock, her belly was an enormous encumbrance, and she looked uncomfortably hot standing there in the heat of the blue August day. But she was radiant, her fair hair shone in the sun, her skin was pink and glowing and the expression in her beautiful amber-green eyes was one of suppressed excitement and anticipation.

'Gracie, Evie,' she spoke their names as if savouring the sound of them, 'I'm being Nellie-ish again, I dinna ken what to say. It's grand – wonderful to see you again.' She laughed a trifle self-consciously. 'I canna get near you – for this.' Lovingly she patted her stomach and they all laughed and surrounded her and then it was all sister talk and breathless giggles of happiness.

'Grace,' she held onto her sister's hand, 'I thought I was lucky to have Evie come to stay, I never expected you as well.'

'I'm a nurse, remember?' smiled Grace serenely. 'I had to come to make sure you are properly looked after and though Evie is a bittie better now, she isna exactly fit enough to go galloping about like a two-year-old.'

'Fit enough?' Nellie turned to her youngest sister. 'Have you been ill, Evie? Nobody said anything. Mam wrote to say you were coming but she never mentioned . . .'

Grace's heightened colour matched that of Evelyn's. 'I'm sorry, I thought you kent about – about – the baby.'

Evelyn shrugged. 'I told Mam no' to say anything, I didna want to steal your thunder, Nellie . . .'

'Steal my thunder!' Nellie was being the big, strict sister

163

again. 'You know, Evie, I've kent you all my life but even yet you surprise me wi' your silly fads and fancies. You behave like a school bairn wi' daft wee secrets you think to keep from the world but I'm no' the world, Evie, I'm your sister, and I have a right to ken what is happening in your life.'

Grace was embarrassed at having given the game away and was glad when Kenneth crooked his arm and invited her to walk up to the house with him.

Evelyn was left with Nellie, a very hang-dog and subdued Evelyn who wouldn't meet her sister's eyes and affected to make a great fuss of a young Border collie who was all waving tail and panting grins.

'Och, Evie.' Nellie put her thumb under the girl's chin and made her look up. 'I'm sorry, I'm a besom, but I worry about you stuck there in the city wi' nothing but drudgery in your wee life. My Evie, the lass who used to run barefoot through the summer cornfields, nothing now but grey streets and smelly chimneys. You belong to the country, quine.' Her voice had grown husky, her heart was sore within her at seeing how white Evelyn was now that the colour was subsiding from her too-thin face. 'You are being stifled slowly but surely by the town, you who were aye so filled wi' life and hope.'

'Ach, Nellie.' Evelyn forced a laugh, dismayed by all this talk of the city when all she wanted to do was forget it for a while and concentrate instead on the wonders of being back in a place where the air was filled with the scents of clover and the beat of the ocean sang in her ears. 'It's no' as bad as all that. There are a lot o' things I enjoy about living in Govan and – well, to tell the truth, I've almost forgotten Rothiedrum, it was all so long ago.' She told the lie swiftly, hoping that her face wouldn't give her away again. 'And the reason I never told you about the baby was because I couldna believe it myself for quite a while. We really canna afford another one but

164

it's happened and we'll just have to manage as best we can.'

'Ay, no doubt,' Nellie said sourly. 'And no doubt either that Davie blamed you for it and conveniently forgot he had an equal part in it, but you're thin, quine, if Grace hadna said anything I would never have guessed you were carrying. You must only be a month or two gone.'

'Nearly five months, but I was sick a lot and maybe that has something to do with it.'

'Five months! Is it an elf you're having?' Her voice was a combination of sarcasm and worry. 'Come on.' She tucked her arm through Evelyn's. 'You're at Croft Donald now and I'm going to stuff you so full of eggs, cream, butter, and meat, you'll break poor old Buchan's back when the time comes for him to haul you away to the station in the cart.'

The rest of the family were in the house, Irene Cameron, Kenneth's mother, sweet-faced and fresh, a bit more grey in her hair but otherwise looking hardly a day older than when Evelyn had last seen her; Isla Nell, and Calum Alasdair, Kenneth's children from his first marriage to Jeannie who had died when she was still only a girl, leaving her heartbroken husband to bring the little ones up as best he could. When he married Nellie she quickly became a mother to his children and they just as quickly accepted her as such. She had always been special to them and it wasn't odd to them that she came into their home and did the same kind of things for them that Jeannie had once done.

They were a credit to Nellie, Isla Nell was now a dainty sixteen-year-old with a cloud of dark hair like her mother's and the same way of smiling, quick and shy, the blushes coming easily to the rose-petal bloom of her cheeks, her young body in repose giving the impression of great stillness but belying a quicksilver nature that could take her to the heights of happiness one minute, the depths of despair the next.

Calum Alasdair, known simply as Cal, had grown into a striking young man with the same build and colouring as his father and the same good nature though he was more reserved; his smile was warm and slow and fooled people into thinking he was a serious lad when all the time he was the reverse. Nellie had known him for most of his life but even yet his soothing presence could lull her into a false sense of peace for he delighted in suddenly picking her up and running with her round the room, not letting her down till he had extracted some ridiculous promise from her, the voicing of which would make them both clutch one another till they were breathless with laughter.

And here was Col, thin and delicate-looking beside the other boy who had looked after him like a brother ever since he had come to live at Croft Donald. Cal had always looked after Maggie's flawed son who was the same age as him and whose poor grasp of knowledge had often tried his patience but had seldom broken it. Col and Cal, the December twins, as they had been known when they were babies. But they bore scant resemblance to one another now, one so fit and bursting with life, the other so obviously frail and withdrawn from the world.

But Col remembered his sisters. When all the fuss and greetings were done with he came over to them, whispered, 'Gwace, Evie,' and putting his thin arms around them in turn he hugged them with such gentle affection each of them was moved to tears.

'Oh, Col,' Evelyn put her hand to her eyes to dash away the tears, 'it's so good to see you again, it's so good to be back.'

He nodded, as if understanding every word, then proudly he turned to Nellie and without any sign of embarrassment he patted her stomach. 'Baby,' he nodded, 'baby in Nella.'

'He kens all about it,' explained Nellie, flushing a little, it wouldn't have been Nellie if she hadn't looked just a little put out at such an intimate subject. 'I thought it best to prepare him and now he's really looking forward to having a bairn in the house. Look . . .' Opening a little work basket she pulled out a crudely fashioned rag doll with yellow wool hair and a big grinning red mouth. 'He made this, all by himself, it took him ages and ages but faith! He surprised us all by persevering till it was done. I dinna ken who was the most proud, him or me, but it's something we'll all treasure for every last stitch was a labour o' love.'

Col's blue eyes gleamed, he smiled and nodded and would have gone on smiling and nodding had not Irene called everyone to the table where a sumptuous tea had been laid in honour of the visitors.

Grace and Evelyn shared the same room, as they had done on previous visits to Croft Donald. In this vast feather bed, Evelyn had given birth to Alex ten years ago, and just a few months later she and Davie had lain here on their honeymoon. Oh, sweet memories, the long, busy days of haymaking, the nights of fun and laughter, great harvest moons hanging like yellow lanterns above the ocean – and the hours she and Davie had spent together alone in this huge soft bed that had happed them round with love and warmth while the sea whispered to the stars and everything that was in their world was mysterious and miraculous and infinite.

It was all so long ago now and even as Evelyn laughed and rejoiced with Grace at being back at Croft Donald, a part of her remained aloof and quiet and a great poignancy swelled in her heart as she lay back on the bed after Grace had gone downstairs. Gazing at the ceiling, those beautiful, happy-sad memories seemed to march, march, before her vision.

'So long ago,' she whispered. 'Where have all the dreams gone? Where is the magic now?'

Where had the years gone, for that matter? They had just passed, one after the other, birthing bairns, rearing them, struggling to keep them decently fed, never enough money to give them the kind of things she felt they ought to have. She would have liked a country upbringing for them, the same kind of childhood that she herself had had. Rachel would have loved it, she so enjoyed it when they went to the park, flowers and trees were a delight to her, her pale cheeks glowed when she talked of the birds they might see and she always took a bag of crumbs to feed to the ducks in the pond. Meg would have been Meg wherever she went, always wanting things she could never have, forever feeling life was cheating her in some way. Little James would have been afraid no matter where he was brought up, it was in that strange, passionate, sensitive nature of his to feel threatened by his surroundings. Alex now – ay, Alex. What would he have liked? He had always sworn to Nellie that he loved the country, that if he lived in it he would help on the croft and become a farmer himself someday. But how could he think these things? He had only been a baby when he left Croft Donald, hardly even a toddler when he had been taken from Dunmarnock to Govan. Yet there was something fathomless about Alex; when he said a thing he meant it. Perhaps he had inherited some of her sixth sense or it might simply be that a love of the country had been born in him.

'He loves horses.' She spoke aloud, not quite knowing why, because, until that moment, her eldest son's feelings towards animals of any sort had never really entered her head. But it came to her there as she lay on the bed, 'gazing at her thoughts on the ceiling', as she herself often put it. He was always drawing horses; other boys drew soldiers but Alex drew horses. He was kind to Dobbie Loan and would grab a carrot from the vegetable box in the scullery to rush downstairs with it and present it to Fishy Alice's tired old nag and while the animal's worn molars crunched the unexpected treat Alex would stand at his head, stroking it, murmuring soothing words into the flicking ears.

'We have that in common.' Again she spoke her thoughts aloud. 'At least we have that in common.'

A picture came to her of her firstborn lying here at her breast just after his birth. He had looked nothing like Davie, he had been big and fat and he had girned from the start. She hadn't been able to take to him, he was a stranger she didn't know and hadn't wanted to know and that feeling existed between them to this day because Alex knew, no one had ever said anything, but just the same Alex knew of her rejection of him as a baby.

She had tried everything she could to bring him close to her but it had all been in vain. Every day of his life, by some innuendo or action, he managed to convey to her how he felt and she knew he was punishing her for what she had done to him. Oh, Alex, she thought wearily, I wish I could give you horses, I wish I could give you the country, I wish you could give me a tiny wee bit of your love . . .

She put her hand up to her face. It was wet, she hadn't been aware of the tears. It was this bed, like a magic carpet it could carry her back into a past that had been so filled with laughter – and with tears.

The baby in her belly turned over, she could feel the hard lump of it under her hands, it might not be big but it was strong. It was in the safest place – the womb. In there it would get nourishment and warmth from her, once it was outside the problems would begin. She smiled; if only it was possible to keep a baby inside its mother's body till outside conditions were suitable for its survival . . .

'Evie.' There was a tap on the door and Isla put her head round. 'Mother Nell is looking for you. She says you've to get outside in the fresh air this minute, and that's an order — Mother Nell's, that is.'

Giggling, the girl withdrew. Mother Nell! How lovely, thought Evelyn. To Cal Nellie was just plain 'Mother' but Isla was at the nonsensical romantic stage and wanted everything to have a poetic ring to it.

Evelyn did get outside in the fresh air. She forgot how ill she had been during the earlier part of her pregnancy and felt herself growing stronger, more alive with each passing sunset. Every spare minute of every day she and Grace roamed the wild, majestic countryside of Scotland's north-west coast; they climbed the braes and followed the hill burns, they explored vast, vaulted caverns into which the sea boomed at high tide; they clambered over rocky shores and paddled their feet in rock pools inhabited by tiny fishes who swam curiously round their legs and nibbled their toes; they visited the tiny tidal island of Soay Bheag where terns swooped and screamed and small, hardy sheep roamed at will. They went out in a boat with Isla Nell and Cal and the four of them fished off Soay Bheag and floated and dreamed on the waves till the sun touched the breast of the ocean, turning it into a vast lake of molten gold.

It wasn't, of course, all thrill and adventure, in fact not one of them ever left Croft Donald till all the chores were seen to and the house was spick and span. Grace made Nellie lie in the quiet of her room for an hour every day and though Nellie protested vehemently at this Grace was adamant in her own unruffled way and Irene breathed a sigh of relief because she hadn't been able to achieve such a thing, no matter how much she had coaxed and, in the end, bullied, or rather tried to. No one ever bullied Nellie Cameron of Croft Donald and got easily away with it.

'It's no' that I want Nellie out o' the way,' Irene explained to the visitors, 'it's just she's such a besom betimes and will not do anything she's supposed to. She's no' able to lift and lay in her condition but she will try and then she follows me around, getting under my feet, telling me how to do things properly – at least how *she* thinks they should be done.' As the days wore on Nellie became fractious and impatient, Kenneth lost his blithe, carefree manner and was tense and curt to everyone in the house so that when he took himself off to the fields one and all breathed sighs of heartfelt relief.

'Oh, I wish it was all over with,' Irene confided to Grace, 'the doctor said the 23rd, Nellie is sure it will be sooner, Kenneth thinks it might be later, Bella Armstrong swears it could come any time since it's Nellie's first and she's so heavy, old Jenny Wren vows it's all water that's making Nellie so big and she reckons both Doctor McDonald and Nellie have got their dates wrong and that the bairn won't arrive till the end o' the month.' She sighed worriedly. 'It's an anxious time for us all, Grace, this baby means so much to Nellie and Kenneth frets and worries about her all the time. She's no' exactly a lassie any more and she's waited so long to give Kenneth a son or daughter.'

'The baby will come in its own good time,' was Grace's quiet opinion. 'We can all drive ourselves to distraction, wondering and waiting, but in the end it all rests wi' nature and it will take its course, you can be assured o' that.'

But despite her brave words she too was as anxious as anyone about Nellie, and when the 23rd came and went without so much as a letter from Donnie the Post's sack to cheer it on, a cloud of gloom settled itself over the occupants of Croft Donald.

The next day four letters came, one from Murn in Australia congratulating Nellie on the forthcoming birth. 'I

told her about it months ago,' Nellie commented scathingly; 'still the same old Murn, aye too busy to be
bothered wi' the affairs o' her family.'

An epistle from Mary was also more concerned with
her own health than Nellie's.

This heat! [Mary wrote] I just sit in the cool of my
room all day and pray for deliverance from this mon-
strous lump. Greg will fuss so and orders me to do
this, that, and the next thing. It's all right for him,
men simply have no idea of what pregnancy is really
about, and doctors are the worst of all. They think
they know everything but in reality they know no
more than the next man, except of course about
hell-inducing things like forceps and scissors and
which end of the baby is supposed to come first.

No doubt you'll be fine, Nell, you were always the
strongest of us all. I used to watch you in the fields
and would think, when our Nell gives birth it will
be as easy as that cow having a calf over yonder.
You have the bones for it, Nell, good and wide and
supple, and though you are certainly not a young
woman, all those years of farm work will stand you
in good stead . . .

'The absolute bitch!' gasped Evelyn. 'Oh, how I would
like to get my hands on her at this minute!'

'She makes you sound like a bloody cart horse!' Kenneth saw the funny side and burst out laughing.

'Ay, the uppity besom has a knack wi' sarcastic words,'
said Nellie drily, 'but at least she put pen to paper, the
first time in years, and though the letter is mostly about
her own self-pitying thoughts she did make the effort to
write.'

'Strange,' said Irene musingly, 'you three sisters, all
pregnant at the same time. Mary will be having hers at
about the same time as you, Nell.'

'Oh, hers will come first.' Nellie's tones were slightly bitter. 'The spoilt madam aye gets her way over everything and she'll make damt sure that Greg will no' let her go over her time.'

A letter from Maggie conveyed all the news of 198, including a very funny account of a fight between Big Aggie and Isa Boag over an incident involving toilet paper in the back-close cludgie.

In common with a lot of tenement dwellers who couldn't afford expensive toilet tissue, both Big Aggie and Isa tore up and hung newspaper squares on the back of the lavatory door.

According to Isa, [wrote Maggie] her habits are very regular and she goes to the cludgie at a set time every day. She swears that Big Aggie was aware of this and that she deliberately sprinkled vinegar on the toilet paper to get back at Isa for telling her the close wasn't done properly. The whole street now knows what the vinegar did to Isa's backside and both targes are so busy battling they're not aware that Willie Dick is having a good laugh at both women behind their backs. He told Jamie that he was drunk one night and went into the cludgie to eat a fish supper in peace. To get rid of the evidence he tore up the newspaper the fish supper was wrapped in and hung the squares behind the door. They were sodden with vinegar and could have been used on ANYBODY'S arse but of course it had to be Isa's and now we're all waiting to see what Isa will do to get back at Big Aggie.

Other than that life goes on the same at 198 except of course we are all anxiously waiting for news from Croft Donald . . .

Enclosed with Maggie's letter was a short note to Nellie from Alex, very much to the point: 'Have you had your baby yet?' he wrote. 'If so, is it a boy or girl or what? I would like a horse myself and when I grow up I will have them instead of babies. Tell my mother I miss her and when is she coming home? Alex.'

'Tell my mother I miss her'. Evelyn experienced a great sense of wonder at these few words together with an unexpected surge of homesickness, and as soon as she could she went up to her room to read the letter Davie had sent her. He too was missing her and asking when she was coming home.

It's been over a week now, Evie, and it's very strange here without you as it's the first time we've been apart since our marriage. The other night I could hardly bear sleeping alone and was so restless I got up and went through to the kitchen to make tea. There was Maggie, making a pot as she couldn't sleep either, and the queerest thing happened. We ended up drinking tea and talking together in a way we've never done and for once I actually felt an odd kind of affection for my mother-in-law.

Stashie never gets any better. He's been coughing his guts out and looks like death warmed up, we haven't had any orders for weeks and according to him no one has paid their bills so he's whining about money again.

I met that funny old crone you work for, Fanny – Something or Other. She was being pushed in her chair by old Curly Ears and the pair of them were wondering when you were coming back. Curly Ears said she understood you would only be gone a few days and I gathered she was having a tough time with Torn Face. So you see, my darling, we are all missing you and the bairns are asking every day for you . . .

With a sigh Evelyn folded the letter and slipped it under her pillow. Her days in Kenneray were coming to an end, if Nellie didn't have her baby soon she would have to leave, but at least Grace would be able to hold the fort for a while longer. She didn't want to go, it had been unbelievably wonderful to be back amongst the hills and the sea but her family, her beloved Davie, needed her, and soon she must go back to that other world of tall tenements and busy streets where no greenery existed except for the trees in the park which she could see from The Room window if she leaned very far out and stretched her neck till it almost broke.

CHAPTER 17

Nellie was being Nellie-ish again, despite her girth, fleering all round the kitchen throwing food into a large picnic hamper lying open on the table. When it was full she ordered Cal to help her carry it outside where it was set down on the step. When two sheepdogs came over to sniff at it she sent them packing with a well-aimed biff on their rumps from a none too gentle shoe and when Cal said tentatively, and for the third time, 'Mother, do you think it's wise going anywhere in your – er – condition?' she snapped, 'Ay, laddie, I think it's wise, a lot wiser than Jenny Wren's suggestion that I should take a long cart ride through Creag Mor Pass. The old bitch wants to kill me, that she does, but I have other ideas, so, if you will get out o' my way I have things to see to.'

Despite his anxiety Cal had to hide a smile. Jenny Wren was the local unofficial midwife, she also went in the capacity of nurse, faith healer and herbalist, depending on which service was demanded of her. On hearing that Nellie had gone over her time she had sprachled along to Croft Donald after breakfast that morning with the suggestion that 'very often a lazy bairn needs a good, rough ride to start it on its way', and 'a good brisk gallop through Creag Mor Pass might easily do the trick'. Whereupon Nellie had just about gone up in a blue light.

Creag Mor Pass was a rough and dangerous track through mountainous country strewn with great boulders that had been brought down from the crags during some tumultuous era in Scotland's past. During winter, avalanches of fallen rock often blocked the pass and the ruts and potholes made it a route to be avoided unless completely necessary.

'Ach, lassie, tis the best bumpy road in these parts,' Jenny Wren had reiterated when Nellie had vehemently rejected her suggestion. 'No bairn could withstand thon.'

'It's the *worst* bumpy road in these parts,' Nellie had returned viciously. 'No human was meant to withstand it, never mind an unborn babe.'

She had been further incensed when the old lady had stretched out a brown hand to lay it on her swollen belly and, in an odd, keening, mournful wail, had chanted one of her strangely primitive incantations. Then, as if that wasn't enough, she had scattered some flower petals round the crofthouse door, a ritual which was meaningless to Nellie but which must have meant something to Jenny since she went on her way looking most self-satisfied.

'I'm no' staying in this house a minute longer, I've had enough o' four walls,' Nellie had decided, and flouncing indoors she had called, 'Right, everyone, we're going on a picnic!' and so saying she had set about gathering foodstuffs together, growing more agitated by the minute as everyone had just stood around watching her in the utmost amazement.

'Dinna just stand there!' she had barked. 'Tis a bonny day, the sun is shining, surely you should all be pleased to go out for the day.'

'Och, Nell,' Grace had said persuasively, 'in the normal way o' things we *would* be pleased, and as soon as you're fit enough after the baby comes, a picnic would be just the thing to cheer you up, but . . .'

'No buts!' Nellie just about knocked Grace over in her hurry to get to the larder. 'I'm going, today, now, and if I have to go alone, well, that's fine by me.'

'Father willna like it,' objected Cal bravely. 'Maybe you should ask him first.'

Nellie, arms akimbo, glared at the boy. 'Is it a bairn you think I am, Calum Cameron? You can get along to the

177

fields and tell him but first I want you to help me wi' this hamper.'

Ten minutes later Cal set off to the fields where his father and grandfather were working, while the rest of the family, Grace and Irene carrying the heavy hamper between them, went off in the direction of the beach. Nellie had decided that she wanted to picnic on Soay Bheag. 'The tide will be going out about now. If we wait a half hour or so we willna have need o' a boat but can just walk across.'

'It might be better to go over in the boat,' said Evelyn firmly. 'Then if we get cut off we can easily row back.'

'Evie, we willna get cut off.' Nellie was very decidedly in one of her stubborn moods. 'Besides, I dinna like boats. I was born wi' my feet on dry land and that is where I want to keep them.'

By the time they reached Shipwreck Rock the tide had already receded so that tracts of glistening sand lay exposed to the sun.

They sat about on the sandy shore, no one speaking very much, not even Col who, sensing the rather strained atmosphere, went to look for crabs in a rock pool, and Nellie was moved to say in exasperation, 'Dyod! It's a picnic we're going on, no' a funeral. Isla Nell, hand me that cushion you're carrying. It was meant for my backside, no' as an ornament. We'll no' have long to wait, the tide is going out quickly now.'

Twenty minutes later saw them tramping over the wet, rutted sand to Soay Bheag, using the highest and narrowest point between the island and the mainland. To the right and to the left of them the sea swirled, lapping the reefs, foaming over the rocks, but they were quite dry and safe on their ridge of land. To Evelyn it was the longest half mile she had ever walked, not just because it took double the usual time owing to Nellie's slow, roll-

178

ing gait, but also because she felt sick, a feeling that had no bearing on her own pregnant state but one that owed itself to the terrible sense of foreboding that had beset her ever since Nellie had announced her intentions of going on this outing.

It was now the 26th of August which meant that she was three days over her time, all the piled up frustration and anxiety had made her jumpy and irritable and it had culminated in this rash move. As well as everything else, Evelyn was experiencing some frustration herself, since she knew she would have to leave Kenneray within the next day or so and she had so looked forward to the birth of Nellie's child. Grace had said she would stay on and if Evelyn was honest with herself, a few days more in the peace of this wondrous place would have suited her very well, but her responsibilities to her own family lay heavily, and she knew only too well that she couldn't ignore them for very much longer.

The wonderful sense of tranquillity on Soay Bheag washed very quickly into the picnic party and it wasn't long before they were all enjoying themselves. Irene and Isla Nell tucked up their skirts and splashed in the cool shallows that skirted the western side of the tiny island, soon followed by Col who rolled up his trouser legs and went blundering into the water, his child-like squeals of joy sending the gulls screaming upwards; startling the terns from their nests so that they too rose up to swoop and dive and hover like swallows in the blue sky.

It was very hot, breathlessly so, the water became like glass, a haze of heat shimmered on the horizon. Nellie, red-faced and uncomfortable looking, sought the cool shadows of the rocks, there to lower herself awkwardly onto the sand and fan herself with her straw hat.

The others joined her there when it was time to unpack the food hamper. Meat sandwiches, buttered oatcakes, scones piled thickly with crowdie cheese, tea and home-made lemonade, all disappeared in no time. Only Nellie and Evelyn seemed off their food and merely picked at the delicacies that had been so carefully, if hastily, packed.

Both women made the excuse that the heat had put them off their food and so saying Nellie put her hat over her eyes and went to sleep while Evelyn took herself off to a shady overhang of rock to write a postcard to Davie. But all the time her eyes were on the water, watching for the turn of the tide. She didn't know very much about the ways of the sea. Like Nellie, she was more used to the land and had no idea how long they could safely remain on the island. No one else seemed very concerned, however. Irene and Isla Nell had gone off with Col to look for wild flowers, and Evelyn began to relax a little and even to enjoy the solitude of that wild and lonely place. She wondered what it was like in winter, when the ocean crashed and roared and the westerly gales came howling over the tiny island . . .

It was peaceful, so peaceful, her heavy eyes closed, she felt herself drifting off into a beautiful state of near-oblivion though part of her remained behind. Through half-shut eyes she saw the sea and the sky and the silhouette of the sheep on the grass-covered dunes; and higher up still, on the sandy slopes leading to the cliff top, a large hare stood up on its hind legs and sniffed the air inquisitively, and she smiled to herself and wondered why she could see it all so clearly in her half drowsing state. Up on the emerald green machair there were more silhouettes, the ruins of an old abbey, jagged and stark against the blue of the sky, and then it wasn't a ruin but a structure that was whole and solid-looking with beside it, and around it, figures that moved and toiled and looked out to sea with eyes that were shaded by loosely-worn hoods. And then the singing came to her, borne on the breath of the breeze, more than singing, a sort of mournful chant that was oddly pleasing to her ears. The throbbing rhythmic beat of it swirled against her eardrums, like the surge of the tide, now faint, now clear, and though she remained neither awake nor asleep she was aware of her senses stirring as the rhythm grew in volume till it seemed to her that the whole world must surely hear what she was hearing.

Then the sadness came to her, the bitter-sweet poignancy of ages that were lost and half-forgotten in the mists of time while, all around her, the tableau unfolded: the Viking longships sailing over the sound, the swish and thud of the oars, the beat, beat of the waves . . . and up above her the terror, the fleeing to places of safety that were never safe enough for the monks of the little abbey . . .

The plish-plash of the oars, coming nearer, the great, fierce, god-like warriors leaping ashore, treading water, their helmets and their shields glinting like gold in the sun . . . Her heart raced, her breath came faster, the Vikings were running, running, swarming over the sands, climbing up to the clifftop. The monks were going to die, she saw the flashes of steel, heard the cries and the pleas for mercy. She sat where she was, immobile, petrified, staring into the blue heat of the day, filled with the dark, black knowledge that serene little Soay Bheag had once been a slaying ground for innocent men who had wanted only to worship their God in peace and solitude. Their bones were here still, interred in the sweet flower-strewn machair that was cropped by sheep, trod by the careless footsteps of the curious visitor . . .

And for all time the monks of the abbey wandered their little island, watching, waiting, singing, crying . . .

Her green eyes flew open, their cries for help were nearer now, she started up, sank back as a wave of dizziness seized her. She heard the sea lapping the shore, there were no Viking longships, no abbey ruins on top of the cliffs, the clean, clear mattress of grass merged into the azure heat of the sky.

'It was only a dream,' she whispered thankfully. For a moment she had imagined that she had witnessed a vision from the past, brought to her by the power of that strange sixth sense of hers. It had been a long time since she had known anything like it. As she grew older the experiences were lessening — then she heard Hinney's voice in her head, as plainly as if the old woman was standing at her side: 'It won't aye torment you, just occasionally, and mostly when you're least expecting it.'

She started up again, there *was* a voice calling on her, only this time it was no ghostly echo but one which belonged very much to the present and which she knew only too well . . .

Nellie's face was wet with sweat, her lips were twisted in pain. When Evelyn knelt down beside her she held out a trembling hand and whispered, 'Evie, something's happened — I — oh, God help me — I think I've wet myself — and — it hurts.'

Old Jenny Wren had been right, much of Nellie's bigness had owed itself to an excess of amniotic fluid, the evidence was there, spreading out over the sand.

'It's all right, Nellie.' Despite her fright Evelyn sounded reassuring. 'It's only your waters that have burst, there's enough there to sink a battleship.'

'My — waters?'

'Ay, you know, when you start into labour that's what happens, for nine months the baby floats around in a bag o' fluid, to protect it from all the bumps and thumps we might experience.'

'Evie.' Nellie gripped her sister's hand tighter, a flush of embarrassment spreading over her pale face. 'I — well, to tell the truth I dinna ken anything about it. I was such a queer prudish quine when I was young I never listened to anything Mam tried to tell me, and now here's you, my baby sister, rhyming it all off like an expert.'

'I *am* an expert,' Evelyn laughed ruefully. 'I've had four – remember? If I dinna ken the facts o' life now there's little hope for the rest o' the world.'

Nellie jumped as pain knifed through her. By the time the others came back she was in great distress, yet hardly a cry escaped her bloodless lips.

Grace took over the situation immediately, all at once the efficient, calm little nurse who was not in the least like the gentle, quiet young woman everyone knew.

She gave out orders, she soothed Nellie, speaking to her in a voice that was like balm on troubled waters, yet she brooked no nonsense from that formidable being, making her lie back and do exactly as she was told for once in her life.

She knew that she had to get her sister over to the mainland as speedily as possible and with herself on one side of her, Irene on the other, Evelyn and Col carrying the picnic hamper, they set off for the causeway. It was a slow, laborious business, in every sense. Nellie was obviously in great pain and though she tried to bear it as silently as possible she was unable to stop the moans that escaped her from time to time. They had to rest frequently as Nellie's distress became more intense, causing her to drag her feet and double up when it seemed to her that her very bones were being wrenched apart inside her body.

The tide was coming in, each of them was aware of it but no one said anything, not even Col, who was more concerned with his beloved Nella's anguish than with anything else. The mainland seemed very far off, more so than it would normally be, the heat haze lay like blue smoke over the land, hiding familiar landmarks.

The beat of the ocean was all around them, hushed, serene, yet oddly ominous. They were only quarter way across when their feet started to sink into the sand and when they looked at the prints they had made they saw them filling with water and they knew that the rise would soon be covered. In front of them the sea was already claiming parts of the ridge, covering it, so that they all experienced the frightening feeling of being surrounded by the ocean. It was all around them and when they looked behind they realized that not only was the mainland cut off from them but that Soay Bheag was quickly becoming an island again.

'We'll have to turn back,' Irene gasped, fear twisting her heart. Nellie was like a ton weight on her shoulder and she saw that Grace too was flagging badly, her beautiful face was drained of colour, her slender shoulders were sagging with weariness.

It was almost impossible to hurry with Nellie in her tortured state. They were treading water now, it had crept over their shoes, in minutes it was up to their ankles, and Soay Bheag never seemed to get any nearer. But Nellie wouldn't have been Nellie if she had just given up and allowed disaster to overtake them. With a heroic effort she shook her helpers off, lifted up her skirts, and began to run, the others panting along beside her.

Treading water, they reached the offshore reefs; half submerged they at last came to the shelving sands; crawling and scrambling they heaved themselves onto the blessed haven of tiny Monk's Bay, there to lie exhausted on the cool white shell sands and allow the hot sun to warm their drenched bodies.

'It's all my fault,' Nellie gasped at last. 'I'm a stupid, selfish besom and it would serve me right if none o' you ever spoke to me again . . . Oh God . . .' A red hot band of pain gripped her, she pushed her knuckles into her mouth and buried her face in the sand to stop herself from crying out. Each time Col saw her like that his face blanched and his blue eyes grew round with terror. It was too much for him now after what they had just come through and crying out, 'Nella! Nella!' he threw himself down beside her and cooried himself into her like a lost puppy.

With a great effort she put her arms around him and hushie-bawed him as if he was a baby. 'Dinna take on so, Col, Nella's fine, it's just the baby coming, that's all. You've got to be a wee man for Nella, just till Kenneth and Cal come, they'll be here soon.'

'It's a good thing the menfolk know where we are,' Irene commented to Evelyn. 'They'll see that the tide has turned and will have the boat out in no time.'

'Ay.' Evelyn shivered. The terrible sense of foreboding that had been with her all day was stronger now, the raw, heavy feeling of doom lay coiled in her belly like an ever-tightening steel cord. Her eyes travelled to the skyline above the cliffs. The sheep had moved off, it was empty of life, be it of the past or of the present. There was no abbey, no soberly dressed beings shading their eyes to the sea where terror stalked in the shape of long-boats, surging, surging, coming ever closer to little Soay Bheag . . . It had only been a dream, it meant nothing, nothing . . .

'Ay,' she repeated, 'they'll be here soon.' And for Nellie's sake she prayed to God that Irene was right.

No one would ever forget the journey over the water in the big, sturdy clinker dinghy, Nellie lying on an assortment of jackets thrown over a tarpaulin that Kenneth had hastily folded across the planks in the middle of the boat. She lay awkwardly, twisted and racked with the crucifying pain of childbirth, her strong teeth biting into the wad of cloth Grace had given her. It helped her to stifle the screams that her tenacious nature would not allow her to utter, though she couldn't suppress the tossings of her tortured body.

Her head was cradled in Grace's lap, Isla Nell held onto her burning hot hand and muttered over and over in her lilting young voice, 'Mother Nell, oh, Mother Nell.'

Kenneth and Cal, assuming that the picnic party had taken the boat over to Soay Bheag and would therefore be able to get on and off the island quite easily, had gone on with their work in the fields, never dreaming that anything could possibly be wrong. They had taken packed lunches with them that morning and had had no reason to go home for anything, so it wasn't till they arrived back at six o'clock to an empty house that the alarm bells had started ringing.

It was now almost seven o'clock in the evening. Far off islands were like golden ships floating on the horizon, Soay Bheag seemed distant and ethereal and might have been a hazy blue cloud merging into the rose-tinted sky. It was difficult to think that the womenfolk had spent so many anxious hours in that tiny idyllic spot and Evelyn sat at the stern, watching the island slipping away, remembering with blinding clarity the cries of the monks as the Norsemen's plundering weapons robbed them of home, and hope, and life.

The boat had barely grounded but Kenneth roared at Cal to fetch the doctor, then he turned his attention to Nellie, lifting her into his arms as if she was no weight at all, treading water, carrying her up the beach, while Iain, who had stayed behind knowing there wouldn't be room in the boat, made to race off to Croft Donald to fetch the cart.

'No,' Kenneth stayed his father, 'Cal will be taking the cart and there's no time to go to Tigh na Beinne and ask for theirs. I'll carry her, just you stay at my side and make sure I don't trip. I canna see anything for this wee mountain in front o' me.'

'An understatement, it's Bennachie itself I'm carrying around,' Nellie managed to joke, 'and put me down this minute, Kenneth Cameron, you aye did take too much upon yourself.'

'Wheest, wife, and do as you're told.' Kenneth managed to sound lighthearted even though the big, Highland heart of him pumped inside his breast in a mixture of anxiety for his wife and the effort it was taking him to carry both her and their unborn child across the fields to home.

She murmured something he couldn't catch and he lowered his head to her lips.

'I said – I hope Cal doesna bring that witch woman back wi' him. I'm in no mood to listen to her queer ravings – and at this time o' the day, knowing her, she'll be drunk and incapable o' anything.'

She said no more, she needed all her air just to breathe – but despite her agony she was jubilant, a longed for baby was about to be born – and she could stand anything with that sort of impending joy to look forward to.

In the early hours of the next morning a baby daughter was born to Nell Christina Cameron, a tiny, delicate little girl with a mop of dark hair and huge blue eyes that opened minutes after she was delivered, eyes that stared and wondered and puzzled at a world so big and strange after the warm, quiet dark of her mother's womb.

It had been a long and terrible struggle for Nellie to bring her child into the world. Doctor McDonald, Grace and Jenny Wren had been in almost constant attendance through the night watch while, down below, the menfolk waited as time passed fitfully and seemed not to pass at all for Kenneth in his heightened state of anxiety.

Then a door opened above, he saw the doctor coming out of the bedroom, his heart leapt and he reached for his bagpipes, ready to proclaim to all and sundry that the child he and Nellie had longed for had at last been born. In such a fashion had he welcomed Cal and Isla Nell into the world, Alex too when Evelyn had given birth at Croft Donald. It had been a glad and stirring sound that, the skirl and chime of the pipes, ringing, ringing, poignant, joyful, powerful, and only a man like Kenneth could have thought to express his feelings in such a way. But this time there was to be no such triumphal expression for Kenneth Mor: the doctor's face was serious when he came downstairs and stayed the big Highlander's actions with just a few quiet words, the uttering of which turned joy to a sorrow so deep and painful it took the feet from Kenneth, forcing him heavily into a chair.

'It – canna be,' he whispered at last. 'Surely it canna be, not now, oh, dear God, not when all that she has longed and prayed for seemed about to come true.'

Doctor McDonald stood there, defeated and weary. 'We nearly lost them both, man, it was touch and go for quite a while but Nell is strong, she'll pull through. The bairn – ' he spread his hands ' – she is too weak even to suckle and has but a few hours. You might like to have her christened, if so I'll arrange for the minister to be here as quickly as possible.'

The baby was christened Jean Christina and barely two hours later she died in Nellie's arms, her tiny limbs relaxing slowly as if she was falling asleep, and in a very short time she peacefully let go of the life that had been so briefly hers.

Everyone was stunned with grief, none more so than she who had so looked forward to having a child that was not of another woman's making. But she was Nellie, she was strong, silent, dry-eyed, putting on the brave face that had become second nature to her over the years. The tears that were never shed remained locked in her heart for all time, to torture and torment her for the rest of her days. She had been given the gift of a daughter, for a little while she had known the sweet poignancy of a downy head resting against her breast that had ached for such a touch. And now that precious moment was gone, cruelly and swiftly carried away on the silent, merciless wings of death that knew no distinctions between young and old.

From the cradle to the grave. Such a short space from one to the next for Jean Christina Cameron. Kenneth himself lowered her tiny white coffin to rest, laying it beside that of her namesake, Jeannie, his first wife who had so long ago and too soon departed this life.

He stood by the open grave, a fine big Highlander whose hair and beard shone in the sun, his kilt lifting in the breeze from the sea, his tall figure upright and strong except for a slight drooping of his shoulders.

He stood there and he remembered, he remembered his Jeannie, his bonny lass who had so pined to come home to her beloved glens and bens and who had died before she ever saw them again. He had buried her here, in this tranquil little cemetery overlooking the ocean, and he had never ever forgotten this first love of his.

At the time he had imagined that there could be no other to take Jeannie's place and in that he had been right; Nellie had never tried to take that special place in his heart, nor had she wanted to, she had been wise enough to content herself just being his wife and a mother to his children. She had known that his was a big heart, that given time she would win her own niche in his affections and, dear God, how right she had been.

She was his life now, she had given him so much of herself and in return he had wanted to give her the world. But she hadn't wanted the world, she had merely wanted to bring their child into it, and now — it had all been in vain, her arms were emptier than they had ever been and he cried for his Nell and prayed to God to give them the strength to see them through this terrible time.

Cal laid a hand on his arm. 'Father, it's time to go.'

Kenneth stepped back, he looked down into the grave for the last time. 'Goodbye, my darling girls,' he whispered. The ocean and the sky blurred and united till they were just a haze of blue in his tear-filled horizon.

It was time for Evelyn to go home. She went outside to gaze towards the sea and wondered how soon she would see it again – if ever. Soay Bheag swam into her vision and she bit her lip. She had to know, she had to find out. Irene came out of the house to take her arm and look at the scene with her.

'Irene.' Her voice was tentative.

'Ay, Evie?'

'Soay Bheag, was there ever a monastery there?'

'Oh, long, long ago, hundreds of years, in fact. There's nothing left o' it now, it fell into ruin, then the wind and the sea took even that away. It only exists now in the memories o' the old ones, the seanachaidhs, they have some gey strange tales to tell o' it.'

'What – kind o' tales?'

'Ach well, wi' it being a holy place there are all sorts o' legends attached to it. The Norsemen invaded the island and plundered the abbey, as they did to so many places around the Scottish coasts. You know what it's like, legends spring up over the years. The one about Soay Bheag is much the same as that attached to Iona. All sorts o' ghostly tales have come out o' the islands and Soay Bheag is no exception.'

'Tell me about it.'

'Ach, there's nothing much to tell, but the old folks say that, whenever some death or disaster is about to happen to a Kenneray family, a member o' that same family will witness a re-enactment of the Vikings' raid on the abbey if he or she happens to be on Soay Bheag at the time. It is just a lot o' myth, I have never . . .'

She saw Evelyn's face, her eyes grew big. 'Evie, I'm

sorry, you have the second sight, Nell said something but I never really took it in. You know Nell, she has no time for that sort o' palaver. Evie, did you . . . ?'

'Ay, Irene, I did, at the time I thought it was only a dream . . .'

She turned away. Only a dream. Oh, would that it had been so simple. Little Jean Christina was dead, that was the stark and awful reality. Soay Bheag had given up its terrible secrets to one who saw and heard with the eyes and ears of the soul. And it was cruel, that: to have the power to know that something dreadful was about to overtake a loved one and to be powerless to stop it happening.

Evelyn didn't look at Soay Bheag again. She left Croft Donald and Kenneray with hardly a backward glance because she couldn't bear to see Nellie's white, tormented face at the window, watching, watching, waiting in vain for the farewell salute, wondering why it never came.

Evelyn stared straight ahead, she swallowed the lump in her throat. Why hadn't she been able to say goodbye? Why at the last moment had she turned from Nellie and ran out to the waiting cart?

The answer came unbidden. She felt guilty, that was why. She was pregnant, Nellie wasn't; she had four children to call her own, Nellie had none. Tragedy had seared an everlasting wound on Nellie's spirit yet still she held her head high and hid her pain from the world.

'Oh, Nellie,' she whimpered, 'I wish I could give you my baby. It isn't wrong, it isn't. You need one so much in your life and I – I'm too tired and too poor to be able to properly look after another bairn. God knows this, and – He isn't angry wi' me, Nellie, because – He understands.'

191

CHAPTER 18

In contrast to Nellie's stoic sufferings the half of Cleveden Mansions must have known that Mary was giving birth. She screamed and she yelled, she ranted and raved, and, forgetting that she was supposed to be a lady, she swore at the midwife and informed her that she was incompetent.

The maids scurried about, fetching towels and hot water and, in one instance, bearing a silver dish piled with pink marshmallows into the bedroom because the mistress had demanded something sweet to keep up her strength.

In between labour pains she gorged herself on the sweetmeats, then was violently sick, a state she immediately blamed on the long-suffering Betty for bringing such rich fare when all she had really wanted was a plain biscuit and a weak cup of tea.

'I should have poisoned them!' fumed Betty to Cook. 'God help the poor wean when it finally arrives, she'll blame it for her so-called sufferings.'

When, some hours later, little Elizabeth Louise made her entry into the world, peace reigned for a while. Without so much as a glance at her new daughter, Mary sank into an exhausted sleep and the entire household breathed sighs of relief.

Only Greg remained wide-eyed and alert in his chair by the library fire. Of all the rooms in the house this was his favourite. He could relax and be himself here, surrounded by the familiar furnishings that he and Mary had brought from Rowanlea Cottage when they had left Rothiedrum. At first she had been glad enough of them but as their circumstances had improved her tastes had become more opulent and she had wanted to get rid of anything that reminded her of humbler days.

Her husband, however, had insisted on keeping his beloved chairs and other items that he cherished.

'Very well,' Mary had finally conceded, 'but it must all go into the library, it's full of dusty old books and your shabby furniture won't matter in there. No one ever goes into that room but you so you're welcome to it.'

So the library became Greg's sanctuary. Into it moved his desk and the fine old walnut bureau that had once belonged to his grandmother. Two big, comfortable arm-chairs sat one on either side of the fireplace. In front of the hearth a beautiful, but worn, Indian rug reposed in all its colourful splendour and on top of this sprawled Ben, a golden labrador who followed Greg everywhere and considered the library as much his domain as it was his master's.

Mary hadn't wanted Ben either. 'Dogs smell,' she had stated, wrinkling her nose at the big-eyed bundle in Greg's arms. 'They cause fleas and cast their hairs every-where. He's only a pup now but he'll get bigger and will eat us out of house and home.'

Greg felt like telling her that Ben wasn't the only one likely to eat them out of house and home but knowing how easily she could fly into a tantrum he held his coun-sel and said instead that she ought to be used to dogs as she had grown up with them and hadn't seemed to mind having one during their years at Rowanlea Cottage.

'My dear Greg,' she had returned with exaggerated patience, 'that was different. I was reared on a croft, I had no say in the matter and when we lived at the cottage I was too silly and young to know better. We live in a real home now and I can't have animals messing it up.'

But for once Greg was adamant. Ben stayed and became a solace to Greg as well as a faithful and constant companion. Everywhere that Greg went Ben went too, even to the surgery to lie quietly and patiently in a little ante-room till the last patient departed, then it was in beside his master and out to the motor car to accompany the doctor on his rounds.

Ben had obediently remained in the library when the mistress was making all that fuss and noise upstairs and when Greg at last came in to lower his weary frame into a chair, Ben knew better than to make more fuss and noise. He sensed his master's need for quiet and lay peaceably by the fire while the clock ticked the silent minutes away.

Greg was desperately tired. He was aware of a tingling in his left arm and a heaviness in his chest but his racing thoughts wouldn't let him rest.

Dear God, he thought, let her for once in her life accept what is and not what might have been. The Mary I knew must be in there somewhere, deep down she is still the girl I loved and married but what, dear God, will it take to bring her back to her senses? At least our child is alive, while Nell, dear, good Nell, has lost her heart's desire. She wouldn't have minded, it wouldn't have mattered to her . . .

There was a rap on the door. Betty entered quietly, concern on her face when she saw the hollow-eyed exhaustion on Greg's.

'Oh, sir, you're done in,' she said kindly. 'Let me just do up the fire, then I'll get you a nice cup o' tea. You could be doing wi' something, I'm sure, it's been a trying day for you.'

'For all of us, Betty.' His warm smile lit his weary eyes and Betty's heart turned over. She was devoted to the master of the house, all the staff were and suffered with him in the rigours of his hard-working days and in the lonely hours of his nights. 'And I'd love a cup of tea, just that, nothing else.'

When the tea came he laced it with a tot of brandy from the bottle in his little drinks cabinet and when he had downed the fiery beverage he felt better and more

prepared for the storm he knew must surely break soon after his wife opened her eyes.

And come the storm did, like a great torrent of thunder from lightning-lit skies. Feeling refreshed after her long sleep and quite well pleased with herself, Mary bade the nurse dress her in a peach satin nightdress, then she demanded to see her newborn infant. But when the child was placed in her arms she took one look at its little face and gave vent to a loud shriek of anguish. And no one could really blame her for that first reaction; her daughter had been born with a cleft palate and a hare lip, a disfigurement so severe it dominated the appearance of an otherwise perfectly formed baby, and the nurse looked sympathetically at Mary's countenance.

But her sympathies were short-lived. Mary pushed the baby away from her as if the poor little blubber of a mouth had somehow bitten her. 'That isn't my baby!' she yelled. 'I could never have given birth to such an ugly creature. It's horrible, horrible! I want nothing to do with it. Take it away this instant! I can't stand the sight of it, take it away! Do you hear me? Don't just stand there gaping like a fish out of water. It isn't mine, I tell you, it isn't. It isn't!'

'She *is* yours, Mrs McGregor,' said the nurse coldly, 'and you'll have to learn to feed her and to love her as she deserves to be loved . . .'

'How dare you talk to *me* like that!' stormed Mary, beating the bedclothes with clenched fists, her black hair falling over a face that was pale and contorted with rage. 'As for feeding her, I could never allow that – that gaping awful mouth near *my* breasts!' She shuddered in disgust and raved on, 'Give her cow's milk, goat's milk, anything, I don't care, just as long as I don't have to suffer the feel of her against my flesh.'

'You will have to learn to feed her, Mrs McGregor,' the nurse continued as if Mary hadn't spoken, 'she has been very good and quite contented with the sweetened water

I fed her but she is hungry now and you have enough milk there to feed two babies. If you don't get rid of it you will get sore breasts and will only have yourself to blame so be a good girl and do as you're told.'

Mary looked at Nurse Allison. She was forty years old, plump, placid and pleasant, but there was a hint of steel in the calm grey eyes and Mary knew that she had a fight on her hands if she didn't obey orders. But what did that matter? Nurses were ten a penny, she would quite enjoy a good argument with this one before sending her packing.

The door opened, Gregor came in. Mary immediately launched into a tirade of abuse and accusations. Why hadn't he told her about the baby? Why had he allowed her to find out like this? He should have been with her when she wakened instead of allowing her, in her vulnerable post-natal condition, to be alone when she was confronted with the awful reality of 'that ugly thing'.

'You weren't interested enough to even glance at her after she was born,' he reminded her when her tirade came to a halt. 'You fell asleep and the rest o' us were also very glad to snatch an hour or so o' rest. I myself went to the library and eventually drifted into a sort of sleep. I had planned to be here when you woke but I'm afraid I succumbed to the human frailties that are common to mankind. I don't know what all the fuss is about anyway. When the baby is older she will have an operation that will make her as good as new . . .'

'As good as new! Older! Meanwhile I have to suffer looking at her ugliness every day of my life! What will my friends think? What will they say? I can't bear it, I can't! And I won't, no one can make me, I don't want to see her till that — that awful face of hers has been made fit for decent eyes to look upon . . .'

'I don't give a damn about your friends and what they think?' Gregor broke in harshly. 'Like it or no', she's our child and you are damned well going to feed her and take

care of her – starting right now! Nurse Allison will show you what to do . . .'

'I don't want Nurse Allison. She's impertinent and incompetent and I want you to get rid of her, Greg, or I'll – I'll have the child put into a home so that we can all get on with our lives and everything will be back to normal.'

Two quick strides took him over to the bed. For a moment he loomed above her, dark and menacing, then in one swift movement he reached out and tore the peach satin folds from her neck. Her breasts sprang out, white, huge, dripping with thick, creamy colostrum. Shocked, she made no move to cover herself, but just lay staring up at him, her eyes wide and black in her suddenly pale face. Never, never, had he ever behaved in such a fashion and though a torrent of protest sprang into her mind she never uttered one single sound. For the first time since his entry into the bedroom she seemed to see him clearly. His clothes were crumpled, his collar undone, a terrible stark weariness glared out of his eyes that were wild in their desperation. His face was haggard and lined, he looked all at once old and defeated and she bit her lip. A strange kind of fear entered her heart in those fraught moments. This was her husband, the man she had once loved, so long ago now, everything had changed . . . Everything? Or was it just she who saw things differently? It couldn't be . . . her heart raced . . . it couldn't be that it was she, who, through her own searching for position and riches, had been the one who had changed everything – even Gregor – that patient gentle man who had once laughed at the little things and who had loved her with such devotion and understanding. But no . . . she pushed such dire thoughts from her mind. They had both changed, everyone did with time, and it was he who had wanted this baby, he who had made her have it, that alien creature with its twisted features and its gaping, whimpering hungry demands that she was being forced

to comply with just because she was a woman with breasts that ached in their fullness.

She looked again at his tortured face and the fear came back to her, engulfing all the resentments that were in her heart.

'Nurse Allison,' she said through tightly compressed lips, 'bring the child to me. I'll feed it if it's the last thing I do, by Dyod I will!'

Nurse Allison smiled a triumphant little smile. She picked up the baby and placed it firmly in the generous folds of its mother's breasts. The flawed mouth searched, found the nipple and clung, Mary shuddered, the child pulled and sucked, milk dribbled and ran down, the baby choked and spluttered but Nurse Allison was there, guiding, caring.

Later, drinking a well-earned cuppy in the nursery, she told Betty, 'Madam won't refuse to feed her bairn again, the doctor will see to that. There's a man for you, the besom is lucky to have his like, she doesn't deserve him but he's not the first man to go to waste on a selfish bitch like herself. If he was mine I'd take good care of him, that I would. If she doesn't watch out she'll lose him, one way or another. He has the look on him of a body at the end of his tether.'

Betty nodded, agreeing with every word, all the while vowing to herself that she would take care of the doctor in any way she could, be it bringing him an extra cup of tea when he was weary or simply warming his slippers by the fire ready for him when he came home. Ay, Betty liked Doctor McGregor, she liked him very much, and how right Nurse Allison was, that self-centred besom upstairs didn't deserve him. Too bad he still loved her, in spite of everything.

'Oh, Evie, Evie.' Mary rocked herself backwards and forwards on the bed, her voice filled with self-pity. 'Have

you seen the baby? Do you know what I'm going through at this very minute?'

'Ay, I've seen the bairn.' Evelyn sat by the bed, not in the least taken in by the look of tragedy on her sister's smooth countenance. 'It looks bad, I must admit, but Greg is quite sure surgery will do wonders . . .'

'Surgery!' Mary broke in rudely. 'It will take a miracle to cure the child. Greg is too optimistic, I'm not stupid, I know he's only trying to appease me with all his fine talk.'

'It isna talk, and a bit o' optimism on your part might work wonders for him. Have you given a thought to what he's going through? She's his baby as well as yours and it's high time you comforted him for a change.'

'Oh, Evie, don't talk so harshly to me, I can't stand any more unpleasantness.' She fell to her rocking again, this time accompanied by a low moaning wail that gave Evelyn the creeps. 'It's a punishment, Evie,' she said in a low voice, 'I'm being punished and I don't know how to cope with it.'

'A — punishment?'

'Evie, you don't know what I've done, the things I had to do to get Greg back on his feet when he was ill and we were so poor.'

Something in her tone made Evelyn's blood freeze. She had made the journey to the west end to see Mary and the baby and had encountered one shock after another. There had been nothing in Mary's letter to Maggie to indicate that anything was wrong with her new daughter and it had hit Evelyn hard when she had seen the child for the first time and had witnessed the despair on Greg's face. Now this, Mary moaning and crying, saying things that didn't make sense.

'What kind o' things, Mary?' She tried to keep her tone as level as she could but was unable to stop herself from staring at her sister's pale, contorted face.

'Oh, nothing too awful.' Mary averted her eyes. 'But

there were men, people with influence, I – sometimes one has to behave in a certain way in order to get on in the world.'

'You dinna mean –' This time Evelyn's voice did shake. 'You canna mean – that wee Beth isn't Greg's bairn?'

Mary forced a laugh, 'Oh, no, nothing like that, she's his all right, but if I had had my way I wouldn't have carried to full term and none of this frightful mess would have happened. Oh, please, Evie.' She grabbed her sister's hand and held it tightly. 'Don't look at me like that, these other men meant nothing to me, I just obliged them with certain favours and in return they saw to it that Greg went up in the world. He wouldn't be where he is now if it hadn't been for me and he'll never know how much I sacrificed for him.'

'No,' Evelyn said dully, 'he'll never know, he trusts you too much ever to suspect that you would sell yourself for power and position. But it's too late to do anything about that now, the important thing is for you to try and make it up to Greg and you can start by stopping feeling sorry for yourself and giving more attention to him and to wee Beth. At least she's alive, while Nellie's baby is dead . . .'

Mary turned her head sharply. 'Of course, Nellie,' she said softly. 'Why didn't I think of that before? She's desperate for a child, she could take Elizabeth and look after her for me. I would pay her, of course . . .'

'Money!' Evelyn spat scornfully. 'You think it can buy everything, don't you? It's all you've cared about for years now, you've neglected your family, your husband, your children, all for your greedy grasping after riches. Well, I'll tell you this, Mary, you're no' going to get rid o' that poor wee mite so easily. If Nellie should have anybody's baby it should be mine.'

'Yours?' Mary stared.

'Ay, mine, I have four as it is, I canna afford another. Nellie could give my baby all the things I can't. There's so much I want to do for the bairns I already have but Davie and I are too poor and likely to get poorer as time goes on . . .'

'Evelyn!' Mary cried. 'If I didn't know better I'd say you were going off your head altogether!'

The other's eyes flashed. 'And if I didna ken better I'd say the fairies took my sister Mary away and left a hobgoblin in her place. What's become of that smiling, happy woman we all kent and loved? What will it take to bring her back to us?'

'Evie! Stop that! You're just jealous, that's becoming more obvious every time you come to visit me. If it's money you want I'll give you some, I'll give you some right now if it means so much to you. I . . .'

Evelyn stood up and backed away from the bed. 'You havena understood a word I've said! You — you silly, blind bitch! I wouldna touch a penny o' your ill-gotten siller even suppose I was starving!'

Mary's lips tightened. 'Please go, Evelyn, and don't dare show your face here again — not until you learn to speak to me with respect — oh, and by the way,' she added icily, 'the child's name is Elizabeth, not Beth. Remember that in future.'

Evelyn went to the door, she was shaking. 'Dinna you worry your selfish head about that, Mary Grant who was,' she said in a low, controlled voice. 'I'll take good care to see that I don't come here again till you have come to your senses. For Greg's and the children's sake I pray to God you will one day come to realize that people are more important than mere possessions, for when your hour comes it will be a human hand you'll want to hold and a loving voice to comfort you. Gold and glitter will be as nothing then because you canna take any o' that with you, and for the sake o' your soul I hope you'll recognize that fact before it's too late.'

The door banged shut. Mary lay back, ashen-faced. She felt no anger, only a renewal of that strange fear that had touched her when she had witnessed the despair in Greg's face, mingling with a terrible apprehension that made her feel physically sick.

Evelyn stood in the quiet avenue of Cleveden Mansions. The autumn leaves were falling from the trees, drifting down, down, all round and about her. The air was damp and tangy, there was a feeling of sadness everywhere. She glanced along the road, foolishly, irrationally, hoping for a re-enactment of that strange, brief interlude during that snowy day last spring. In her mind's eye she saw Gillan striding along in front of her, his dark head bowed, never knowing that she watched and waited in vain for him to turn round and see her there . . .

She stared and stared into the distance till her eyes were aching and dry, but there was nobody, nothing, only the dead leaves of summer falling all around her, reminding her that the days were shortening and winter would be here all too soon.

PART 3

Winter 1928

CHAPTER 19

It was dismal and depressing in the yard at the top of The Sac. Evelyn stood outside the workshop door, listening, digging her cold hands into her pockets while she plucked up the courage to go inside. Davie didn't know she was here, he was ill in bed with a bad bout of colic and would have been furious if he thought she was interfering with his working life. But she was desperate, hardly a penny had come into the house these last two weeks. She was in her eighth month of pregnancy and had been forced to leave Fanny's employ at the end of October.

Both Fanny and Lizzie had let her go regretfully. 'You come back to us when you're able,' Lizzie had said kindly. 'You're the best lass we've ever had working here and are more like one o' the family than just a good house-keeper.'

But Fanny wasn't so magnanimous. 'I'm sorry to see you go, of course, Evie, but I cannot promise to hold your position. Lizzie is all very well but she can be very unsympathetic to the needs of an invalid like myself. If I can get someone worthwhile to live in I won't hesitate to take her on, though I hope you won't forget us and will come back to visit us from time to time.'

Looking very martyred, every wizened inch of her oozing the gracious philanthropist, she handed Evelyn two pound notes that were over and above her usual wage, patted her hand and told her to 'buy something nice'.

The family ate comparatively well for a week but all too soon it was back to porridge and soup and bread with dripping, for, no matter how much he argued with

Stashie over money, Davie had managed to bring very little into the house.

Now he was ill, unable to eat, the crushing pains in his stomach making him irritable and unreasoning. No matter his mood, he would certainly never have agreed to Evelyn 'fighting his battles for him' as he would have put it, and for a long time she stood in the cold outside the workshop, wondering if she was doing the right thing. If Davie ever found out . . .

The wrenching open of the door made her start violently but it was only Joss Coburn who appeared, his thin young face as startled as her own in the fitful light filtering onto the yard from the grimy smiddy windows opposite.

'Joss,' she acknowledged breathlessly, 'I thought you had left, Davie said you –'

'Ay, I've left,' he returned bitterly, 'or rather, I was given my marching orders two weeks back. I came to see if he –' he inclined his head backwards – ' – would gie me the money he owes me but no such luck.' He looked at her. 'If that's what you've come about you're wasting your time, the old bugger is on his last legs by the look o' him and hardly heard a word I said.'

'Joss, you won't tell Davie you saw me?' she said anxiously.

He grinned. 'Saw you? No' a hope. There's no' a woman in their right mind would face that heap o' bones in there, and from what I know o' you, Mrs Grainger, you've got your head screwed on.'

'Thanks, Joss.' He moved off, she waited till his footsteps had died away then resolutely she pushed open the door and marched bravely inside.

The consumptive raspings of Stashie Dunbar filled the workshop. The frightening sounds made Evelyn shudder and she stared about her, hardly able to believe the squalor that met her eyes. Dust and cobwebs were everywhere, the stink of grease mingled with the odour of

unwashed clothes and rising damp, only the pleasing tang
of cut wood diminished the vicious assault on the nostrils,
but even so, Evelyn took a gulping breath. Poor darling
Davie, no wonder he was often moody and bad tempered,
anyone could be excused anything, having to come in
here every day to work in such an atmosphere. She hesitated, and might easily have gone away again had not
Stashie's harsh voice stayed her.

'Who the hell's that now?' he groaned. 'Come over
here where I can see you, whoever you bloody well are!'

In a daze Evelyn moved through a tangle of ramshackle
furniture to the bed where Stashie lay, his wasted body
sunk into the lumpy tick of the sagging mattress, covered
by a tea-stained blanket and a filthy great-coat.

His death mask of a face glared up at her, his eyes were
black pits in their hollow sockets, the skin that covered
his bony skull was waxy white and shining with sweat,
his chest was thin and sunken and looked as if it might
easily collapse at any moment, blood stains had dried on
the grey collar of his shirt and he was altogether a dreadful and pitiful sight to behold.

Involuntarily, Evelyn took a step backwards, her
thumping heart making her feel faint and sick. She knew
she should never have come, Stashie Dunbar was a dying
man, too far gone to care about himself, never mind
about the welfare of anybody else.

His mocking grin leered up out of his shrivelled flesh.
'Davie's wife, eh? Come about the same thing as that
young bugger I've just shown the door.' His exhausted
eyes raked her face. 'By Christ! You're a beauty! How the
hell did you land up wi' such a raw deal? Bairn after
bairn, misery after misery! You're no' the usual sort we
get around here. Gave it all up, eh? For love, for
romance? Poor, silly bitch, found out too late it was all
just a dream. You'll get nothing but heartache married to
Grainger. Weak, stupid sod, he knows nothing, nothing,
fancy setting himself up as my partner . . .' He gave a

weak, derogatory laugh, 'And now it's all gone — every-thing — finished — like me.'

A bout of coughing robbed him of further speech. When it was finished, a blob of red glistening blood hung on his lower lip, his labouring lungs heaved and fought for air. Turning, Evelyn ran from the place, never stop-ping till she reached the corner of Lewis Street where she leaned weakly against the wall, struggling to get breath into her own lungs.

By the time she reached Camloan Road she had com-posed herself sufficiently to bid a fairly normal greeting to Big Aggie's Man as he sauntered homewards. In the street outside 198, Fishy Alice had stopped her barrow. Hanging in his traces, looking half dead, Dobbie Loan seemed not to have enough strength to raise his head as she approached.

'Poor old lad,' she soothed, rubbing his nose with a gentle hand, angry at herself for not having a tit-bit for him in her pocket. There were no tit-bits these days, but Dobbie Loan showed not the least interest in her or her empty pockets.

'He's for the knacker's yard, lass.' Fishy Alice drew a holey sleeve over her nose and sniffed loudly. 'The poor old boy's done in, I'll be lucky if I see another day's work out o' him. When he's gone it'll be a barrow in the Gallowgate for me. My wandering days are done when old Dobbie kicks the bucket.'

'He isn't finished.' Alex's voice came defiantly from behind Fishy Alice. 'I want to buy him, Mother, I could *make* him well again and when he's strong enough I know he could earn his keep. I'll *make* him strong again.'

Evelyn looked at her son. In his arms he clutched a great parcel of fish and in amazement she said, 'Alex, where did you get the money to buy all that?'

'I saved it,' his tones were still defiant, 'out o' the

money I got selling kindling round the doors and from doing old Dunbar's books before he fired me.' He paused, resentment in his eyes at the memory of Stashie growling at him to keep his bloody nose out of the books in future, as he never had earned his money anyway. 'I know how things are — with Father and Stashie,' he continued, 'so I bought fish, you're always saying how good it is for us. You or Grannie could make it into a sort o' tattie and fish pie. And I have enough left over to buy Dobbie Loan. Say I can, Mother, I could winter him in Dunky the smith's shed, I could do odd jobs for Dunky every day after school to help pay for Dobbie's keep. In the summer he could graze in Dunky's field and later on I'll think o' other ways to make money so's I can keep him.'

He stared at her, willing her to say yes, even though the expression in his eyes told her that he expected opposition. Her first instinct was to refuse her permission, the idea of her ten-year-old son buying a horse being so utterly ludicrous it took her all her time not to smile at the idea . . .

Then she remembered how he loved horses, how he spoke of them and drew pictures of them, how kind he had always been to poor old Dobbie Loan. And she remembered her own childhood, surrounded by animals . . . surrounded by horses that she had adored and whom she still thought of with the greatest longing and affection . . .

They had something in common after all, she and Alex, and reaching out she put her hand on his shoulder and said softly, 'Ay, Alex, you can buy Dobbie Loan if you can afford him, but remember, he'll be your responsibility and your father must have the last word on the subject. If he says no then no it is and you'll just have to thole it. And dinna forget, you will also have to see Dunky and find out if he's agreeable to you keeping the horse in his shed.'

He looked at her for a long moment, saying nothing,

then he put his hand on her arm and squeezed it gently. Something happened between them in those brief moments, a bridge had been crossed, each of them knew that and silently acknowledged the fact with a small, tremulous smile.

'Mind now,' Fishy Alice was saying, 'you'll have to match what I would have got from the knacker's yard. Only a couple o' pounds like as no' but it will be enough to set me up wi' a barrow in the Gallowgate.' Her watery old eyes softened. 'I'm glad Dobbie's getting another chance, he deserves it after all the faithful service he's given me over the years. Come for him in a couple o' days, laddie, that will give me time to sort myself out.'

The cart trundled away, Alex gave a little whoop of joy and tucking his parcel of fish under one arm he took his mother's hand and walked with her into the close, being careful not to rush her up the stairs since, by now, he knew only too well that ladies in 'her condition' had to take things easy and it was a case of one step at a time.

That night Evelyn couldn't sleep. She tossed and turned and was unable to get Stashie's deathly white face out of her mind. It had been cowardly of her to turn and flee like that, she should have stayed and tried to help, made him something to eat, at least given him a cup of tea. He had no one, no one to care for him or even care *about* him. How awful to be dying and to know that not one person in the whole world was in the least bit concerned. The next day she was quiet and withdrawn, another sleepless night followed. When she arose she was exhausted and pale with dark circles under her eyes. When Maggie asked anxiously if she was feeling all right she replied, 'I'm just a bit tired, Mam, I havena been sleeping and there's something I have to do before I'll ever get a night's rest again. Would you look after the bairns for me this afternoon!'

'Ay, Evie, but when you get back I want to ken what all this is about. Both Jamie and myself are worried about you, lassie, this has been a difficult pregnancy for you and you're not getting the proper nourishment to feed two. I'll make some fish soup for your tea tonight. Alex bought enough Finnan Haddies to feed an army, he's turning out to be a decent laddie after all.'

A faint smile touched Evelyn's white lips. 'Ay, he is that, only ten-and-a-half years old and already he's behaving like a wee man.'

This time she didn't hesitate when she reached the workshop at the top of The Sac. Opening the door she went straight inside and made her way to Stashie's mean bed with its filthy coverings. The cloying stench of death was heavy in the air. She was too late. The realization hit her like a blow and she swayed on her feet as she forced her eyes to focus on the dead man's face.

But he was still alive – just – his sunken eyes gazed up at her out of a chalky mask that was laced with purple-blue veins, his body was a rickle of twisted bones and sickly yellow flesh.

Beside him, on a small, scratched wooden table, the pitiful remains of bread and cheese lay mouldering beside an empty, tea-stained cup.

When he saw her he opened his mouth but no sound came, then his hand came out of the blanket, a skeletal claw that trembled and appealed as it hung suspended in mid-air. A bout of weak coughing seized him, blood gushed from his mouth. Repulsed though she was, Evelyn seized the bony hand and held on to it. A few moments later he died with her there in the room and she stepped back, letting go of the wilted hand, shock and horror curdling in her stomach till she had to rush over to the grease-encrusted sink where she was violently sick.

When she had recovered slightly she glanced once

more at the man in the bed but tore her eyes quickly away from the forbidding sight. A wad of papers on the table attracted her attention and going over she leafed slowly through them. They were bills, demand notes, claims for payment from just about every conceivable source. Stashie had been in debt up to his ears, no wonder he hadn't been able to give either Davie or Joss their due. It had all been in vain, she had sold her precious necklace for this and now there was nothing. Then she saw a ten shilling note protruding from under the cup.

For a long time she stared at the money, sorely tempted to take it. Her hand came up from her side, her fingers uncurled, she seemed to stop breathing altogether as she stood there, looking in mesmerized fascination at the note. Her breath exploded from her lungs with a gush, tears sprang to her eyes. How could she have sunk so low? How could she, Evelyn McKenzie Grainger, even consider stealing money from a dead man? Where was her sanity? What had happened to that dignified pride that she had always believed would never desert her.

'Oh, Lord, forgive me,' she whispered, 'I forgot myself, I forgot that I'm a Grant with Ogilvie blood in my veins, Gillan is my cousin, oh, dear Gillie! Where is he now? I need him so.' She shook herself. 'Forgive my self-pity, Lord, and bless this poor man who lies here in death. Take his soul unto you, Lord, and grant him peace.'

The simple prayer seemed to give her strength for she went quite calmly from the workshop and walked out to the yard. Alex was coming round the side of the smiddy, leading Dobbie Loan. Davie had been amazed when his eldest son had first broached the subject of buying a horse, then he had laughed, and had granted his permission. Dunky too had been good-natured about the whole thing and had obligingly made a space in his shed in preparation for Dobbie's arrival.

'Though you'll have to make yourself useful about the place,' he had warned Alex. 'Every day after school and 'no shirking, my lad, or the old horse could still find himself at the knacker's yard.'

'I'll be here, Dunky,' Alex had promised with shining eyes. 'I'm big and strong for my age and I can pump the bellows and feed the fires and later on you can show me how to make the horse's shoes. I'll fetch and lift and lay and . . .'

'Hey, steady on, son,' Dunky had laughed. 'First things first. Get the horse here, then we'll decide what you can and can't do.'

'Look, Mother,' Alex called when he saw her approaching. 'Dobbie's here at last. I'm just taking him into the shed to give him a rub down and a feed o' hay then I'll be home to fill the coal buckets and empty the ashcan and maybe help Rachel wi' the tea dishes . . .'

He was full of good intentions, highly delighted with himself and so excited he never thought to question his mother's reasons for being in that particular spot at that particular hour.

His mood was infectious. She rubbed the old nag's nose, then walked home to seek out Davie and say, 'Stashie's dead, he died while I was there. I went to see him two days ago to ask him for money and found him dying. It is finished, Davie, you have no job, we have no money. I am tired of it all, I am carrying a child who will have no future, no chance, no opportunities, and I want you to agree to let Nellie have it.'

He stared at her, too stunned at first to be able to speak. When he found his tongue he was almost too inarticulate with anger to be able to say the things he wanted to say. 'You're raving,' he told her bluntly when at last he had calmed down. 'You know what happened before when Nellie kept a baby of ours. To this day Alex hasn't forgiven you for leaving him as you did.'

She pushed her hair away from her face and said

evenly, 'It willna be like that this time. I want Nellie to have the baby for keeps. She can give it all the things we will never be able to give it. With her, and Kenneth, our child will have its chances and with a bit o' luck our other four children will survive this time o' poverty and grow up as well and as strong as any bairns reared in the post-war years.'

He lay back, the pains in his stomach claiming all his attention for a few minutes. He had suffered the complaint on and off for years but wouldn't see a doctor. 'I don't trust any o' them,' he had told Evelyn, 'and I trust hospitals even less, neither did me any good in the war and I wouldn't thank you for the muck they call medicine.'

When he opened his eyes he took her wrist in a painful grip and rasped, 'Our baby stays wi' us and no' other word about giving it away to Nellie or anybody else. As for Stashie, alive or dead the bugger owes me. As soon as I'm up on my feet I'll go to see my lawyer. I put good money into that business and expect to salvage something from the wreckage.'

But there was nothing to salvage. It came to light that Stashie had been a compulsive gambler. Every penny he had ever made had gone to satisfy his compelling habit, there was nothing left and everything in the workshop that was sellable had to be sold in order to pay off some of the debts.

Davie was devastated and in his despair he had no time to notice that his wife was growing more withdrawn, more hopeless, in hers.

CHAPTER 20

Christmas was just a week away and it was snowing. Evelyn awoke from an exhausted sleep and looked towards the window. 'Rothiedrum!' she whispered and forgot for a moment the tenements and the closes and the grey, poverty-stricken streets of Govan.

But it wasn't Rothiedrum, she had only been dreaming about it, and now that she was more fully awake she was aware of a dull, aching throb at the base of her spine which brought her quickly back to reality.

'Davie,' she murmured, turning her head on the pillow. But he wasn't there by her side and she remembered it was his day for signing on at the Exchange where he would queue to put his name to the necessary forms in order to draw his unemployment money.

At first he had refused to believe that he wouldn't find a job. 'I'm a qualified carpenter,' he had told her, his jaw tightening in that defiant way she knew so well. 'I'll have no bother finding work – and I'm damned if I'll join that hopeless mob at the Exchange – even if I have to go on halftime.'

But he soon discovered that work wasn't so easy to come by, even for the skilled worker with a trade, and with pride choking him he had been forced to sign on and to draw unemployment benefit amounting to thirty-four shillings a week. It was a pittance; after rent and fuel had been paid there was very little left over for food and the outlook for Christmas was very bleak indeed for the Grants and the Graingers.

With no money to buy drink, Jamie had been forced to abandon the bottle, and instead turned his attention to his lasts in an effort to forget the gnawing pangs clawing at his innards. But no one could afford the shoes and boots he produced. For a long time they lay in a rejected heap in the kitchen cupboard, then one morning he gathered them up and went round the doors, giving them away, and it was back to the old story as drinks were bought for him by grateful neighbours in the pubs where men went to drown their sorrows and never mind the wife and bairns waiting at home for the reprieve from poverty that never came.

Maggie had ranted and raved at Jamie, she had told him he was worthless and weak and when she was finished she wept in the solitude of the scullery before putting on her hat and coat and going out to seek employment as a washerwoman. Thereafter she travelled to Jordanhill thrice weekly to wash clothes for the posh houses of that area, earning three shillings a day for her labours and a reputation for thoroughness that soon become second to none. She always returned home exhausted after a hard, hot day spent over a wash-tub, but her weekly nine shillings bought food for the family and kept the wolf from the door.

But today she was at home, and when Evelyn didn't appear for breakfast she went ben The Room to find her lying quite still in her bed, her brow bathed in perspiration and an unnatural flush high on her cheekbones.

'Mam,' she struggled to get up, 'I dinna ken what time it is, am I late . . . ?'

Maggie pushed her gently back into bed. 'Lie you still, my lass,' she said kindly. 'I'll bring you a cup o' tea, you dinna look too well. Are you in pain?'

'My back,' gasped Evelyn as a band of red hot pain gripped her. 'I think maybe the bairn has started.'

The pains came in earnest after that, tearing her innards apart till The Room became filled with her cries of agony. Outside the snow whirled, blotting out the grey tenements, draping the rooftops in blankets of white that effectively took away the harshness of angular silhouettes.

The midwife came followed by the doctor. When the children came home from school they heard their mother's frightening screams and went about whitefaced and silent. James was so upset by the idea that his mother was going to die he lapsed into one of his caterwauling tantrums, his head thrown back, his mouth gaping wide in his contorted face.

Meg and Rachel were so scared by this they both began to cry but Alex wasn't so easily upset.

'Shut up!' he yelled. 'Shut up! Shut up! Shut up!'

So saying he drew back his hand and landed the open palm on James's cheek with a mighty blow.

The little boy immediately stopped his loud wailing, so stunned with shock he couldn't say anything for quite a few minutes. Then he began to sob, hopelessly and soundlessly, his breath catching in his throat, his body growing rigid till even Alex was afraid and Rachel made haste to take her little brother on her knee and rock him backwards and forwards as if he was a baby.

Maggie was in The Room with the doctor and the midwife. Jamie, unable to bear his daughter's pain, had gone out to pace the streets. Davie, feeling helpless and useless, was sitting in Jack's house, biting his immaculate nails and smoking one cigarette after another while Jessie Jack stomped around the tiny room, grinning her inane grins. Old Mrs Jenny Jack made tea, most of which she slopped into the saucer as her palsied hands laid it on the table beside Davie.

So the children were alone in the upstairs kitchen, narking at one another in their uncertainty, none of them being very kind to the other because anger gave them a certain strength and they all needed to feel strong in such a fraught situation.

'You'll have to make our tea, Gypsy,' Alex growled at

his sister. 'James won't let go o' Rachel and I'm no' going to do girls' work.'

'Make your own,' returned Meg sullenly. 'I don't see why girls should be servants to silly boys. I don't know how to make anything and there's no food in the house anyway.'

'Fetch the toasting fork,' directed Rachel. 'We all know how to make toast and can take turn about holding the fork.' Soothed by the heat of the fire, fortified by hot toast running with melted margarine, they gradually became amiable towards each other. Anxiety united them and soon they were talking in low voices, confiding their fears, discussing what they knew about mothers having babies and making up the things they didn't know.

'I'll never have any,' declared Meg, her young face serious. 'They come out o' some secret part o' your body, tearing you up and making you nearly bleed to death.'

'But what part?' Alex wanted to know, his face set and earnest. 'Nobody has an opening big enough for a baby to get through so how do they get out?'

'Well, they grow in your belly,' Rachel spoke speculatively. 'We all know that because we've seen Mam getting bigger and bigger but Nancy Docherty in my class says that it's only mothers who have a special place in their bodies for babies to come through.'

'Maybe they have a pouch like a kangaroo,' Alex said hopefully. 'My teacher told us about how kangaroos carry wee baby kangaroos in a sort o' pocket attached to their bellies. When girls get old like our mother they could easily grow a kind o' skin flap that a baby could climb into till they are old enough to be born.'

'But – how does a baby grow in the first place?' Rachel wrinkled her brow. 'And if a baby is able to climb into a flap surely it should just get itself born right away without having to go to all that bother.'

Meg, looking slightly superior, gave a sniff. 'Babies can't climb, you're both wrong, they're all soft and wrinkly when they're wee and take ages to start crawling about, never mind climb.' She lowered her voice and gazed round at the others in a conspiratorial fashion. 'It's something to do wi' men. Maisie Thomson's big sister got married a while back and Maisie heard Molly in The Room, telling her man no' to go too far cos she didn't want to have bairns for a while yet.'

James stirred on Rachel's lap. 'Mammy,' he whimpered. 'I want to see her. Why is she crying? Will the Big Black Bogle Man take her away? Will she go into a coffin like Witchie Winnie and be carried off forever by the black horses wi' the black plumes on their heads? If she does she'll never come back, she'll be dead forever.'

He buried his head in Rachel's lap and began to weep softly. His words struck fresh dread into the hearts of his sisters and brother.

'I don't want our mother to die,' Meg stated, her face devoid of colour. 'I love her, she's a good mother and she promised me a yellow ribbon for Christmas.'

'Is that all you can think about?' Alex said scathingly. 'All you ever think about is yourself.'

'What about you?' Meg returned with asperity. 'For weeks you've hinted about a grooming brush for that old nag o' yours, you don't love our mother, you've never loved her, you look at her wi' they marble eyes o' yours and never a smile does she get. Maybe I do want things she can't afford but I still love her, even though I don't get them.'

There was a long silence. Alex fought some inner struggle with his emotions, he opened his mouth, shut it, then said in a rush, 'I do love her: I love her more than you, more than anybody, I just can't show it – that's all.'

Rachel buried her face in James's thick black mop. 'My mother is the best in the world and I don't want her to die. I'm going to say a prayer: "Dear Jesus, please make Mother's pain go away, don't take her to live wi' you, Gentle Jesus, because we like her living here wi' us and we need her to make the cocoa in the morning. Father also needs her to make him happy when he's grumpy and Grannie and Granda need her because she's their daughter. Amen."'

'That was a selfish prayer,' grumbled Alex. 'You're old enough to make the cocoa, you should have told Jesus we need her because she's beautiful and sings bothy ballads when she's happy and has a laugh on her that makes other people happy.'

'You tell Him,' said Rachel, hurt.

Alex placed his hands together and shut his eyes. 'Rachel didn't say that right, Jesus, we want our mother to live because we don't want her to die, that's all for now, Jesus. Amen.'

'That's daft!' exploded Meg. 'If she lives she won't die, Jesus won't know what you're talking about. Boys are just stupid, they don't know how to pray or . . .'

Alex quelled her with a look just as a single terrifying scream came from The Room. The children eyed one another, they said no more but lapsed into a silence that was filled with dread.

Evelyn haemorrhaged twice after the birth of her third son but had already lapsed into a semi-conscious state during the delivery. Together, the doctor and the midwife laboured to bring the child out of the bruised and torn body of his mother, and little wonder that the task was so difficult for he weighed all of ten pounds and yelled his head off the second it popped out of the birth canal.

When the doctor had delivered the rest of him, he shook his head and said grimly, 'Little wonder she's in a bad way, he's sucked all the nourishment out of her and left her with little strength. Take him, nurse. It looks as if I have a fight on my hands to save his mother.'

Davie was devastated when he learned how ill his wife was and made no effort to defend himself when the doctor told him that this child ought to be the last or he would answer for the consequences.

'Evie, my darling girl,' he wept when he was allowed to be alone with her for a little while, 'I'm sorry, forgive me for doing this to you. I just can't stop myself from wanting you, you're so lovely. You've always driven me mad with feelings I can't control.'

But the young woman who lay so still and unresponsive in the bed was very unlike the beautiful Evie he knew. Her tumble of rich red hair framed a face that was deathly white, the skin of it so transparent that the delicate fretwork of blue veins on her temples could plainly be seen. Her breathing was so shallow there were moments when he thought her heart had stopped beating altogether and it was then he gathered her into his arms and kissed her pale lips, as if by doing so he could breathe some of his own life into her. 'I love you, Evie,' he whispered into her hair. 'I've never told you that very often these past years, but – you're my life, please, please, my dear, dear, Evie, don't leave me.'

Maggie found herself with a new baby on her hands but she had reared so many of her own she was equal to the challenge and this big, bonny boy was a good baby. He accepted cow's milk with gusto and when he wasn't eating he was sleeping, contentedly lying in the spacious, cosily-lined bottom drawer of the family dresser because there wasn't enough room in the kitchen for his crib.

The children were fascinated by him and took turns to hushie baw him, even little James sitting quite still and patient by his side to purse his lips and copy the soothing sounds Maggie was so skilled at making.

'Shoo, whoo, shoo, whoo.' For days it seemed there were no other sounds in the kitchen but these for, after his first mighty yells of greeting to the world, the new

221

arrival made hardly a whimper and was quite happy just being fed and rocked and changed.

'At least he's a good bairn,' said Jamie. 'We can thank the Lord for that.'

'Ay, but he's got a big appetite,' said Maggie ominously, and left it at that.

Evelyn floated and dreamed in her world of delirium. Sometimes she was aware that Davie sat by her bed, that he kissed her and held her and murmured sweet things into her ear, but when she tried to talk to him she couldn't get the words out and then she was afraid because the blackness kept pulling her down till it engulfed her altogether and she wept her silent tears into a blanket of emptiness that was nothingness yet smothered her with its thick, dark folds.

Visions came to her, of people that she knew and loved, her mother and father, Grace, wavering there in front of her, transient and unreal, like an angel with skin as pale as alabaster and delicate hands that touched her brow and made her feel that the cool, sweet air of beloved lands had swept over her.

Gillan came to her out of a deep, dark wood filled with memories that were written on gossamer-thin paper hanging from trees that swayed in the breezes of life flowing gently down from a golden sky. At first he was just a slim shadow far off in the distance, then he came closer, wavering through the trees, his face becoming clearer with each light step until he moved into a sun-drenched glade and stood looking at her, just looking, saying nothing. But he didn't need words to tell her that he was close to her and that he cared. He had promised that he would come to her in dreams, in that way, he had vowed, they would always be together and it would be their secret, one that the rest of the world would never find out.

But was it a dream? He was smiling at her, his dark, handsome face lit by his gladness at seeing her.

'Are you real, Gillie?' she whispered. 'Are you there?'

'I'm here, Evie.' Grace's voice seemed part of the dream and suddenly Evelyn was afraid, for no one, not even her beloved Grace, could be allowed into dreams of Gillan and she cried out, 'Grace, come out of there, you'll get lost in the woods, only Gillie knows the way.'

'I'm here, Evie, I'm not a dream,' Grace reassured her, and Evelyn sunk back into her pillows, glad that it was Grace who spoke to her and not Davie, he must never find out that she met with Gillie in dreams because she couldn't hurt her Davie, not ever, she was his to the end of his days . . .

And then Nellie came, hovering there in front of eyes that saw a room filled with half-light and flurries of white things whirling down beyond great panes of glass. But then the light and the windows were blotted out by a fair head that she knew so well, but it couldn't be Nellie, Nellie was far away in a country of sea and sky, only she never saw beyond Croft Donald now for she sat alone in a dark corner of life, weeping, weeping, for a little girl who had gone far away beyond the light.

'Nellie.' Feverishly she held out her hand, never expecting to feel that strong, well-remembered touch because this was just a dream like all the others. But it was real, her fingers knew the grasp of warm flesh, and she heard Nellie's voice speaking to her.

'Ay, Evie, I'm here, Nellie's here, you're getting better now, dinna be feart any more.'

'Nellie, Nellie.' Desperately she tried to raise herself up. 'Nellie. I want you to take my baby, I'm too tired to look after it myself and I want you to take it and keep it for your own. Please, Nellie, please . . .'

'Oh, wheesht, my babby,' Nellie soothed, the tears

falling unheeded out of her eyes, 'dinna try to talk any more, you're going to get better and Nellie will stay by your side.'

Exhaustion engulfed Evelyn but before she sank into the abyss once more she murmured, 'Take it away before I see it, put your name upon it, it's your baby, Nellie — yours and Kenneth's . . . My Christmas gift to you, mine and Davie's . . .'

Nellie stepped back from the bed, her face ashen. On hearing how ill her sister was she had made the long journey from Kenneray, risking the blizzards that were sweeping the countryside. On arriving she hadn't even waited for a cup of tea but had gone straight into The Room to see Evelyn. Davie led her to a chair and made her sit down by the fire that had been kept burning day and night since Evelyn took ill.

Nellie leaned back gratefully and held her cold hands to the heat. 'I dinna suppose Mary has been to see Evie,' she said grimly, 'yet I ken fine that Evie went to see her when her baby was born.'

'There was some disagreement between them,' Davie spoke absently. 'Evie gave her a piece of her mind and Mary told her not to come back.'

'Ay, she would, Evie wouldna have minced words wi' the spoiled madam. It's Greg I feel sorry for, him and the bairn, it was a shame she was born as she was but it's no' as if it's the end o' the world. Things like that can be sorted but our Mary likes everything to be just so and canna thole being put about in any way.'

Davie leaned forward and spoke imperatively. 'Nell, Evie wasn't ranting just now, she meant what she said. A month or two back she spoke to me about letting you have our baby but at the time I was too taken up wi' myself to see the sense in what she was saying. Nell . . .' he took her hand in his, an action which surprised her since he had never been a demonstrative sort of man, 'I've changed my mind, I agree wi' Evie, I want you to

224

have our son and to bring him up as your own, you can do it legally, adopt him, so that you need never fear he will be taken away from you . . .'

A shocked Nellie drew her hand away. 'Do you ken what you're saying? Give your child away! But how can you? He's your flesh and blood. I could never even consider stealing him away, it's a baby we're talking about, no' some possession to be handed around the family!'

'Och, Nell.' He grabbed her hand again, his voice vibrant with emotion. 'If things were different I would never have dreamed of letting go of a son o' mine – but consider the facts. Evie has had enough, she's ill and weary and it takes her all her time to look after the bairns we already have. I don't have a job, your mother has lowered her pride to go out and slave at a wash-tub in order to earn a few bob, we have very little food, very little of anything. Compared to us you live in a land o' plenty and you could give the boy any opportunities that are going, also he would be reared in the clean air o' the country. It breaks Evie's heart to know that our children couldn't have a country upbringing like herself, and even if you can't do this for me then please, please, do it for a sister who loves you and trusts you wi' the life o' her son.'

Nellie stared at him. She noticed how gaunt his face had become, how his dark eyes burned with the pain of having to lower his pride and admit that he couldn't support his family. But it was an earth-shattering thing that he was asking her to do and she was silent for a long time while she absorbed the full import of his passionate plea.

'I would have to ask Kenneth,' she said at last. 'I canna just walk into Croft Donald wi' a new baby in my arms and expect him to feel as I do – because –' she looked Davie straight in the eye '– I canna deny it, nothing else in the world would give me more pleasure than having a baby I could call my own. Since I lost my own darling wee girl I have felt empty and useless . . .'

225

'Then, you'll do it.' Davie jumped up to go to a drawer and bring out some writing paper and a pen. 'Write to Kenneth, Nell, now, this minute, don't stop to even think about it.'

When Maggie came ben to fetch Nellie through for some hot soup she found her eldest daughter writing away industriously, her face crimson with excitement.

Later, when Maggie could get her daughter alone, she said thoughtfully, 'It is a rare and precious gift that you are being offered, Nellie. Take the bairn and bring him up as your own. Jamie and myself agree it is the best thing for everybody concerned, your arms will be filled in the way you've aye dreamed, the lad will have a good life at Croft Donald, and both Davie and Evie will get the chance to raise their other four bairns to be healthy men and women.

'I've watched Evie this last year or two, she's no' the same blithe lassie she used to be. Poverty and despair have taken away her strength. When she found out she was having another baby it was the last straw for her. This is what she wants to do, Nellie, for you, for herself and Davie, and most importantly, for their son.'

'Oh, Mam.' Nellie collapsed into her mother's arms and like a child she allowed herself to be soothed and comforted. It was not at all like Nellie and Maggie stroked the fair head, her heart so full she shed a silent tear or two for this eldest daughter who had always pushed her deepest emotions into her heart where they remained locked – till moments like now when she proved that she had the same frailties as anyone else.

Kenneth's answer to the letter came three days later. He would be delighted to have Evelyn and Davie's child, if that was what they wanted. The cradle was waiting, no baby would receive a warmer welcome.

Nellie's hands shook so much she could do nothing

for some time and for the rest of that day she went about in such a daze it was all she could do to speak rationally or even to eat any of the simple fare that was set before her.

It was decided that she should leave for home as quickly as possible. Evelyn was getting better and it would be too cruel to allow her to waken to a sight of the child she could never hold.

Alex had been very silent since learning of his baby brother's fate and before Nellie left he managed to get her alone to say, 'Take me instead o' *him*, Nellie, he's too wee to be much use to you but I'm big and strong and would be a good help to you on the croft.'

'Oh, Alex, Alex.' She took him to her knee and stroked his hair. 'You've aye been special to me, you ken that well enough, and you're right, you are big and strong and your mother needs you very much just now. She's been very ill, as fine you know, for a whilie there we thought we were going to lose her. She's getting stronger now but it will be a long time before she's fully back on her feet. You'll have to help your father to look after her because you're old enough now to be a big help to them both. The baby is coming wi' me because he's too little to look after himself. I lost my own baby, Alex, she was very precious to me but I only had her for a few hours before Jesus took her away. Now I've been given the gift of another child and he'll be just as dear to me as if he was my very own son.'

'A kind o' Christmas present?' Alex's voice was husky.

'Ay, a Christmas present, the best I have ever had, and you will remember what I told you, Alex? You must be strong and good for your mother's sake and help her all you can. You can do it, I know you can, you're growing into a fine wee man, I'm proud o' you and so too are your parents.'

Alex visibly puffed with pride. 'I'll look after my

227

mother,' he said gruffly and went off at once to fetch a cold cloth for Evelyn's brow.

The baby was happed warmly in the shawl that had served his brothers and sisters, Nellie's bags were piled in the lobby, and hidden in the kitchen press was a small mound of gaily wrapped parcels she had brought to fill the children's Christmas stockings.

Handing the baby to her mother she went ben The Room to say goodbye to Evelyn. Her eyes were closed, the lids and the delicate skin beneath them were smudged with purple. She had only that morning taken her first real meal since her son's birth; she was still very weak and inclined to drift off to sleep at any given time.

Nellie bent over her and kissed her brow. 'Thank you, my darling sister, you have given me a treasure beyond compare. Your heart and your soul conspired together in this act and I'll never, never be able to find the words to thank you. No sister could do more than you've done and to the end o' my days I'll never forget your kindness.'

'Nellie.' Evelyn opened her eyes, a tear trembled on her lower lashes. 'Please go, go quickly, for I canna bear to say — goodbye.'

Nellie understood. With a last lingering look at the young woman in the bed she turned and went blindly out of The Room. A few minutes later she left the house, carrying a white bundle that was already more to her than the world.

That evening Davie played Richard Tauber on the gramophone he had made for his wife two Christmases ago. The haunting voice filled The Room.

'Davie.' Evelyn held out her hand, he went to take it. 'I love you, Davie,' she whispered.

'And you — you, Evelyn McKenzie Grainger, are my heart's delight, my star in the darkness . . .' His voice broke, he couldn't go on.

'Davie,' she sighed, one trembling finger coming up to stroke his hair, hair the colour of the earth, she had always loved it. He was only thirty-three but already it was sprinkled with white – like little bits of snow patching the rich soil.

Her eyes grew misty, she felt close to him, closer than they had been for years. 'Davie, was it – a boy – or a girl?'

He stared at her, then he remembered, she couldn't possibly know, she hadn't been fully aware of what was happening when their son was born.

'A boy, a fine boy, Evie.'

'Did Nellie give him a name?'

'Kenneth David Cameron.'

'Oh, it's perfect, Kenneth will be so proud, and I'm glad his other name is yours.'

Davie took a deep breath. He was glad also – and proud that the child would grow up with the name David in his title.

PART 4

Summer/Autumn 1929

CHAPTER 21

'Roll up! Roll up! A penny to see the Wonder Horse!'

Alex's boisterous cries echoed round the yard at the top of The Sac, accompanied by a gay burst of gypsy music from James on his grandfather's old fiddle. His big brother had persuaded him to come to The Sac that day with the hope that some lively music might help to attract the crowds to the grand opening of 'Dobbie's Debut'. Today was the day that the old horse was leaving his winter quarters in favour of the open fields where the grass was growing green and the horses waiting for Dunky the smith's attention grazed and browsed under the trees.

It was a warm Saturday in May, the sky was blue, the sparrows were chirping noisily from the tall eaves where they were building their nests. The heat was bringing out the unsavoury smells from the backcourt middens, a Friday night drunk was sleeping off his excesses in a corner of the yard, but nothing could take away Alex's exuberance.

He had waited a long time for this day, mainly because he was finding it harder and harder to keep Dobbie adequately supplied with hay and oats, but also because he was genuinely excited about showing off his 'wonder horse' to his contemporaries.

Dobbie's health had certainly shown a marked improvement, his coat shone, his eyes were no longer lacklustre but were bright with interest, he held himself well and felt so good these days he was wont to utter little snorts and grunts of pleasure in Alex's ear as if to thank him for his new lease of life.

He was the love of the boy's life, a 'wonder horse' in every one of Alex's senses. Often he had shared Dobbie's shed during the long winter evenings, grooming him, talking to him, feeding him tasty titbits he had brought in his pockets. Never mind where they came from, old Charlie the grocer never missed a carrot or two from his boxes, it was enough that Dobbie's molars crunched them with the greatest of pleasure and that he had learned to nuzzle the boy's pockets till he was adept at extracting a tasty morsel from the folds of cloth.

One night Alex hadn't come home at all and his father had gone looking for him, eventually finding him in the shed, fast asleep, his head resting peacefully on Dobbie's patient flank.

Now the long winter was over, the skies were wide and light, and Alex had planned this little 'coming out' ceremony because to him it was only right that his horse should have a memorable send off into a world of greenery that he had never known in all the years of his work-filled life – and if a few pennies were earned in the process, that was all to the good as far as Alex was concerned.

James hadn't been too keen on the idea of playing his fiddle in front of a crowd. His thin little body was as taut as the strings of the instrument he held in his nervous grasp, and an annoying tic in his right eye made him blink continually, but as the moments passed and no unruly mob appeared, he began to relax a little and even to enjoy his playing.

'Nobody's coming to see your silly horse,' Meg told her big brother. 'What's there to see anyway? Only an old cuddy wi' brown teeth and flies biting his bum.'

'Ach, you don't know anything,' Alex retorted with a twist of his lips. 'You're just a daft gypsy and no' a very nice looking one at that.'

Meg opened her mouth to retaliate just as Mad Monkey Morrison appeared on the scene, tearing into his flamed-red hair with broken fingernails, an action that made both Meg and Rachel move out of his vicinity, having been well warned by Evelyn about the amazing acrobatic feats of head lice.

At sight of Monkey, James's new-found confidence plummeted, his bow scraped the fiddle strings which emitted a loud screeching wail.

'Is this a backcourt concert?' Monkey grinned sarcastically. 'I could get the same results tying two cats together and setting them alight.'

'You wouldn't do that!' Rachel faced Monkey, her fists bunching. Though she was the most placid of all Evelyn's children she was also the fiercest protectress when it came to animals and small children.

Monkey saw the fire in her grey eyes and backed down awkwardly. 'Naw, you know I wouldny do that, Rachel, I like cats, I hate it when my Da throws beer bottles at them when they scream at one another in the middens.'

'Liar!' jeered Meg. 'I've seen *you* throwing things at them *and* I saw you jamming a tin can over the nose o' a poor wee kitten.'

'No' me.' Monkey's face turned bright red. 'Somebody else did that, I was trying to get it aff – and I did – though I couldny help tearing out some o' its whiskers, that bloody can was stuck tight and I'd a helluva job gettin' it aff.'

Alex looked at his flame-haired friend with something akin to dislike. He was growing away from Monkey and no longer thought it fun to tease and torment helpless animals as once he had done, though never to the same drastic extent as the other boy. Just recently two cats had been found dead at the foot of a stairhead window, their tails tied together, the fur cruelly scorched from their bodies.

Monkey had boasted to him that he had committed the foul deed and Alex's dislike and disgust of his one-time inseparable companion became very strong indeed.

'Get away from here, Monkey,' he ordered. 'You're

only out to cause trouble and I'm no' having any o' that today.'

'Naw, I'm stayin',' Monkey stated baldly. 'See if you can make me go.'

Snotters Monroe came onto the scene, followed by half a dozen of Alex's classmates, their timely arrival almost certainly preventing a fisticuffs between the glaring-eyed pair. Monkey shuffled away, turning at the last minute to draw his fingers across the holey seat of his pants before holding them up to Alex in the V sign.

Snotters was reading the untidily scrawled poster attached to Dobbie's shed.

'A penny to see the wonder horse!' he guffawed. 'What's wonderful about a broken down cuddy wi' calluses on his knees? I've seen mair wonder in a greasy poke filled wi' chips!'

The other youngsters nodded their agreement, sniggers and jeers broke out.

'A penny to see him and another penny to ride him round the trees,' Rachel said hastily, seeing the look of thunder on her elder brother's face.

There was a short silence. The children were intrigued, none of them had ever ridden a horse before, the novelty of such an event was appealing.

'Tuppence, that's a lot o' money,' objected one of the girls. 'I could buy a lot o' sweeties for tuppence.'

'Tuppence or nothing,' stated Alex, seizing delightedly on Rachel's idea. Grumbles and moans followed but everyone wanted a ride on Dobbie's broad back. In minutes he was being led out of his shed and over to the field where he lowered his head and ecstatically buried his nose in the dewy grass.

'He thinks it's a heaven for horses.' Alex was completely carried away, his good temper was restored, willingly he helped the first in the queue to mount Dobbie's bare back. The horse remained placid and obliging, and for the next hour, with a rest and a carrot in between, he plodded in and out of the trees as if he had been carrying children all his life.

The morning was a great success. At the end of it Alex jingled the money in his pocket and the children unwillingly dispersed.

'Can we do the same next Saturday?' they called on the way out of the field.

'Ay, as long as you bring your money,' Alex agreed, with admirable restraint.

But as soon as the last customer was out of sight he seized his sisters and brother in turn and waltzed them round and round his contentedly grazing horse. Then he grabbed Rachel and kissed her soundly on the nose. 'You're the best sis in the world,' he laughed, 'and I'm going to buy you all a treat!'

So saying he raced them round to the Tallies at the corner of Younger Park Street where he bought them each a large ice cream cone running with raspberry syrup. They sat at the edge of the sun-warmed pavement to savour each delicious mouthful, utterly at peace with the world.

Meg finished first and wiped her mouth with a corner of her frock. 'What will you do wi' the rest o' the money? By rights you should divide it up between us, we all helped you today.'

Alex stood up. 'By rights you didn't even deserve that ice cream cone you've just gulped up like a greedy pig. Rachel and James helped and they've had their payment, the rest o' the money goes to Mother. She needs it more than any o' us.'

Evelyn was touched when her eldest son presented her with a pile of warm pennies straight out of his pocket. Explaining how they had been earned he promised, 'I'll get you more next week, everyone loved riding Dobbie, he doesn't mind, he's strong and well now.'

'Alex,' Evelyn looked at the mound of coppers on the table, 'I'm really glad o' these, we'll have fish suppers for our tea tonight, but listen, Alex, you'll never guess, I went to see old Miss Gillespie this morning and I've to go back and work for her. She says things have never been the same since I left and I start on Monday.'

Fanny and Lizzie had indeed been delighted to see her. They had had one girl after another, they told her, and none of them had been suitable. They had been on the verge of sending for her but instead she had come to them like an answer to a prayer, and could she please start as soon as possible? Monday? Ay, Monday would be just grand, and Evelyn went home feeling happier than she had done for a long time.

But Alex looked less than pleased. He had come to enjoy having his mother at home every day, to knowing she would be there when he came home from school and that she wouldn't be too tired to talk to him as she had sometimes been when working for old Fanny Gillespie.

Evelyn saw his face. 'I have to do this, Alex,' she explained. 'You ken how much we need the money and it means that anything you make can be put towards winter feed for Dobbie. You have to prepare well ahead for that, so when next Saturday comes just you keep any money you've earned.'

'Ay,' he said a trifle sulkily, even though he saw the sense in her words. But nothing could take away the euphoria of that day and by teatime his good spirits were fully restored.

An hour before bedtime he set out to fetch Dobbie from the fields and lead him to his nice warm shed at the top of The Sac. The nights were cold still and he was taking no chances with old Dobbie – not now.

Early next morning, well before the Sunday School that Evelyn insisted her children attend, Alex ran to The Sac in order to let Dobbie out to the field. But a terrible sight met his disbelieving eyes, one so earthshattering that he couldn't quite take it in at first. The shed had disappeared, and so too had Dobbie! All that remained was a smouldering heap of wood and bits and pieces of singed leather, all the things he had worked so hard to acquire during last winter.

'Dobbie.' He breathed the name in a dread whisper before rage and grief swamped him, forcing his legs forward, making him open his mouth and yell, 'Dobbie! Dobbie! Dobbie!' over and over till the yard rang with his voice.

Dunky the smith appeared then, coming out of a small, rickety shed attached to the blacksmith's shop.

'Over here, lad,' he called. 'Dobbie's in here.'

Half sobbing Alex ran into the dingy little building, blinking his eyes after the brightness of the morning. Dobbie was lying on a pile of old sacking, his eyes closed, his breath coming in strange little grunts. He made no move when Alex appeared and the boy went over to him to fall on his knees and lift the heavy head onto his lap.

'It was a good thing I came by this morning to finish a job,' Dunky said, getting down beside Alex. 'I found smoke billowing from the shed and was just in time to get Dobbie out before the damt thing went up in a blue light. Some bugger did it deliberately, I could smell paraffin everywhere.' He put a sympathetic arm round the boy's shoulders. 'He's in a bad way, Alex, not too badly burned, but I think his lungs are scorched and he's suffering from shock, of course.'

'Dobbie, Dobbie.' Tenderly Alex stroked the horse's soft nose. 'You'll get better, I'll be here, Alex will be here, but first . . .'

Drawing his sleeve across his nose he jumped to his feet and went to fetch an old blanket to cover Dobbie before saying to Dunky, 'Would you look after him for a wee while, Dunky? I know who did this, and I'm going to *kill* the swine!'

He was off before Dunky could speak. In the yard he espied the same old drunk of the previous day, this time sleeping off his Saturday night's indulgences. Grabbing the grizzled creature by the collar he shook him and shook him till he grunted and cursed and opened one bloodshot eye.

'Get off me! Away tae hell! Leave me alane, ye bloody wee upstart!' Alex flinched as the stench of stale sweat and second-hand alcohol bathed his face, but grimly he hung on to the old boy's collar, forcing him to emerge from his stupor.

'Listen,' he ordered imperatively, 'you've been here all night. Did you see a fire? Over in that shed there?'

'Gerroff! Gerroff or I'll have the law on ye! Can a body no' get a bit o' shut-eye wi'out one hooligan after another pouncin' on him? Where's yer pal? The one wi' the carroty hair? Mad Monkey, they call him. He's already had a go at me and noo you think it's your turn. Gerroff, I tell ye, before I call the polis!'

'The fire!' persisted Alex. 'Did you see Mad Monkey over at the shed?'

'Bloody hooligan.' The drunk wiped saliva from his mouth. 'He came at me wi' a can o' paraffin and said he would set fire to *me* as well if I didna give him money. I only had a few bob and the bastard took it, every last halfpenny . . .'

Alex didn't wait to hear more, he had all the proof he needed. When he finally ran Monkey to ground, the boy, seeing the half-mad expression on his face, backed away from him.

'It was a' your fault,' he whimpered. 'You winna let me play wi' ye yesterday. Don't hit me! Don't hit me! We're pals — remember?'

Although Alex was barely eleven, he had the well-developed muscles of a fifteen-year-old. In five minutes

240

flat he had reduced the snivelling bully to a bloody-nosed, frothing-mouthed mess, then, breathing hard, he ran to the nearest police station to report what had happened, ending, 'I nearly killed him for what he did and if you want to take me in for it I'm no' coming till my horse is better.'

He stayed with Dobbie all that day, tending his wounds, speaking to him, soothing him in every way he knew how. When he didn't come home at dinner time Meg was sent to look for him but nothing she could say would make him leave his horse.

An hour later Evelyn herself appeared with a flask of soup and a thick doorstep of bread spread with dripping. Putting the food beside him she got down on her knees without a word and quickly examined the horse. He was in a bad way, she only needed to glance at his dilated nostrils and his staring eyes to see that.

But she didn't tell any of that to her son, instead she just sat there with him while the minutes passed and the sun rose higher and higher outside.

Eventually she had to go but she didn't press him to go with her, instead she sent Rachel with some food at tea time along with a message that he wouldn't be doing Dobbie any good if he allowed himself to get ill through lack of nourishment. At that the boy wolfed down both his dinner and his tea and as soon as he had done that he curled up beside Dobbie and refused to move.

At midnight a soft footfall outside made him sit up, his pulses pounding, but when the door opened it was to admit his mother, her arms piled high with blankets and a pillow.

'I'm staying with you,' she informed him, arranging the bedding as she spoke.

He stared at her round-eyed. 'But – Mother – this is no place for a – lady. And what could *you* do anyway?'

He sounded so old-fashioned she smiled. 'I ken something about horses, Alex, dinna forget I was reared on a croft and rode bareback on a Clyde when I was two. So I think I'm perfectly capable of helping you to nurse Dobbie.'

Secretly he was glad of her company. It was eerie in the lamplit shed, the slightest sound had set his heart racing, and when there had been silence from Dobbie he had thought the old horse had breathed his last and once or twice he had gone into a panic.

His mother's presence was wonderfully comforting, she didn't speak much, that was one of the things he liked most about her: she never fussed or got out of hand like some mothers he knew and she was also sensible. The way she handled old Dobbie was a treat to behold and when sleep became imperative to him he allowed himself to drift off, knowing that she was there, watching over Dobbie and him.

At dawn he awoke with a start; something was happening, there was movement, noise. His heart thumped. Dobbie was dead! He knew it, he knew it! He raised his head and saw a sight that made him cry out. Dobbie was rising to his feet, snickering a little, tossing his head as if to clear it . . . And his mother was there, helping the old horse, talking to him, giving him every encouragement she could.

'*Dobbie!*' Throwing back his blanket he thrust himself at his horse, taking the big head in his hands and covering it with strokes and kisses. Then he turned to his mother. She was pale and very tired looking – but she was beautiful. Her rich red hair had escaped its pins, it cascaded over her shoulders in a waterfall of waves and curls and her green eyes were shining, like twin lamps in the darkness.

He thought of all this before he put his arms round her waist and buried his head in her bosom. Unable to do a thing to stop them, he let the tears burst out of him and he was ashamed even while he cried and held her so close he almost smothered himself in the folds of her dress.

It was the first time since babyhood that he had cried in her arms. She felt moved and – it was the only way she knew how to put it to herself – honoured.

She touched his hair and allowed him to cry himself out and when he eventually thrust himself away from her with an indistinct surly murmur, she wasn't offended but knew that it was the act of a young boy trying to uphold his manhood.

'He *is* a wonder horse, isn't he, Mother?' he questioned gruffly, not looking at her.

'Ay, Alex, he is that, and it's all thanks to you.'

Dobbie got rapidly well after that and was soon returned to the fields beside the other horses. He munched clover and sweet grasses and was such a favourite with all the children he never went short of carrots and the occasional piece of apple.

Mad Monkey was brought up before the juvenile courts for fire-raising, damage to property, and grievous injury to a helpless animal. Because it was his first time in court he was severely reprimanded and allowed to go free.

Soon after that his parents moved away from Govan, taking their rebellious son with them – along with his eight brothers and sisters, one maiden aunt and a dottered grandmother. They had all of them lived in a room and kitchen and it was little wonder that poor old Mad Monkey Morrison had become a rebel with just a touch of genuine madness in his make-up.

That was a happy summer for the Graingers, one of the best that Evelyn could remember. Davie was more contented these days, he had found part-time employment with a cabinet-maker in Glasgow, the result being that he no longer felt the same sense of degradation that he had while drawing unemployment benefit. With Evelyn also in employment there was a sense of quiet security in the home which rubbed off on everyone. Whenever they could afford it, Davie and Evelyn took their children on inexpensive little outings such as picnics to local parks; tram rides to Glasgow Green; a visit to the Kelvingrove Art Galleries; ice cream cones in Kelvingrove Park; paper bags bursting with juicy Victoria plums from the Barrows; evening visits to the nearby picture-house for the adults; the Saturday matinee for the young ones.

Sometimes Maggie, Jamie and Grace accompanied them on their outings but mostly it was Evelyn and Davie with their children, united and carefree in their enjoyment, somehow happier than they had ever been before.

A bond had sprung up between Evelyn and her eldest son. He was still silent and stern of eye when he looked at her, but he did things for her, thoughtful little gestures that made their relationship a special one even if it was different to that which she enjoyed with her other children.

The happiness itself she put down to the change in Davie which had come about after the birth of their third son. When she had lain so ill, Davie had seen the kiss of death on her and when she had gradually risen up out of the Valley of the Shadow it was as if he himself had shaken off the fetters that had bound her during those terrible days.

But he was a man of lustful passions and tremendous physical needs and while he never forgot the doctor's warning that Evelyn shouldn't have another child, it was beyond him to deny the cravings of his body. But he was careful during their lovemaking and she often worried that such self-restraint might lead him into the arms of another woman. The days of his selfish indulgences seemed very far in the past now but even so she knew he suffered when they were together and he couldn't possess her fully, and that was the only blot in her happiness all during that long, idyllic summer.

Towards the end of July a letter came from Nellie who often wrote, reporting on the progress of little Kenneth David, but the contents of this letter were different, and so astonishing that Evelyn stared at the words for several moments before taking in their import.

'Nellie's pregnant again,' she said at last, 'and the baby's due at the end o' September!'

Maggie put on her glasses to read Nellie's letter for herself. It bubbled and sang with delight and happiness.

Here I am, nearly forty-one years old and I'm to be given another chance. I didn't say anything till now because I had to get the first months over with before I felt really safe, and now, here I am, with a belly on me like an expectant cow (to quote Kenneth). The doctor thinks it has something to do with me being relaxed and happy having my darling wee Kenneth D. at Croft Donald. Isla Nell and Cal are fussing over me like a pair o' broody hens and Wee Col looks at us and thinks we're all daft.

CHAPTER 22

On the third day of October 1929 Nellie gave birth to a healthy baby girl. Neither Grace nor Evelyn had managed to be up north for the event but as soon as the anxiously awaited letter came from Kenneth Mor, Davie told his wife, 'Away you go to Kenneray. You know you would love to see Nell and I'll look after things here till you get back.'

She stared at him, hardly able to believe her ears. 'But, Davie, we canna really afford it and Kenneth never said anything about Nellie wanting me there. Perhaps she's afraid o' me seeing our baby son. I dinna even ken what he looks like though I canna deny it, I often wonder about him. Sometimes I canna seem to get him out o' my mind and I go cold inside when I realize how easily I gave him away.'

'You never gave him away easily, it must have taken a lot o' soul searching for you to decide on a thing like that.' He took her in his arms and ran his fingers through her hair. 'And it was the right thing to do, Evie, at the time we could never have afforded another bairn.'

'At the time! But we could now, you have a job, I'm working again, we would have managed.'

'Oh, Evie, Evie,' he murmured, holding her very close, savouring her perfume and the softness of her body. 'Would we? Babies grow up quickly, remember, they need more and more, and with another one in the house we would have neglected our other children. Think o' the wonderful summer we've all had together, we're closer to each other than we've ever been and none o' it would have been possible if Nell hadn't taken our son. So you go there and see for yourself the kind o' life he has. He'll grow up big and bonny in the country and besides, he's no' our son any longer, he belongs to Nell and Kenneth, and you must tell yourself that when you see him for the first time.'

It was easy to believe all this when she was in the comforting circle of his arms. Such a different Davie now, warm and considerate, all his old moody tempers and irritations gone, or at least held well in check, because she was wise enough to know that people didn't just change overnight and when he was tired and frustrated she often saw flashes of the old Davie. But it was enough that he was more understanding, more patient than he had ever been and she left for Kenneray with his words of wisdom held tightly in her heart.

It was more than a year since her last visit to Croft Donald but it hadn't changed. It stood there against the couthy blue hills, giving the impression that it would still be there when everything around it had fallen apart; a banner of welcoming smoke billowed from the chimney; the nets at the windows were snowy white; two fat brown hens preened themselves on the window-ledges; a black and white collie was sunning himself on the warm stone paving outside the door.

Iain had come to the station to collect her in the cart and for the last mile of the journey, along a pot-holed track that ran along beside the sea, Soay Bheag had seemed to follow them, that blue, tranquil little island inhabited by sheep and – she couldn't forget – by the ghosts of monks who had lived there long, long ago – and who had died there under such cruel circumstances.

But today Soay Bheag looked just like any of the other islands that were scattered like green and blue jewels over that stretch of the Atlantic, and after a while she could look at it with the wonderful quiet enjoyment she had always felt when driving home to Croft Donald.

Home! Ay, in her mind it was that, a place to come to when she needed the country in her soul again, a second home that made no noisy demands on her time and her strength.

The cart had no sooner stopped than the door of Croft Donald was thrown wide and Kenneth came striding out, playing his pipes, the gay skirl and ring of them echoing far and away over the hills and the sea. Her breath caught in her throat, she laughed and half-cried as he came marching towards her, the tunes from his pipes never faltering nor stopping till he had piped her out of the cart and up to the door and thereafter into the kitchen.

And if that wasn't welcome enough the one that awaited her inside Croft Donald made her feel like royalty instead of one travel-stained young woman with flyaway hair and a thirst on her that she felt could never be slaked.

'Ach, Kenneth,' reproved Nellie when he looked inclined to raise the chanter once more to his lips, 'will you stop deaving our lugs wi' that din and let the poor lassie catch her breath.'

But she didn't mean it, in her mind she relived again that wonderful moment when the chimes of Kenneth's pipes had welcomed their daughter into the world. She had lain back on her pillows, her beautiful baby in her arms, and she had allowed the tears to flow out of her, all of those she had never spilled for the little girl who had been taken from her, mingling with those of happiness and thankfulness for the perfectly healthy child who looked up at her with wondering blue eyes and suckled hungrily at its own chubby fist.

After everyone had eaten a huge farmhouse tea of soup, fresh eggs, crusty warm bread, scones, pancakes, butter, cream and jam, Evelyn was taken upstairs to unpack. When she came back downstairs the babies were there in the kitchen, one in its cradle, one in Nellie's arms, a fine little boy of nine months with fair hair and laughing brown eyes.

'Take him.' Nellie put the child into her sister's arms. For the first time Evelyn looked into the face of her youngest son. He gurgled, he smiled, he reached up an eager hand to grab a handful of rich red hair, and promptly stuffed it into his mouth.

'Everything goes into his mouth.' Nellie's laugh was slightly forced. 'He eats everything, even the cat's tail and Kenneth's socks. But Isla Nell and Cal are aye there if I'm not and Irene's there at every turn. Wee Col rocks him when he's sleepy and Kenneth walked the floor wi' him when he started teething at three months.'

'Ay.' Evelyn nodded, thinking she might not be able to trust herself to speak. But it was all right, her heart felt sore and strange within her but there were no tears. Davie was right, this was Nell and Kenneth's son, she had had no part of his first days, the bonds had been formed between him and the people who had held him and loved him in his early awakenings and with a smile she handed him back to Nellie and tiptoed over to the cradle.

The little girl had a mop of dark hair — so like . . . Evelyn paused, remembering that other scrap of life with her huge eyes and her black hair. Jean Christina, such a brief visitor to the world, what a wealth of happiness she had held in her new and innocent soul, how beloved she would have been if she had lived. And now this, a pink and white bundle of health and strength — what a beautiful little sister for Kenneth David.

Nellie came over and stood looking down at her daughter's sleeping face. 'She shall be Grace, Grace Evelyn Cameron, Kenneth loves it, what about you, Evie?'

She shall be Grace! It rang out like a benediction, spellbinding in its simplicity. Her eyes grew misty; turning, she took Nellie to her breast to hold her tightly and for once Nellie didn't protest or struggle away. Some occasions needed 'palaver o' that sort' and this was very much one of them.

One night, when it was just Evelyn and Nellie sitting by the fire, the latter stood up suddenly to gaze down into the flames and say, 'About wee Kenneth, Evie, I dinna ken how you feel after seeing him, I dinna need to tell you how much we all love him but you – you're his mother, I would hate it if I thought you were unhappy about him, I would try to understand if – if . . .'

'No, Nellie, you're his mother, he's your son, yours and Kenneth Mor's. Even if you hadn't adopted him it would still be the same. I have no claim on him now.'

'But – that's just it.' Nellie leaned against the mantelpiece and put her head in her hand. 'Both Kenneth and myself decided no' to adopt him until – until you and Davie were sure about your decision. He's still yours, Evie, and if . . .'

But Evelyn shook her head. 'I have no claim on him now, Nellie,' she repeated. 'I have never forgotten what happened wi' Alex when I left him here after he was born. Only now is he starting to trust me and nothing like that must be allowed to happen again. Wee Kenneth is no more mine than Col is Mam's or Father's. You have a son and a daughter, Nellie, and they're going to have a wonderful life here at Croft Donald.'

'Oh, Evie.' This time it was Nellie's turn to display a 'bit o' palaver' but she was not ashamed to kiss the sister who had so unselfishly given her a Christmas gift beyond compare.

With the passing of summer it seemed to Evelyn that everything that had been good about those days had passed away also. But she was the only one of the family who felt like that, everyone else got on with their lives

250

as usual: the children laughed and grumbled, Maggie and Jamie argued and made up as they had done for years now, Davie had long forgotten his earlier dreams of travel and had lost many of his old resentments.

Tenement life had its ups and downs for everybody. No one had much money but made up for it with resourcefulness and good humour; Jessie Jack still nipped babies in their prams and stole hard-won sweets from young children; Jack Jack continued to enjoy a flutter on the nags 'and that wasn't a' he enjoyed', according to the neighbourhood spies who, with very little evidence to go on, had branded him a womanizer 'while that poor auld wife o' his sits at her window and sees nothing that goes on under her nose'.

Jenny Jack saw plenty from her window, mainly she watched the world go by but occasionally she saw things that were outwith the normal code of tenement conduct though never once did her dapper little husband do or say anything that brought him into that category.

Big Aggie and her man remained an avid topic of gossip for Isa Boag; Creeping Jesus still crept about on 'carpet slippers' while her shy and retiring husband kept himself to himself and stayed mostly indoors, therefore upholding the belief that the pair o' them were 'keyhole snoopers' when all the time they were just a sad old couple who had lost their only son in the war and had never really gotten over it.

The colour and life of Govan went on but for Evelyn the clouds were gathering. With each passing day the sense of foreboding grew stronger within her, she felt afraid and very lonely as she struggled to present a façade of normality to her family.

In bed she cried when she thought Davie was asleep but one night he awoke and held her close in his arms. He kissed away her tears and she cooried into him like a lost child and murmured, 'Davie, my Davie, always be with me, always be mine.'

251

'I'm not going anywhere,' he had laughed. 'You're no' going to get rid o' me that easily.'

After that he had plumped the pillows behind her back and they had both sat up to talk the night away, remembering the youthful years of yesterday, reliving their meeting in Cobbly Wynd with the sad leaves of autumn falling all around them, the leaves of summer dying while they, in their hungry young eagerness, were only just beginning to live.

And now the summer leaves were dying again, taking with them all the hopes and dreams of warm days and love-filled nights.

Desperately she strove to hide her feelings from the world and she must have been successful for no one suspected anything was amiss, not even Jamie who had always been sensitive to her moods.

Then one day, when she was alone in the house with little James, a surprising thing happened, one so unexpected and frightening, some minutes passed before she could bring herself to cope with it.

'Mam,' James said, gazing up at her with dark, secret-filled eyes, 'who's going to die?'

Her breath constricted in her throat, she clutched the table top while she fought to control her senses.

'Die, James?' she got out at last. 'Who said anyone was going to die?'

'No one said it, Mam, I just feel it.'

She looked down at him, his face was upturned to her and in his eyes she saw reflected the same expression that had gazed fearfully back at her from a mirror when she had been a receptive child living at King's Croft.

'James, my baby.' Getting down on her knees she had cradled his thin little body in her arms, she had talked to him and had soothed him but never once did she tell him he was imagining things. He would have known she was lying, he was six years old and he had the second sight.

It was Friday and it was raining. But Evelyn didn't stop to think about the weather, Davie was taking her to the cinema that evening and he had told her to be home sharp so that she would have time to 'make herself beautiful for him'.

'Can I go now, Fanny?' she called from the kitchen. 'I've finished in here.'

There was a squeaking of wheels on the polished hall lino as Fanny propelled herself along. She appeared in the kitchen doorway, more wizened, more imperious than ever, her eyes looking fearsomely large behind the bottle-glass lenses of her specs.

'You're in a hurry,' she observed sourly. 'You've buzzed around so fast today I've hardly seen you for the stoor. Are you going somewhere special wi' all that haste you have on you?'

'Ay, Davie's taking me to the pictures.' Evelyn was peeling off her apron as she spoke, unpinning the white cap with its long streamers from her hair. Fanny still liked her to dress up in her black and whites for afternoon callers though these were thin on the ground lately owing to the fact that the last girl Fanny had had working to her had made the tea so thick you could 'jig on it' according to Lizzie, 'and never crack the skin'.

The girl had also been ungracious and rude to 'my ladies'. Fanny had pursed her lips at the remembrance before continuing, 'She was also a slut in the kitchen and handed Mrs Bryce Lomax a cracked cup wi' tea slopping all over the saucer. A cracked cup, I tell you; no wonder I sent the sloven packing.'

People like Mrs Bryce Lomax had stopped visiting Fanny Jean Gillespie but gradually the old cronies were returning now that Evelyn was back with her happy, pleasant manner and her undoubted prowess in the kitchen.

Fanny knew that she had a treasure in Evelyn and was wont to allow her some small concessions in order to keep her happy but she never forgot her father's adage, 'You must be careful with hired help, if they think you're soft they'll play on it.' Therefore she always made certain to assert her position of authority in the home. At Evelyn's words she sniffed and said, 'The cinema, Evie, is that what all the fuss is about? I don't hold wi' that kind o' thing myself. It's a very false world these film stars live in wi' their painted faces and their wiles wi' men. The theatre now, that's different, my father used to . . .'

Lizzie appeared, her cheery face wreathed in smiles as she announced, 'I've looked out that picture book you like so much, Fanny, the one wi' the photos of all the famous film stars. I thought you might like to look at it tonight when you're all nice and cosy by the fire.'

Fanny's face was a study. Lizzie winked at Evelyn and saw her to the door. 'You enjoy yourself the night, lass,' she said warmly. 'I'm glad your man is taking you out for you deserve it. You're still in love wi' him, eh? I see it in those bonny eyes o' yours whenever you mention his name.'

Evelyn smiled. 'Ay, Lizzie, I'm still in love wi' him — and I always will be.'

It was cold in the raw wind funnelling through the dark streets. Flickering gas lamps made blue reflections on the wet pavements, beams of light from shop doorways spilled outside to alight on shadowed figures hurrying along on various pursuits, some to the pub for a quick pint before going home to a noisy house filled with the weans and the missus; others were making for Greasy Joe's at the corner to pass the time in the queue whilst

254

waiting their turn for the Friday night fish suppers; one or two walked with stealth, hands buried deep in coat pockets, their assignations no more sinister than a meeting with the bookie on the next street corner.

But despite the shadowy darkness everyone recognized a passing neighbour and Evelyn had been hailed at least a dozen times before she reached 198 Camloan Road. At the close mouth she hesitated even while she knew every minute counted if she was to get her tea and make herself ready in time.

A shudder went through her, one so chill she felt herself trembling as if icy fingers had clutched at her heart.

Slowly she went on, into the vaulted cavern of the close with its inadequate lighting and its intangible spectres riding the black shadows that invaded every nook and cranny. Mrs Boyle had been busy with her pipeclay, the garish white squiggles and whorls leapt up out of the surrounding dimness in startling contrast.

Creeping Jesus was gliding downstairs on soundless feet, just another spirit of the night, without substance, a floating vapour that spread out and loomed large and terrifying as it came on and on, down and down . . .

'It's yourself, Mrs Grainger.'

Evelyn gasped and took a step backwards. She had been smothering in some nameless dread that walked hand in hand with her most terrible nightmares, and she stared wildly at the poor, surprised woman as if she was a demon personified.

'Oh, Mrs Conkey, it's you, good – good evening.'

Mrs Conkey blinked at her, she seemed grateful to be addressed in such a mannerly fashion, she also looked – sad. The notion flashed into Evelyn's mind and for a moment she wondered about this stringy, half-starved-looking woman with her strange silent ways and her timid ventures into the harsh world of children-dominated backcourts, busy streets and gossiping neighbours.

Mrs Conkey moved on, drifting into the blackness of the back close with her ash-can clasped to her aproned bosom like a trusty friend.

Gone and forgotten. Evelyn thought no more about her, all her thoughts were concentrated on getting herself upstairs, on raising herself out of the pit that had been hers for a few heart-stopping moments.

Imagination, fantasies, her mother had always maintained she had too much of both.

CHAPTER 23

As soon as Evelyn stepped over the threshold all her fears came together in an explosion of emotions that made her feel weak. Davie had come home before her and one glance at his pale, sweating face was enough to tell her that he was very ill.

He sat spreadeagled in the old rocking chair by the fire, racked with pain, his hands clutching his stomach, every so often bringing his knees half up to his chest whenever his agony tightened and deepened.

'Evie, thank God you're home!' Maggie greeted her daughter. 'He's been like this ever since he came home an hour ago and he'll no' let me call the doctor. Maybe you can persuade him.'

'No!' The cry of protest ripped from his gaping mouth. 'I don't want a doctor! I won't go to hospital! It's only another bout of colic. I'll be fine in a wee while, just leave me alone, the lot o' you.'

'No, Davie.' Evelyn could be just as stubborn as her husband. 'I won't leave you alone, you're going to bed – this minute! And if you're no' any better soon then I *am* calling the doctor.'

Despite his objections he allowed her to lead him ben The Room where he fell onto the bed as if the effort of moving from one place to the next had been too much for him.

It was freezing in The Room, the fire was never lit there except on festive occasions and during illness, simply because the household budget couldn't stretch to more than one fire.

But Jamie was a dab hand at spinning out the fuel and while Evelyn undressed Davie her father brought through a shovelful of glowing coals straight out of the kitchen range so that an instant blaze was soon leaping up the chimney.

With the curtains drawn and the firelight flickering on the blood-red tiles of the hearth, The Room soon took on a cosy aspect. Davie seemed easier now that he was in bed but he refused to eat anything, and Evelyn, her own appetite gone, drew a chair over beside him, and took his hand in hers, shocked to discover how cold and clammy it was when the rest of him burned with fever.

All her instincts told her she ought to call the doctor and never mind what Davie said but, as if reading her mind, he held on to her tightly and they both stayed like that for a long time, not speaking, she listening to the rapid sound of his breathing, the blatter of rain on the window panes.

'Evie.' Slowly he turned his head and looked at her, his eyes glazed with pain. 'Evie, I'm sorry about tonight, I know how much you looked forward to going out.'

'Ach, I'm glad to be indoors on a night like this,' she said as lightly as she could.

'The gramophone, play Richard Tauber – "O Mädchen mein Mädchen".' He spoke urgently, almost as if he was hurrying off somewhere.

The golden voice filled The Room, Davie's body relaxed, his muscles moulding themselves into the pillows, his breath coming easier.

'Evie, do you remember the Christmas I gave you the gramophone?'

'Ay, Davie, I never forget it.'

'I made it for you with my love in every grain. I knew I was sometimes a selfish bastard to you and it was my way o' saying "sorry". I am sorry, Evie, I failed to give you all the things you deserved to have in life. Sometimes I think o' that lad you were always so fond of, Gillan Forbes. If you and he had married you would have had so much more than you ever got from me. There was aye something o' the lady in you, Evie, you were born for better things. He could have given them to you, I was aware o' that and that was why I was always so jealous o' him.'

'Davie, stop that!' she whispered, shaking her head as if she couldn't bear to hear the things he was saying. 'You're all I ever wanted or needed, I've always loved you and only you.'

'Ay, and loving me was your downfall. I made a mess o' everything, I even lost you that necklace that was so precious to you. Strange about that, I never really paid much heed when you told me who gave it to you. Why would someone like old Lord Ogilvie give you a thing like that, I wonder?'

She held her breath. She could never tell him the truth, he must never know that Gillan was her cousin or that Lord Lindsay Ogilvie was her grandfather – yet – the thought came to her – Davie was part of the family, why shouldn't he know the truth about the past? Who could it harm now? None of it could ever be forgotten but it was over and done with a long, long time ago.

She began to speak, he appeared to listen. Once she had started explaining about the connections between Megsie, her grandmother, and Lord Lindsay, her grandfather (affectionately and naturally she referred to him as 'Old Oggie'), her mother, Lady Marjorie, Gillan, she lost her self-consciousness, the years were bridged, she knew again the wonder that she had felt when Maggie had told her what these people were to her . . .

The door opened, startling her, plucking her away from the path of remembrance and bringing her very forcibly into the present.

Little James stood there, solemn and big-eyed. 'Mam,' he said in his childish lilt, 'can I see my father?'

She glanced quickly at the bed. Davie's eyes were closed, he seemed to be asleep. With a finger to her lips she motioned her son to come in and close the door.

He climbed onto her knee and lay back against her breast, his thumb in his mouth, a habit common to him from babyhood and one which she had never forcibly tried to break. He didn't speak, but was quite content just to be there in The Room with his parents.

Some minutes went by, the fire crackled in the hearth, she was lulled into a sense of peace and was therefore all the more taken aback when James said suddenly, 'Mam, when is the Big Black Bogle Man coming for my father?'

She stiffened, her heart went cold within her. The Big Black Bogle Man was James's childish way of alluding to death, which in his young mind was the ultimate spectre of darkness.

She glanced again at the bed. Davie was very still, too still. Hoisting James into her arms she started up, her hammering heart hardly allowing her to breathe.

'Davie.' She touched him, his hands were icy but his brow was burning. Oh God, she had thought . . .

Maggie came through bearing a cup of tea for her daughter. 'Mam,' she said urgently, 'take James through, I'm going to the doctor. Davie has lost consciousness.'

Maggie laid down the tea and rushed the little boy away and the door had no sooner closed on her when a burst of weak coughing from the bed made Evelyn hurry to take Davie in her arms and sit him up in order to stop him choking.

The attack left him spent, he lay in her arms like a rag doll. Gently she settled him back on the pillows only to see a stain of red spreading over the front of his nightshirt.

Her hand flew to her mouth, a terrible vision beset her mind: Stashie Dunbar, dying, blood congealing on his pillow . . .

But Davie couldn't have TB. He had never shown any signs of a cough, his weight hadn't altered and, except for occasional bouts of colic, he had always been quite well and strong.

Even so . . . She recalled the squalor of Stashie's workshop. Davie had gone there every day, he had worked close to a consumptive man, one who hadn't been too fussy about personal hygiene nor about any sort of hygiene, for that matter.

She didn't know what to think, she only knew she had to fetch the doctor quickly and throwing on her coat she let herself out of the house and ran through the wet night, never stopping till she reached the doctor's house.

An hour had passed. Davie had lapsed into a state of delirium, he tossed and turned and rambled in his own private torment but occasionally an odd word made sense. It was obvious he had gone back in time to the trenches, his feet were cold, he said, bloody cold, all this buggering mud and wet . . . 'Socks, Evie, send socks.' He muttered the words yet they were so clear it was as if he really meant what he said.

Evelyn sat on the edge of her seat, so tense her knuckles were white and stiff, so long had she held them clenched to her face. The doctor had been out on a call, his assistant was at a confinement, the doctor's wife had promised to send her husband the minute he got in.

'Please, God, make him come,' Evelyn prayed silently. 'Don't let Davie die, don't let him die.'

Doctor McBain folded his stethoscope and put it away. His examination had been thorough and the face he turned to Evelyn was grim. 'I can't really be certain but everything points to the fact that your husband has a ruptured appendix and is suffering from peritonitis.'

He glared into her white face. 'Tell me, Mrs Grainger, has he ever complained of stomach pains?'

'Yes, sometimes he has colic, last year he had a really bad bout.'

'And who told you it was colic?'

His severe tone unnerved her. 'Davie — my husband did. He's been bothered with it since — since the war.'

He saw her strained face, his tone softened. 'Why didn't he call a doctor, Mrs Grainger? That's what we're here for.'

She twisted her hands. 'After the war he — he never trusted doctors. He was a POW and became very ill. He imagined everyone was poisoning him — even the doctor at the camp. His mind was — sick.'

'I see.' His eyes were kind now and he put his hand over hers. 'Well, he hasn't done himself any good by not calling me out sooner, I'm afraid. Most likely he's had a grumbling appendix for years and this is the result. Also, do you know if he has taken a fall in the last day or so?'

'A fall? Ay, he did say something about tripping and falling coming home from work last night.'

'Well, he must have landed heavily, he's cracked a rib which has punctured his lung, hence the bleeding. He'll have to go to hospital. I'll send an ambulance right away.'

It was ten o'clock, two-and-a-half hours had elapsed since Evelyn had first run for the doctor. In that time Davie had rambled and raved before finally falling into a sleep that was too deep and too still.

Maggie stayed with the children leaving Jamie to accompany Evelyn in the ambulance. And it was good, that, to have her father beside her at such a time, perfectly sober, entirely capable, not saying too much but just being there to take charge of things.

On arrival at the hospital Davie was rushed up to the surgical ward where he was bound in bandages and a tube put down his throat in an effort to drain away the poison that had invaded his body.

An hour elapsed before Jamie and his daughter were

allowed in to see Davie. He lay very still, his face was a waxy yellow colour owing to the impurities in his system. When Evelyn spoke to him he didn't stir and she knew that he was beyond hearing her.

A doctor came to them to explain that it was doubtful if Mr Grainger would come round before morning and that the best thing for them to do would be to go home.

'Is he going to get better?'

Evelyn sounded calm though every fibre in her was tensed as she waited for the doctor's answer.

'Mrs Grainger,' he looked at her over his glasses, 'your husband is very far gone, his entire bloodstream is affected, not to mention his abdominal tract. If we had caught the appendix in time we could have operated – as it is . . .' He spread his hands.

Jamie took his daughter's arm and led her away. The night was black and chill, and the hours that followed were endless for Evelyn. Lonely and afraid she slept only fitfully and was angry at herself for sleeping at all when her Davie was so ill.

He lingered for three days, sometimes waking, mostly sleeping, that deep unnatural sleep that gave him no rest from memories unearthed from the dark, secret recesses of his mind.

Evelyn knew that he was dying, yet once, when he opened his eyes and pleaded with her to take him home, he sounded so rational and normal a cruel hope rose in her breast.

'Ay, Davie, I'll take you home,' she breathed, holding his hand, willing him to stay awake so that she could talk to him, tell him how much he was missed, how much she loved him.

But he had no sooner made the urgent request than his lids drooped and the hand in hers became limp and uncaring.

On the third day she went to see him with faltering footsteps. He had torn off all his bandages trying to get out of bed.

'Evie, Evie!' he cried, his hand outstretched to her in urgent appeal, 'I must go home, please take me home, I'll die if I stay in here!'

He fell exhausted against the pillows. She took both his hands in hers. He was barely breathing yet life stark and aware was there in his eyes.

She didn't know how long she sat there with his hands in hers, it could have been minutes or hours, something as intangible as time didn't matter to her then.

Suddenly he stirred and looked around him. 'Evie,' he whispered, 'is it getting dark? I can't seem to see clearly – any more.'

She stared at him, his eyes, those beautiful velvet-brown eyes that had captured her heart at their very first meeting, were growing dim and distant as his life ebbed away.

'Davie?' She gathered him to her breast and in her arms he died without ever speaking to her again. Gently she laid him back on his pillows and kissed his brow before she fled sobbing from his deathbed.

The corridors were long, endless, she couldn't see them for tears but she knew that she was running through black unending tunnels without any glimmer of light to show her the way. Her heart was thumping, thumping, she heard the powerful thud of it inside her head but she wanted it to stop beating so that she could have respite from her grief . . .

A hand on her arm stayed her even while the black, enclosing corridors whirled on. 'Mrs Grainger, you'll have to come back, the doctor wants to see you.'

Dazedly she stared at the nurse's young face. What did she know? How could she ever understand about a love that had begun long, long ago in a homely little teashop in Cobbly Wynd?

'I loved him, Nurse.' She spoke slowly, as if trying to convey something of herself to this girl who watched her with the cool, detached eyes of a stranger. 'He was my — Davie.'

The mask of efficiency fell from the girl's face. 'I know you did, Mrs Grainger, and I'm sorry if I sounded a bit harsh just now — it's just — well — I've still to learn how to handle people who have been bereaved. Seeing the doctor is only a formality, he won't keep you long.'

Back through the cold, clinical corridors, back to a place where death had taken Davie a long way from her. In the end the Big Black Bogle Man only came in one guise and he never went back alone.

Maggie sat very still by the fire, her thoughts taking her backwards and forwards in a restless procession. Except for the children asleep in bed, she was alone. Evelyn, unable to bear being in the house, had gone to see Grace. Jamie, feeling that she needed someone beside her, had accompanied her. Her grief was absolute, yet she had been so silent and dry-eyed since coming back from the hospital that afternoon with the news of Davie's death, it was as if she didn't want to speak about him any more than was necessary.

Maggie herself wasn't quite sure how she felt, she was trying to picture what it would be like not having him in the house. He had often made life miserable for her and Jamie, particularly her; he had always been fond of his father-in-law and had displayed affection towards him along with a resigned forbearance over his drinking. Davie had never been a drinking man himself, declaring that he loathed hard liquor, therefore it was all the more surprising how patient he had been with Jamie, even to the extent of going out to look for him when he didn't come home at night. But he had never taken to his mother-in-law and she had reciprocated his feelings. Yet, away back in the beginning he had tried to win her over only to meet hostile resistance time after time.

She had sensed the selfishness in him and hadn't wanted him for her daughter, but – perhaps if she had tried a little bit harder, she might have learned to accept him for what he was.

But by the time they had all moved to Govan it was too late and hardly a day had passed but they had niggled at one another.

She stared into the fire and sighed, her pride resisting certain facts but her inherent honesty making her face them. It couldn't have been easy for him having his in-laws continually around him, and – she couldn't deny it – any man would have rebelled at being caught up in such a situation. He had never had any privacy in his marriage, she herself would have rebelled if she had found herself in the same boat as he – and far more forcibly than he had ever done.

Evelyn had never stopped loving him, she had been loyal right up to the end, and in some strange way Maggie could understand why her daughter had loved him. He had been a very handsome man but there must have been other qualities that had made her so fiercely devoted to him.

Maggie sat back and thought about it. She knew he had had a weakness for other women but even then, when Evelyn must have known what was going on, she had remained staunchly faithful to him. Her allegiance had been a shining thing to behold, even though there must have been times when her love had faltered and faded a little.

Love needed love to sustain it and it came to Maggie that Davie had loved her daughter too, deeply and truly, those amorous adventures had meant nothing to him but he had needed them in his life, perhaps to boost his morale, perhaps as an escape from the monotony of his existence. Marriage and children hadn't figured largely in his earlier plans, he had wanted to travel, to know what the rest of the world was like – and he had died without ever seeing further than the dug-outs in France, or of knowing what lay beyond the high wire of a prison camp.

Now he was gone, and – Maggie couldn't stop the thought – there would be no more waiting in bed in the morning till he came through to eat his solitary breakfast and let himself out of the house.

But, she had to admit this too, no one could ever accuse him of being lazy, he had risen with the birds and was gone from the house before anyone knew it and – strange – she had grown used to having that extra time in bed. When she was younger she had rebelled against it but in the last few years she had been glad to turn over whenever she heard him creeping into the kitchen, knowing that she could savour an extra twenty minutes before the day began.

Her glance came to rest on her Monday washing hanging on the pulley. What a bone of contention that had been between him and her, both of them stubbornly refusing to give in on the subject, each of them hanging on to their separate arguments, the whys and the wherefores.

He had been right, of course; in the close confines of the kitchen the motley assortment of clothing was not an attractive sight. She had hated having to display her washing for everyone to see, the knickers, the combinations, the vests; holes, patches, darning. It was so undignified, far more natural an outside line on a windy day, the clothes gaily blowing hither and thither, never staying still long enough for the patches to show.

But outside in the backcourts? No! Decidedly not! It was bad enough having the family see the signs of wear and tear in things she would once have given to the rag-wife, but for the neighbours to see them as well, the very idea was an outrage!

Davie or no Davie, she would continue to use the kitchen pulley till the day she died and that was an end to the matter.

She smiled, she had been arguing with herself in the exact way she would have argued with Davie and, the thought struck her, she would miss those altercations with her son-in-law. Mondays would never be the same again.

A knock on the door brought her out of her reverie. A young woman stood on the landing, one who had only recently come to stay in Camloan Road.

She introduced herself as Mrs McLean and said she was round collecting money for a wreath for one of the neighbours who had died that day.

Word had certainly got round, Maggie reflected, it only needed one or two to hear a piece of news before it spread like wildfire.

'I didn't want to do it,' the girl said nervously, mistaking the expression on Maggie's face as a refusal to contribute, 'but Mrs Boag said it would be a good way for me to get to know people.'

It was unfair, Maggie thought, to send a newcomer on such a delicate task, one who was as yet too new to know one family from another.

The girl's eyes fell on the two brass nameplates on the door, one inscribed J. Grant, the other D. Grainger. She coloured with embarrassment and stepped back. 'I'm sorry, I didn't know, Mr Grainger was the one who died today so I won't ask you to put anything towards his wreath.'

Maggie began to laugh. The girl threw her a shocked look before scuttling away downstairs, the rest of the inhabitants of 198 temporarily forgotten. Maggie went on laughing for a few moments more, then she went back to the kitchen and cried.

*

Every bone in Evelyn's body ached with weariness but she was glad of that, exhaustion meant sleep, sleep meant freedom from grief, but then she remembered the dreams and knew that she couldn't escape her sorrow so easily.

She lingered in the dark lobby, unwilling to face the empty room. It had become an alien place to her, chill and unwelcoming, yet with Davie there she had somehow never noticed the cold.

But Maggie had lit the fire, it was only a small glow but it took away the harshness from the hearth and made everything seem more homely.

She couldn't sleep, the hours came and went and all she could think about was Davie, Davie, Davie . . .

Quite suddenly she remembered her diary. She couldn't recall when last she had written anything in it but her life was recorded in those hand-bound books she had once treasured: her life — and Davie's.

She lit the candle, found the tin box, unlocked it, and took out the top volume. She flicked through the pages, a mist of tears blurred the words. She wrote:

November 1929. I look back over the years, fifteen of them have passed since I met a young soldier in Aberdeen. He called me Bright Eyes because I was always so eager to see him, I called him The Ghost Soldier because he was always so elusive.

That was how it began. Today Davie died. It is finished.

Nellie and Kenneth came south for the funeral. A rock was Kenneth in the few days he was there, his strong shoulder ever available for a sister-in-law who was very dear to him. And Nellie, so good with the children, capable and kind, keeping them amused when they became restless, driving away their tears with her stories and her little songs. She had never had much tune to her voice but it was the content that mattered to childish ears. Even Alex, who had gone off for two nights after his father died, finding solace in the undemanding company of old Dobbie, listened to Nellie's stories and songs and laughed despite himself when his favourite aunt spoke in a deep, man's voice or lisped her lines in a high-pitched cackle that was meant to portray a witch.

Gregor arrived on the morning of the funeral but Mary was conspicuous by her absence.

Nellie was furious at this and was about to tackle Greg on the subject when Maggie shook her head warningly. 'No, Nellie, look at his face, he's ashamed for his wife, no doubt they had a row about it. Forbye that, he's no' the same Greg I remember, he's unhappy-looking and fair done in by the look o' him.'

Nellie studied her brother-in-law. He *was* unhappy-looking and he did look tired, tired and dispirited.

That bitch! Nellie fumed to herself. If a good hiding would knock some sense into her I would go over there and do it myself but it would take more than that to bring her to her senses!

Davie's last journey from 198 Camloan Road was well attended by neighbours who had gathered to see him off, for though he had been a private sort of man he had been well respected and no greater accolade than that would he have wished for.

Events like funerals and weddings were meat and drink for people like Mrs Boag and Big Aggie, they could criticize and comment to their hearts' content and many little observances were made that morning.

Hannah Todd was getting fat, she was too lazy for her own good; Maria Leckie was terribly thin, it was rumoured she had a cough and was never away from the doctor; could it be the galloping consumption?

It was reckoned that white-faced Mrs Galloway had pernicious anaemia; that Mary Craig's unmarried daughter was growing stouter every week and that Mr Craig had gone storming round to Govan Cross to order Jimmy O'Brien to marry 'that tart' before she became the talk of the neighbourhood!

Pre-school children were also much in evidence and jigged excitedly at their mothers' skirts while they waited for the horse-drawn hearse to arrive.

'My big brother went away in one o' those,' boasted one young innocent. 'The horses took him away to heaven.'

'Mammy, Mammy.' A four-year-old girl tugged her mother's sleeve. 'Will they throw pennies when the cart moves off?'

'This isny a weddin', ye daft wee bugger,' came the fond reply, 'it's a funeral, nobody throws pennies at a funeral!'

Little James's Big Black Bogle Man was there that day, the undertaker himself, black coated, top hatted, nailing down the coffin, helping to shoulder it and carry it down the stairs.

'I hate him,' James wept in his mother's arms, 'he's taking my father away like he took Witchie Winnie. He's a greedy Bogle Man, he wants everybody for himself, he'll never bring my father back.'

'God has taken your father.' Evelyn kissed the top of her son's head. 'He won't hurt him.'

'Will his soul go to heaven?'

'Ay, he loved the earth but he'll be happier in heaven.'

She didn't go to the window to watch Davie's coffin being driven away. She had said her goodbyes at the hospital when he had died in her arms.

'He wasna old, Mother.' Alex scrubbed his eyes with his fists.

'No, Alex, he wasna old.'

Her heart filled and almost burst with her pain. His span had been short. He had been thirty-four years old.

CHAPTER 24

Greg had never been so glad to reach Cleveden Mansions as he was now.

Bringing his bullnose Morris to a jerking halt he opened the door and got out. Every movement he made felt heavy and unnatural, his arms were like lead, his legs a ton weight.

The bitter November air hit him like a blow, the shiver that went through him was even more intense than those that had beset him for the last few hours. Not even the hot soup that Maggie had served to the funeral party had been able to dispel his tremors.

It had been cold in the cemetery. The raw wind, the dampness, had bitten into his marrow. The chill had remained with him long after the mourners had dispersed from that lonely grave laid bare to the elements. It was full now, Davie was the last to go in, his mother, his grandparents, one or two other relatives had all gone before.

So cold, that grave, so young was Davie, poor, dear, darling Evie, he had been the love of her life. Greg would never forget her sad, pale, lovely face, yet she was strong, even in the very depth of her sorrow she had remained dignified and in control and had thanked everyone for coming to the funeral that day.

Everyone? He shuddered. Try not to think of that. Try not to think of – her.

But how could he help it? He had been so ashamed; Evelyn's very own sister, absent at such a time. Little wonder that Nellie's face had been like thunder, that Evelyn's greeting to him had wavered when she saw that he had come alone . . .

The gate, thank God! The steps. How many? He had never counted them but they seemed to go on forever, on and up, to black eternity. One flight, slippery, dank with moss and wet leaves. Only five more to go and he – was home.

That familiar tingling was in his left arm again – his leg too. His vision was blurring – but – he had to reach out – ring the bell.

He lurched forward and met the wall with a mighty thump. His shoulder set the bell ringing. He had to keep up the pressure as long as he could. That was his last thought before he slithered down the wall and lay in a huddled heap on the top step.

Mary was entertaining Mrs Janeta Kerr-Campbell to afternoon tea. With the heavy velvet drapes shutting out the darkening November day and the firelight glinting on the best silver tea-service, the room wore a cosy air of genteel refinement that was very pleasing to Mary.

It was like a balm to feathers that had been badly ruffled by the row she and Greg had had last night owing to her refusal to attend Davie Grainger's funeral. What a row it had been, more a showdown, really; because of it she had barely slept a wink all night and even thinking about it now made her inwardly cringe at the cruel things Greg had said to her.

Eyes blazing, face contorted by outrage, he had accused her of being self-centred, selfish, heartless and mean. He had told her that she led a useless, self-indulgent life, that she cared for nobody but herself. He said he had put up with it all these years because he had truly believed she would one day waken up to the meaninglessness of her existence and come to her senses.

Also, he had added – and there had been a tinge of pathos in his voice – he had hoped she would start to see him as a human being in his own right and not just someone whose place it was to provide her with all the possessions she seemed to look on as her due.

He had gone on and on: she took him for granted; she showed him no love but displayed towards him the same kind of amused tolerance she might show to a caged pet canary; she had no time for their children; she had no time for her family; her silly, empty-headed friends got more of her than her own flesh and blood; forbye them she cared only for expensive clothes and jewellery and keeping up appearances.

'And now this — this latest insult!' he had fumed, his face so congested with anger she was afraid he was going to strike out at her. 'Refusing to go to a family funeral! Never mind people like that, eh? Too ordinary? Not important enough? A waste o' your precious empty time! Ay, that would be more to the point. Folk like the Grants and the Graingers could never be instrumental in helping a fine lady like yourself climb the social ladder.'

'Greg,' she had pleaded, frightened by this side of him she had never before experienced, 'David Grainger was nothing to me . . .'

'NO!' he roared, towering above her, his eyes half-bulging out of his head. 'But he was everything to your sister! Evie knows about love! She might not have had much of anything else in her life but she had love and she gave love back. She's a warm, caring, loving woman and because o' that she'll have more in her life than you'll ever have — you — you selfish, Godforsaken *bitch*!'

She had known real fear then. This wasn't the gentle, kind, patient man that she knew. This was a stranger who looked at her with eyes full of hate and an anger so black it was terrifying.

She had backed away from him, blustering, stuttering, saying anything that came into her head, and they were all the wrong things. Thinking to win him round she had harked back to Evelyn's last visit, her cheek, her rudeness.

275

'Ay, and it was all because o' you!' he had roared. 'You told her never to come back here simply because she was honest enough to tell you a few home truths about yourself.' He paused to stare at her before continuing in a low, controlled voice that was even more frightening than his shouted words.

'So, that's it?' he had spat. 'She dared to oppose you and for that you haven't forgiven her. You never went near her when she almost died in childbirth. Her husband is dead and you refuse to pay your respects, if not for his sake then at least you could make the effort for her — your sister — your own flesh and blood. She never let you down. She visited you. It must have cost her to have to listen to you yabbling on about frivolities when she and her family could barely make ends meet. She came to see you after the birth o' our daughter and tried to give you advice and make you see reason. Evelyn Grainger has a big heart but you — you have none. You're childish and mean and petty and if it wasn't for the children — I'd finish with you, by God I would.'

His words had come to a breathless halt. He looked spent and ill — and something else. For just a few moments a trapped, wild animal glared out of his eyes, then he turned away from her and she was glad — so glad — because not for one second more could she have borne to look at that beast in the eyes of her once-gentle Greg.

Just thinking about it now made her hands shake so much she overfilled the tea cups so that the hot liquid slopped into the saucers.

'Bother!' She rang for Betty and ordered her to bring fresh cups. 'And make sure they're the correct ones, Betty, from the same set.'

Betty brought two more cups and saucers made of exquisite bone china decorated with delicate rosebuds. Clattering them onto the tray she stood back and said politely, 'Will that be all, Mrs McGregor?'

'No, Betty, that is *not* all. You almost broke those cups

276

just now and I'll thank you to be more careful in future. You have grown very careless of late and I hope I won't have to remind you again of your slipshod behaviour.'

'Quite right, dear,' applauded Mrs Janeta Kerr-Campbell when the door had closed on the girl. 'Servants must be made to know their place, give them an inch and they'll take a mile. I keep mine on their toes, they don't like it but then, we don't pay them good wages to like or not to like, as the case may be.'

She lifted her refilled cup to her red-painted lips to sip daintily, yet despite all her care she made little gulping sounds as she swallowed.

Her Adam's apple, thought Mary absently, is too big.

Mrs Janeta Kerr-Campbell was wearing peacock-blue silk that afternoon. Privately Mary thought it was too gaudy and wasn't at all becoming to her carefully corseted figure. Then Mary gave herself a mental shake. She too was clad in somewhat colourful green taffeta which, if it wasn't for her own metal-boned stays, would have been bursting at the seams.

Her visitor reached out for a cream cake topped by a juicy peach slice.

'My dear,' she beamed, 'how naughty of you to tempt me in this way. You will simply have to learn that I never can resist anything with cream in it.'

Mary noticed her podgy hands, bedecked with at least half a dozen glittering rings, all set with precious stones of some sort. A fortune must be there on those fat hands – another was strung round her neck: pearls, hanging down to her amply swelling bosom – and this was her afternoon wear. What she must look like on a formal evening out was almost beyond the realms of fantasy.

A Christmas tree! Mary thought idly and smiled to herself.

'Janeta,' she said mechanically, 'do have another cake, there's plenty and they will only go to waste. Greg never eats cream cakes and they're far too good for the servants.'

Janeta! She wondered about that name. Had it once been just plain good old Janet, with an 'a' added on later to give it some style – or should that be 'swank'?

'My dear, how is that adorable little daughter of yours?' enquired the visitor. 'I hear she's been through some operation or other to have her poor mouth straightened.'

Mary flinched. Mrs Kerr-Campbell had been repelled when first she had seen baby Elizabeth. She had made no attempt to hide her feelings but had just stared in a most rude manner before exclaiming, 'Oh, poor little thing! You *do* have problems there, Mary dear. Is it an inherited defect? Oh, I know you are perfectly normal but someone in your family, perhaps?'

It had taken Mary all her control to remain pleasant on that occasion. Now she took a deep breath and said, 'Yes, she has had two operations and each time she has shown an improvement.'

'Oh, good, I'm so glad. You have hopes of her growing up to be a normal child, then?'

Mary's nostrils flared. 'She *is* a normal child, Janeta, her mouth defect does not affect her brain or any other part of her body. She is an intelligent, good and loving little girl and there is no reason not to believe that she will grow up to be beautiful as well.'

Mary digested her own words for a moment. It was true, everything she had said, her daughter was affectionate and even-tempered and in spite of all her own early fears and resentments she was growing to love the child more and more with each passing day.

Automatically she reached for a cream cake but stopped the action as her fingers touched the plate. Momentarily frozen into immobility she saw her hand, as plump and dimpled as that of her visitor, and with an intake of breath she drew it away as if she had been scalded.

'My dear,' Mrs Kerr-Campbell looked inquiringly at her hostess, 'are you feeling yourself today? You seem distant, worried somehow.'

Mary made haste with her assurances, the other woman made some suitable remark and helped herself to another cake. Her large teeth bit into it, cream squelched and oozed, Mrs Kerr-Campbell made great play with her napkin, she was in her element and was supremely happy.

She began to talk about clothes, she told Mary about a forthcoming trip to the Paris fashion houses, about another nearer to home in Edinburgh.

Mary nodded and tried to look interested. If the truth be known, she was growing rather tired of Mrs Kerr-Campbell whose favourite topic of conversation, other than clothes and jewellery, was herself.

Her opinions, *her* ideas, *her* feelings, *her* emotions, self, self, self, a seemingly bottomless well of self-adoration, self-concern.

Mary was stifling a yawn when the doorbell started ringing – and went on and on ringing, and ringing . . .

Ben was the first to reach the door, in a scrabble of paws he slithered to a halt on the polished floor and began to whimper and whine, his nose pressed to the frosted glass panels. Betty was behind him and they both rushed outside, Ben to paw and lick his master, Betty to get down on her knees and take Greg's head in her lap.

'Greg, my dear,' she whispered, then remembering her place, 'Doctor McGregor, oh, God, what's happened to you, what's happened?'

She wasn't long in summoning help. Cook was called, together with Bob Adams who tended the boiler and did all the heavy jobs around the house.

Between them they got Gregor into the living room where they settled him on the couch before Betty ran to the sitting room to announce breathlessly, 'Mrs McGregor, it's the doctor, he collapsed at the front door. He's in the living room now and — would you come quickly, please?'

Mary stood up, the room swam as she did so and she would have fallen had not Mrs Kerr-Campbell hurried to her assistance.

But Mary shook off the supporting arm. 'I'm fine, Janeta, if you'll excuse me I must — I must see to my husband.'

'My dear Mary, are you sure you're all right? You look so pale. Is there anything I can do? I'm very good at first aid. I was with the Red Cross during the war, you know, and my services were greatly . . .'

'No, no, Janeta, we can manage, perhaps if you'll just — go — I'm so sorry, you know where to find the door . . .'

'Oh well, in that case —' Mrs Kerr-Campbell sounded rather hurt but Mary had neither the time nor the inclination to appease her.

'Betty, phone for the doctor,' she ordered before hurrying away to the living room.

Betty rushed to obey. Her heart was heavy with dread. She prayed that there was nothing wrong with Gregor that a good rest wouldn't cure. Then she remembered the dreadful row he had had with his wife the night before, everyone in the house had heard it. But even before that he had looked strained and ill, he had been on the brink of something terrible and last night's happenings had pushed him over the edge.

Evelyn found the letter in the inside pocket of Davie's best suit. It bore a Canadian postmark, dated December 1928, and must have come when she had lain so ill after the birth of Kenneth David. It was from Davie's father. In it he told his son that there was a job waiting for him in Canada.

You come out first, [wrote Douglas Grainger] then when you are settled you can send for Evie and the children. If you're willing to work hard it's a good life out here, son. The job I have lined up for you is with a flourishing cabinet-maker who is only too anxious to find good, qualified carpenters.

Say the word and I'll send the fare. You can pay me back when you can.

I think about you a lot, Davie, you and me always got on well and I would love to see Evie and my grandchildren again.

I know things are hard over there and I'm sure Maggie and Jamie will understand that you and Evie have to grab hold of opportunity while you're both young. Let me know soon . . .

Evelyn folded the letter and put it away. She stood for a long time with the smooth material of the jacket held to her cheek.

'Davie,' she murmured, 'you gave up your dream o' a better life because you thought it wasn't what I wanted. But I would have gone with you, my love, we were both ready for a new beginning, and now it's over and there is nothing. I see no future, only a dark road filled with loneliness, and I am afraid.'

Mary came to 198 Camloan Road a few days before Christmas. For the first time in many years she set foot in a house she had tried to shut out of her mind, but she came only with a humble heart and a great desire to seek forgiveness from a family she had shunned.

She also came to tell them about Greg. 'He had a stroke,' she explained quietly, sitting there in the old rocking chair by the fire. 'Four weeks ago now, I didn't write, I didn't want to worry you, I know how much you all like him, and to be truthful I was so worried and upset

I seemed not to know what I was doing from one week to the next.

'He spent some time in hospital, but he's home now. His speech wasn't affected, thank God, but he's partially paralysed all down his left side. The doctors say that with rest and quiet he may completely recover but for now it's a case of one day at a time.'

She glanced from one to the other of the quiet faces around her. 'It was all my fault, everything, I know that now, I was a blind, selfish woman who cared for no one but myself and when I look back and see what I had become I hate myself for it.'

'Ay, you were all o' these things,' Maggie said bluntly. 'There was nothing in the woman you became to the healthy, happy lassie we all kent and loved.'

Mary put her hand to her eyes. 'I didn't want to be the Mary of the old days, I wanted only a fine house and beautiful things, I couldn't see what I was doing to my family – or to my dear, dear Greg. He was so good, so patient with me, until he finally – snapped. It was a silly, false way of life, I was already growing tired of it when – when Greg took ill. Oh, I'm so looking forward to being myself again, it's like coming out of prison, being natural, not having to put on foolish airs and graces.' She glanced up at Evelyn. 'What did I do to you, my dearest sister? When you were so very sick one part of me longed to run to you but the other selfish part wouldn't let me. And then – there was Davie's funeral. Greg and me had such a row about it because I refused to go. It was the last straw for him, the very next day he had a stroke and I'll never stop blaming myself for that. Can you forgive me, Evie? Will you ever forget what I did to you?'

Evelyn knew she would never forget her sister's neglect of her, but she had already forgiven and with tears in her eyes she stooped to hug a very subdued Mary before rushing into the scullery with the excuse of filling the kettle for tea.

'I'm taking Greg to Nellie's for Christmas,' Mary announced when they were all settled round the fire drinking tea. 'I wrote telling her what had happened and she answered by return of post, saying that the country was the sort of tonic Greg needed and we could stay indefinitely if we wanted.

'At first I was horrified at the idea, three babies creating mayhem, Donald, Wee Col, two other youngsters, six adults, it sounded like hell on earth. Then I remembered what you told me about Croft Donald, Evie, the peace, everyone going about their business and bothering no one, Nellie so good with babies but disciplined and firm just the same. And Nellie said Greg could have the parlour as his sanctum and needn't be bothered with anything or anybody if he didn't want to be.

'When I told Greg about it he smiled that nice smile of his and said it would be lovely to be with a family again. I realized then how much I had deprived him of — normality.'

She went bubbling on, full of enthusiasm, her face animated, in her excitement occasionally lapsing into the dialect of her native tongue.

She was selling the house in Cleveden Mansions, they could never afford to keep up such a place now, it was in the hands of lawyers, they would stay with Nellie till they found a suitable house, somewhere in the country, Greg had always loved the country and if he should fully recover from his stroke he wouldn't be short of pursuits to keep him occupied.

Gardening, for instance, he had often spoken longingly of growing his own vegetables 'when he had the time'.

'Painting too, he used to dabble a bit when we stayed in Rothiedrum, and fishing, walking, oh I can hardly wait for it all to happen! Do you know what I've missed most these last years? Lighting my own fires! I've watched Betty doing it and there were times I simply longed to get my hands dirty again; to roll the papers into twists like Father showed us, setting the taper to the ends and *voilà*! Lovely crackling wood and coal, the sparks flying up the lum. The whoosh of the paper catching, the smell of the kindling smouldering.'

Her face was alive, the flush of excitement bloomed in her cheeks, she was the Mary of old, so carried away she could hardly sit still in her seat. When at last she got up to go she kissed them all in turn and left behind a great pile of presents for Christmas.

The door closed on her, the kitchen was suddenly very quiet. Maggie, Jamie and Evelyn all looked at one another.

'She's come to her senses — at last,' nodded Maggie, and gathering up the parcels she went to hide them on the top shelf of the kitchen cupboard before the children came home from school.

CHAPTER 25

The snow was falling thickly in Cleveden Mansions. Evelyn went to the window to look for the taxi that was taking the McGregor family to the station and she lingered for a moment to watch the big fat flakes whirling down.

This was her second visit to the house in the last few days. The first time she had come to help Mary pack china and books into boxes ready to be stored till she and Greg were settled into a new home. Bob Adams and Betty had already carried out much of the work but there remained all the little personal bits and pieces that were far too numerous for one person to manage, and Evelyn had been glad to offer her assistance.

Since Greg's illness the household had been snowed under by an avalanche of mail from patients and colleagues, all wishing Greg a speedy recovery, all a testimony to his enormous popularity, both as a medical man and as a valued friend. Callers had come and gone in a near constant stream. Mary had coped admirably but was very relieved when Evelyn said she would answer some of the letters.

She had taken a large bundle home with her and as well as warming her heart, they had helped her to take her mind off herself. Now the day of departure had come, Donald, home for the Christmas holidays, was in a fever of impatience to be on his way, Mary was in a state of continual motion, Betty kept running in and out of the room, her face blotchy as if she had been crying.

Greg was the epitome of composure. He sat quite still in a chair, the debris of packing all around him, Ben propped on one side of him, his sticks on the other, only his shining eyes showing how much he was anticipating Christmas in Kenneray.

'Evie,' he said in his deep, pleasant voice, 'come over here, I want to say goodbye before the bustle of departure.'

She went to stand by him. His strong right arm came out to pull her down to him so that he could kiss her cheek. 'Thank you, Evie,' he murmured huskily, 'for everything. I want to tell you how much you mean to me — as a sister-in-law and as a dear friend. I feel your heartache as if it was my own. I want you to write to me and tell me how you are.'

'Greg.' She touched his cheek with her finger. He had grown a beard since his illness, it suited him and made him look distinguished — but older. In just a few weeks he had aged but he had never looked happier. 'Of course I'll write, though what I'll find to write about is another story.'

He was surprised. 'Evie, you mustn't think o' your life as being empty. You have four lovely children to fill your days. They are Davie's legacy to you, every day you'll see something in them to remind you o' him. You have also been blessed with great strength o' character, you are a very attractive and intelligent young woman, you have a lot of living to do, Evie, and never again do I want to hear you implying that life is over for you.'

'Oh, Greg.' She fumbled for her hanky and held it tightly to her eyes. 'I'll miss you so, you were aye so good for me.'

'Hey,' he laughed, 'we aren't going to the moon, you know, we'll still be here, in Scotland, and when we're settled I want you to come and visit us — doctor's orders!'

He had made her smile, his own heart lifted at the sight of her sad, sweet face lightening and brightening. Into her hand he pushed a small package. 'Merry Christmas, Evie, I'll drink a toast to you on Hogmanay. We'll all be thinking o' you then.'

There was no time for more. The taxi had arrived. Mary came rushing in to help Greg to his feet and say to her sister, 'Och, Evie, I wish you were coming with us, I know how much you love Croft Donald. Oh, Betty, there you are, will you take these bags? Has Bob cleared the steps! I don't want any accidents, not now.'

'Everything has been seen to, Mrs McGregor.' Betty's voice wasn't quite steady. The contingent had reached the hall and before her dear Doctor McGregor was lost to her forever she reached up to hug him.

'Betty!' cried Mary, aghast. 'How dare you take such liberties!'

Betty turned away. Liberties indeed! That poor, blind besom would never know, never even begin to imagine how much she and the doctor had been to one another this last year. She had given him comfort when he most needed it and he – he had given her joy that she would carry in her heart for the rest of her days . . .

'Thank you, Betty, for everything.' Briefly his hand was in hers, conveying his affection for her. Mary looked at them both with swift appraisal, a frown on her brow, but the moment was soon over. Nurse Allison was coming downstairs with little Elizabeth Louise who was a picture in her fur-trimmed coat and hat. Her creamy skin was dewy fresh from her bath, her huge dark eyes gazed tranquilly at the world, one fair curl had escaped the hood and hung like a golden penny over her high, smooth brow.

She had suffered in her short life; further operations would follow the two she had already undergone, but she was equal to pain and challenge and change, a brave, good-humoured little girl who was her father's delight and her mother's new-found pride.

Her mouth wasn't perfect by any means but before the passing of many years she would be beautiful. More important than that, she would be loved. At just one year and four months she had captured many hearts, amongst them that of Nurse Allison and, more recently, that of her brother who, since he had come home from school, had never tired of playing with her and especially enjoyed reading to her when she lay big-eyed and dreamy in her nursery bed.

Nurse Allison had refused to part with her. She was travelling with the family as far as her sister's house near Inverness where she was spending Christmas but 'the minute you find a suitable house I'll be there at the double' she had told Mary, not giving her any opportunity to speak. 'All I want is my bed and board and a few shillings to keep me in stockings. The doctor won't aye be laid up and you're fit enough and young enough for at least two more bairns. Don't worry, I'll be at hand to see to them and to you. I've tholed you all this time, I'm used to your tantrums, you won't find another to put up with them.'

Mary had been speechless, then she had almost burst her stays laughing. She had met her equal in Nurse Allison, there was no question about it, the woman had become part of the family and it looked as if they were stuck with her.

The taxi was ready to go: in a flurry of tears and farewells, Mary kissed and hugged Evelyn, said her goodbyes to Betty and Bob, and then it was just faces at the windows, peering out, waving, Ben's wet nose pressed against a pane, making a moist, steamy circle.

Betty, her apron to her eyes, half fell up the steps in her hurry to be out of sight that she might cry in peace. Evelyn followed more slowly, experiencing a great sense of deflation.

The house seemed so empty, void of life that had been there only minutes before. The furniture and other items would be sold at auction, the lawyers would arrange that, everything else was in store till it was needed.

She helped Bob and Betty check the rooms and put dust sheets over the furniture, then they left and it remained only for her to lock up and leave too.

When finally she turned the key in the lock she stood for several minutes, her back to the door, letting the flurries of snowflakes drift onto her lashes, melt in her hair. Something wonderful was in the air, she sensed it keenly, as if some sort of vibrations were winging their way to her over space and time.

Her previous feelings of depression dissipated as easily as the flakes of snow that touched the warmth of her face. She was seized with a wonderful euphoria, her heart throbbed with the strength of her emotions, she knew she had to hurry down the steps to the avenue – someone was there – someone who was very dear to her . . .

She had no memory of negotiating the steps, she was just suddenly there – in the avenue – the snow falling all around her, as it had done that March day almost two years ago – and she knew even before she saw him that Gillan was there, striding along in front, his body bent into the wind, his coat collar pulled up to his ears.

He was moving swiftly, with that lithe grace she knew so well, the whirls of snow were blotting him out – and this time she wasn't going to let him get away from her.

'Gillie,' she whispered his name, then, 'GILLIE!'

He stopped, turned, peered along the avenue. She began running towards him and in seconds was close enough to see his dark, handsome face, his eyes, disbelieving, incredulous.

'Evie, it can't be you, I don't believe . . .'

She stood there in front of him. He was shaking his head, half-laughing, then his arms came round her and he pulled her in close to smother her in a muffle of damp tweed and warm wool.

They said nothing, there was nothing to say that could

express the wonder they both felt at that moment. The snow wrapped them round, covered their clothes, their hair, it blinded them and caressed them. His lips were cold against the warmth of her neck, his nose was like a frozen cherry pressed into her cheek.

A minute later they were talking as if they would never stop, pausing every so often to gaze at one another with sparkling eyes.

'Was it sheer coincidence that brought you to Cleveden Mansions,' he asked, 'or do you know someone who lives here?'

She told him about Mary and Greg, ending, 'They won't be back, Greg took a stroke and they're looking for a house in the country. What about you?'

'My old friend, Lord Quigley-Jameson, lives here. I always look him up when I'm in Glasgow. He retired in the summer and is moving to Edinburgh in the spring. This was my last visit to Cleveden Mansions.'

'Mine too.' The import of her words made her draw in her breath. Neither of them would return to this place. If they hadn't met today . . .

'I know,' he took her hand. 'I was thinking the same thing. Come on, let's go where we can really talk, I know a good place, not too noisy.'

He took her to Charles Rennie Mackintosh's Willow Tearoom. She remembered little of the taxi ride, and even when it was over and they were seated in an intimate little corner of the elegant establishment, her sense of unreality persisted.

He ordered tea for two with hot buttered muffins but so taken up were they with one another they weren't aware of eating or drinking.

She told him everything that had happened in her life since last they had met. The minutes passed, he hung on every word, eager to know about Maggie and Jamie and all those other members of her family that he remembered so well. But somehow she couldn't bring herself to tell him about Davie, the wounds were too raw, too new.

'I've thought about you all so often,' he told her, 'and wondered where you were, how you were faring. Mother still talks about you as well, she grew very fond of the Grants, particularly of Maggie.'

'And Mam loved her too, that sounds a bit strong but it's true, it *was* love in the end.'

She glanced at him. 'We're cousins, Gillie, did you know that? I only found out fairly recently and suddenly it all made sense, the things that old Oggie used to say to me, the hints of family ties.'

He laughed. 'Ay, we're cousins, Evie. Mother told me soon after you left Dunmarnock, she was feeling a bit low, missing Maggie, and suddenly it all came out, and it was right somehow, blood kin, ties that bind forever.'

His hand reached over the table to take hers, she blinked back her tears. 'Gillie, I canna believe this has happened today, there's so much I want to ask. How is Lady Marjorie? Evander? Dear old Oggie?'

'Mother is hale and hearty and spends her time between Rothiedrum, London and Capetown, Father died some years ago, a heart attack, old Oggie is still going strong and still takes an active interest in his business affairs. He's never forgotten you, Evie, and always hopes the families will get together again some day.'

'Ay, someday,' she said shakily. She took a deep breath. 'And you, Gillie? What about you? Did you ever make sense o' these fusty old books you used to talk about?'

He smiled. 'Not much. I became a barrister. For years I buried myself in my work, it was the only way I knew how to forget a red-haired girl who took my heart and never returned it. Mother was worried about me, she said I was living an unnatural way of life. She nagged, coaxed, berated. In the end I gave in to man's basic instincts and got married four years ago. We live and work in London. My wife doesn't like the country, she's a fashion editor

291

with a large publishing house and also does some design work. No children, two Siamese cats, hers, one aquarium, mine. I visit Rothiedrum whenever I can, I love the old place.'

She wanted to talk about Rothiedrum, about the couthy farmtoun folk that had been so much a part of their childhood, but she was afraid that if she did, the floodgates would open and she would never again be reconciled to tenement life.

He understood, his hand tightened over hers. 'Davie's dead, isn't he, Evie? You haven't spoken his name once.'

'Ay, he's dead,' she said quietly. 'It happened just over a month ago. He was only thirty-four.'

'I'm – so sorry, my darling Princess, you must ache in your mourning, yet I have never seen you looking more beautiful than you do now.'

For a long time he gazed at her. She was free now, while he . . . 'Evie, Princess,' he whispered, 'I'm joining Mother at Rothiedrum for Christmas before we both go to London for New Year. Come with me: if you can't come alone bring your children, bring Maggie and Jamie. Mother would love it, she might suffer a few mild fits to begin with but in the end she would adore to see you all again. Think of it, Evie, Rothiedrum in the snow, the parks smothering in virgin white; the old speak in your ears; the faces of the folk you've never forogtten.'

The pain of longing stabbed her heart. Oh, to revisit Rothiedrum? To see once more the lands of her birth! To feel the cold wind tugging her hair; to smell the frost-rimed winter earth; to hear and see again sights and sounds that she had dreamed about for years. The old speak! The old ways! The old folks! Always remembered, forever cherished.

It was cruel! Such temptation! Because for her it could never be.

'Gillie, please.' She lowered her head so that he wouldn't see her brimming eyes. 'I can never go back, never, it would be too much for me to thole, knowing that I would have to leave it all again.'

'Then give me your address and let me visit you,' he urged. 'I — can't let you go again, Evie, we can't waste any more years being apart. We were meant for one another, you and me. Destiny brought us together today, we can't deny it any longer.'

She threw back her head and shut her eyes. 'No, Gillie, it would never work, you have a wife, one day you will have children. We must forget one another.'

'Forget!' He was angry now, his dark face was taut with pain. 'How can you say that? Forget! As if all these years of thinking of one another meant nothing. Because you have thought about me, Evie, I've come to you in your dreams, just as you've come to me in mine! Can you deny that?'

'No, Gillie, I canna deny it, you have always been with me and always will be, but dreams are fleeting, real life is what matters — and your life is with your wife, mine is with my children.'

A faint smile touched his mouth. 'Funny, I had forgotten how stubborn you can be. Very well, have it your way.'

Reaching into his pocket he took out some cards and pushed them over the table. 'Take these, you can reach me at any one of these addresses, Edinburgh, London and, of course, Rothiedrum. I want you to promise me this, if ever things get too much for you to bear, you will contact me. Promise me that, Princess, even if you can't promise me anything else.'

She picked up the cards. 'Ay, Gillie, I promise.'

He stood up. 'I must go, I have a train to catch, Rothiedrum and Mother await.' Unpinning the red carnation from his buttonhole he fixed it to her coat. 'Merry Christmas . . .' His breath caught, he took her hands. 'My darling girl, I would give you the world if you would let me . . .'

Regardless of his surroundings he took her face in his hands to gaze deeply into her eyes before his mouth met hers in a long, lingering kiss.

They drew back from one another, then side by side they walked to the door.

'Can I get you a taxi?'

He sounded polite, already a million miles away.

'No, I can easily get a tram from here.'

Fiercely he lifted her hand to his lips and kissed it. 'Our paths will cross again, Princess,' he said firmly before he strode swiftly away, soon to be lost in the snow-filled darkness.

She stood for a moment, her mouth burning with his kiss, her fingers caressing the carnation from his button-hole. It was wet – stained with her tears.

She walked away in the opposite direction he had taken, and in minutes she too was swallowed up in the night and in the snow that swirled down to cover her footprints.

Rhanna
Christine Marion Fraser

A rich, romantic, Scottish saga set on the Hebridean island of Rhanna

Rhanna

The poignant story of life on the rugged and tranquil island of Rhanna, and of the close-knit community for whom it is home.

Rhanna at War

Rhanna's lonely beauty is no protection against the horrors of war. But Shona Mackenzie, home on leave, discovers that the fiercest battles are those between lovers.

Children of Rhanna

The four island children, inseparable since childhood, find that growing up also means growing apart.

Return to Rhanna

Shona and Niall Mackenzie come home to find Rhanna unspoilt by the onslaught of tourism. But then tragedy strikes at the heart of their marriage.

Song of Rhanna

Ruth is happily married to Lorn. But the return to Rhanna of her now famous friend Rachel threatens Ruth's happiness.

Storm Over Rhanna

The 'islanders' popular minister, Mark James, mourns the tragic loss of his family, and turns to Doctor Megan Jenkins for comfort. But Megan has a post from which she cannot escape.

'Full-blooded romance, a strong, authentic setting'
Scotsman

FONTANA PAPERBACKS

Autobiography
Christine Marion Fraser

In addition to her immensely popular RHANNA series and KING'S series, Christine Marion Fraser has written three bestselling volumes of autobiography, in which she recounts her own remarkable story with characteristic warmth, observation and humour.

BLUE ABOVE THE CHIMNEYS
ROSES ROUND THE DOOR
GREEN ARE MY MOUNTAINS

'Christine Marion Fraser happens to have a wonderful gift for conveying the joyousness of her daily round. We are privileged to share her joyfulness in this remarkable fashion; her narrative is fresh and genuine throughout. Happily her tumble of words has been harnessed into fiction too.'

Jersey Evening Post

'Enthralling, superb, admirable . . . a refreshing book from an extraordinary lady.' *Edinburgh Evening News*

'A warm and touching story . . . captivating humour.'

Book Preview

Fontana